Jumping Judiciary Corruption

A Sharp Investigations Novel

Book Nine

BY: E. N. CRANE

EDITED BY: A. O. NEAL

US Print ISBN: 978-1-957539-29-4

US eBook ISBN: 978-1-957539-28-7

Keep being Pawsome!

PERRY DOG
PUBLISHING

POWERED BY COFFEE
& DOG FUR

To everyone out there protesting, fighting, and tired of watching the hateful people win, I see you. This one is for us. To see what it looks like when just once, justice is served to those who deserve it.

Foxtrot Delta Tango—History cannot be erased while we remember and refuse to be silenced.

Chapter One: Dearly Departed

A tear splashed against the folded computer printout in my hand, landing on Trigger's name. Somewhere ahead of me, a military chaplain was making words about God and sheep, but I just stared at the paper in my hand.

Someone had printed off the memorial program on generic computer paper, haphazardly folded hundreds of them in half, and left them sitting in a box lid at the church entrance. His military portrait, a ridiculous picture of a man with overly large ears taken decades before I was born, didn't look like the man that I knew. Trigger's service record was detailed inside, leaving out his most interesting and classified missions. The items chosen for inclusion carefully downplayed the military's role in his wheelchair days as a gun range owner and dog father.

Whoever had written this drivel hadn't even included the large black husky-mix who was currently lying beside the empty wheelchair, forlorn and listless. Not as a loved one left behind, a footnote, a snapshot, he was altogether forgotten by whoever had composed the mindless factoids of a man's life ended too soon. Ruger's entire world was just gone, and no one had even mentioned him. They'd mentioned Trigger's time with the Marines, his work on joint ops with the SEALs and the Rangers, but not his sole surviving family member.

Another tear slid down my cheek and landed on the ridiculous legal name.

Clyde "Trigger" Sampson.

"When God calls our shepherds home, it is with the triumphant..." I wanted to scream at the man in black. His asinine comment that somehow this death should be celebrated had earned him at least a gut punch. The military hadn't celebrated him when they'd unceremoniously kicked him out, a punishment for losing his ability to walk and dispatch death at their whim, but they were more than willing to pretend now that he couldn't spill their secrets. "Trumpets will blare as his wings carry him..."

To crap on your stupid head.

Winnie leaned her 90-pound fur frame against my leg, weighing me down. The German shepherd Malinois mix, a retired and un-celebrated military reject herself, could sense I needed to be kept in line. Normally, Sgt. Winnifred Pupperson was the one who needed to be contained, restrained or placated, but today… Today the leash was more to keep my six-foot, size 18 ass from catching assault and battery charges than the other way around.

It was why our team worked.

"Amen," the church coursed, and I made a snarling, lip curled face at the back of the bald head in front of me.

Winnie and I had a seat at the back, the wooden pews nearly filled to capacity with every service uniform I could imagine. Trigger owned a military veteran's only gun range, Shots Fired, an establishment that brought together service members and their families to shoot and heal. Be it from shattered bones or shattered psyches, he made sure there was a place for them to feel connection and belonging. Though I didn't believe in God or an afterlife, I believed in the work Trigger was doing in this one. I could only pray that someone with "esquire" in their title had a document to make sure that the mission continued.

Without the aforementioned belief in God, I wasn't sure who I was hoping would hear me.

Taylor Swift, maybe?

"Well, you look like murder and despair had a baby." A woman slid onto the bench beside me, her husky voice a rasp courtesy of the elements and a few explosions. Winnie's tail thumped the underside of the wooden bench, her collar jingling as the woman pet her. "Good turnout."

"Never really understood that comment," I wiped tears and snot from my face using the sleeve of my dress greens. My brain flashed back to a dumb joke about a girl with a runny nose and green hair she claimed was natural. It was like even my brain would do anything to be somewhere else. "The dead person is dead. Do they really care how many people showed up to their funeral? A better compliment would have been to show up for them in life."

"It's usually to comfort the family, I think…" May questioned her own hypothesis. "Actually, it's a pretty dumb thing to comment on. Like bragging about crowd sizes at a rally or telling a lesbian how hung you are."

I snorted and looked over at the woman. Her hands still shook, but she seemed to have more control over the gross motor skills required for day-to-day life. Dark hair that was once matted around her face was now smoothed and pulled back into a tight bun at her nape, her Marine uniform crisp and clean. Instead of shifting uncomfortably, her back stayed tall as mourners passed by and eyed the pair of us with mixed expressions.

"You look… better, May," I remarked, unsure if it was a compliment to comment on her transition away from homelessness. "Did they do something about the shrapnel messing with your nerves?"

"Thanks. Your… when you helped Arturo, he worked to come back and help a lot of us. They put me on a new medication, and yes, found a treatment to reduce the effects of the shrapnel. Worked on helping me find a job that wasn't… triggering. Housing, all of it. It was a turning point." She kept her hands threaded in Winnie's fur, brows creased, and lips pressed together.

"Are you happy?"

Silence answered my question, and I joined her in it. Around us, the church had emptied and an electronic gurney was moving the casket out of the rear of the building. Winnie whimpered, and May released her, watching as my partner advanced to the front of the church to nudge Ruger with her nose.

The Pitbull Husky mix didn't move.

"Ruger?" I stood up, click clacking in my black heels toward the front of the room. May followed behind me, and we arrived beside the dog at the same time Winnie placed her head over his shoulders. The black dog's nose was dry, his energy levels low, but he was breathing, even as my heart stuttered in my chest.

"What's wrong, baby? Who are you here with?" I looked around but there was no one besides me, May, and an empty wheelchair that once held his most valued friend. Fresh tears ran down my face, my fingers sinking into the thick black fur and rubbing at the white undercoat. I wanted to squeeze him into me and take away his loss, bring back his entire world, but there was nothing left I could do.

Nothing any of us could do.

May sat down on his opposite side, holding space while I cried into the top of the dog's head. When he raised it, ever so slightly, to lick my salty tears, I let out a soft hiccup. He gave me another kiss and I sighed, trying to sit up and wipe the snot off my face for the second time.

"Where's he been staying?" I whispered, trying to cross my legs. The pants portion of my dress greens hadn't gone on comfortably with my post service eating habits, but the skirt was a bit more forgiving. Unfortunately, it was also not pants, making sitting without showing the world my undies a challenge. "Why isn't anyone here for him?"

"I'm not sure. I know he was in the room when they found the body-"

"What do you mean 'found the body'? Trigger wasn't at home?" I asked, eyes narrowing. There hadn't been any mention of an investigation. No one had mentioned murder or that he was at a different location than his usual 2 haunts.

No one had mentioned a damn thing, and my sadness quickly evaporated under the anger of being kept in the dark.

"Trigger was serving jury duty. That big case at the federal courthouse with the campaign manager to the politician who was accused of attempted murder? Tommy Stump, the guy who tried to accuse the other candidate of voter fraud and was then found to have actually committed voter fraud, but somehow his attorney and campaign manager were arrested when the opposition was found nearly beaten to death and the weapon in the attorney's car? But the attorney was exonerated and it all got pinned on the campaign manager who is now on trial. Marius something?" May summarized, and I blinked at her, completely oblivious to the scandal on my state's soil. "It's my understanding it was a sequestering situation because of the media surrounding the trial and no one was permitted to leave the premises except to go to the courtroom."

"That sounds illegal as fluff." I stroked Ruger's head, watching the black fur shift to brown and white as I went against the grain. "Don't you have any rights when someone else commits a crime? Like that's basically prison for people suckered into doing their civic duty."

"Honestly, I have no idea what is and is not legal. I only stopped being considered a criminal for living on the streets four months ago."

It was the sad truth of society that needing help and not being able to access it was criminalized. The number of people who'd come home from combat and been too damaged by the experience to function in society as a result was heartbreaking. The number of suicides and arrests in the same group... none of it made sense. But it also wasn't something I could fix beyond showing up, showing support, and lending an ear and some snacks.

"Excuse me?"

May and I looked up together. Standing in front of us was a gangly redhead with limbs like an octopus. He had curly hair, nearly no waist, and freckles you couldn't count with a microscope. My best guess would put him at sixteen.

"Are you Cynthia Sharp?"

May and I exchanged a look that said, *how does he not know?*

"Yup," I answered, popping the P at the end.

"Sweet. My dad is Mr. Patterson, Mr. Sampson's attorney. He asked me to help track you down today." The kid pulled a card out of his pocket and held it out toward us. May and I exchanged another look, neither of us reaching for the card. Winnie let out a sneeze, and the card fell out of his fingers to the floor. It landed neatly by the toe of my heel, face up.

We all stared at the piece of paper, Patrick Patterson, Attorney.

He was named like a Stan Lee character.

"So… uh…" Patterson junior swallowed hard, taking a step back. "There is a will reading in a few days which I obvs need to invite you to. But the deceased left custody of that…"

He gestured toward Ruger.

"You did not just call him a *that*, Patrick junior," I snapped, preparing to murder him and find a spare casket. There was no scenario where dogs didn't rank above humans as the best thing ever.

"N-no. I meant… that dog. He left you custody of his dog." The kid fumbled backward a few more steps. Ruger snuffled forward a few more inches, and I realized my hand was no longer stroking his fur. Returning to my task, I relaxed back into the steps and looked at Winnie. Her head was still laying protectively across Ruger's shoulders, but she didn't sense anything off about this guy.

"The official reading and paperwork will happen on Thursday, but the dog isn't doing well. He was with my dad, Patrick, for the past couple of days, but he's not eating or really drinking… so my dad sent me to the funeral hoping to find you and pass him off."

"You wanna come home with us?" I asked Ruger, pinching the thick triangles of his ears and rubbing them between my thumb and index fingers. His black nose sniffled closer and when he reached my leg, gave it a lick. "I'm going to take that as a yes. And you going to be a good older sister?"

Winnie's tail thumped twice, and I kissed the top of both of their heads.

"So…" I rolled my eyes back to the kid. He just wouldn't go away. Bending over, he grabbed the business card off the ground and held it out again. "The address for the will reading is on here and you need to be present for the whole legal transfer."

A long-suffering sigh slipped out, and I took the business card, pocketing it.

"Yeah, sure. Whatever, kid."

"Charles. I'm Charles Patterson. Do you by chance know a Helena May?" he asked, back to looking like a toddler in a grown-up costume.

"Maybe, what's it to you?" I asked, not daring to look at the woman beside me who'd gone still. Her first name being Helena was weird, and I didn't really like learning she had a first name. Or maybe a last name. I wanted her to be May, like Zendaya or Siri.

"I need to invite her to the will reading as well, but I can't find any contact info for her."

Nodding, I held out my hand for another card.

"Just put the date and time on the back of a card. I'll see that she gets it."

Chuck hesitated.

"Couldn't you…"

"Nope." I answered, assuming his request involved somehow giving over R2-D2 and C3PO to the Empire. These were not the droids he sought, and I would not aid in the destruction of Alderaan. "You can give me the info to share or tell your dad the Stan Lee character you failed. Up to you, Chuck."

"Charles."

"Do I look like I give a fluff, Chuck?"

"Charles!"

Winnie and Ruger let out rumbly grumbles at his outburst and he walked back another step.

"Ugh, fine." He handed me another card, and I tucked it in my pocket. "Are you guys heading over to the grave?"

May and I exchanged a look and then looked at the canines. Winnie nosed at Ruger, who whimpered with a long look at the empty wheelchair beside him. He hadn't looked at the casket the same way. Either the embalming process had altered his smell, or he didn't need any further confirmation his person was gone.

"I think we're done paying our respects. Perhaps we'll see you Thursday," I said, dismissing him from our company.

"Nope, I have school. Good luck with the dogs." He shot us with double finger guns and walked out backward, stumbling slightly on a hymnal left on the floor. Once he turned around, I handed May her business card.

"Guess I'll see you on Thursday too?"

She looked at it and shrugged.

"Got nowhere else to be."

My phone alarmed, reminding me I needed to be at work in two hours.

"Sadly, I cannot say the same."

Chapter Two: Growing and Growling

"What do you wear to the reading of a will?" I asked the dogs lying on my bed. "I don't own a suit anymore, the greens are still dirty, and I don't want to look like I'm trying too hard..."

Winnie was once again resting her head across Ruger's back. The barrel-chested black dog was resting his enormous head on crossed paws, a dignified forlorn. But neither of them offered wardrobe advice and I flopped on the bed beside them. Reaching for my coffee mug, I drank the life-giving liquid with one hand and petted the dogs with the other.

Cursing my lack of a third hand when I had to alternate between their floofs or forgo the coffee.

"This is why Persephone went mad, I'm sure of it. Cerberus had 3 heads, and she only had 2 hands... also did the ancient Greeks have coffee?" Neither answered me, but I hadn't really expected them to.

Ruger still hadn't returned to normal. Winnie had encouraged him to eat, his water intake and output at least close to the same as hers, but his energy was lacking. No thanks to an evil killer corporation, Ruger had sustained a leg injury that left him with a limp and limited what he could do on the farm, so he was definitely getting enough rest. Though a few months had passed, and he was fully healed, he was not going to be able to herd sheep, chase goats, or tick off temperamental old mares.

Which was actually perfect, because doing all those things had landed Winnie her costumed photo spot in front of the ice cream parlor. Though my former canine partner could still detect bombs and take down bad guys, she was also now the proud owner of several glitter tutus, fairy wings, and tiaras. The farm manager, Joseph, had plotted to recruit Ruger to be her co-host, but my newest fur-child wasn't having it. The second he saw the children, their parents, and the ridiculous hat Joseph wanted on his head, the dog turned tail and hid in an empty barn stall. When the farm hands needed that stall for a pregnant cow, he'd simply moved over and made room for her without vacating the premises.

Pretty sure they were besties now.

"We have thirty minutes before we need to head out. Anything you guys want to do?"

Neither dog said anything, so I took that as a good sign my coffee was working.

Beside us, my phone buzzed with an incoming text, and I picked it up to see a message from my best friend, Mo. Mary O'Connor had been with Teach for America and now owned and operated a popular bakery and coffee shop in town. She'd been on vacation with her boyfriend for the past week, and this was the first message I'd seen from her.

Mo: Hey! We just got home; do you want to come over? I brought you something!

I looked at the two dogs on the bed and then back at my phone.

Me: We're about to head out, but you can come over here if you want. I've got some news.

Mo: Is it about Levi and how you two are getting married? Or having a baby? Or doing sweet nasty things to each other????

Rolling my eyes, I sent her a picture of the two dogs. My best friend was a little too obsessed with the idea of me being happily paired off. A normal person might think it was sweet, but I was pretty sure she wanted me pair-bonded with someone in the area so I wouldn't pick up and leave again.

Hypocrisy in my opinion, as she also picked up and left, albeit not to a war zone.

Mo's inconvenient reasoning aside, I wasn't sure I wanted to pair bond with anyone long term. Other people had the potential to disappoint you. If the primary concern was me leaving, then I was fairly certain the sight before me should convince her I had to stay. Dogs never let you down, but they did have a fondness for couches, food, and air conditioning, so I wasn't so sure leaving was really an option anymore.

ME: TRIGGER DIED... HE LEFT ME RUGER IN HIS WILL, AND THIS IS NOW A TWO DOG HOUSEHOLD. WE'RE FINE BUT I HAVE TO GET READY FOR THE OFFICIAL READING OF THE WILL. ANY CHANCE YOU KNOW WHAT PEOPLE WEAR TO THAT?

Texting dots appeared in our chat. Then they disappeared, reappeared and finally my phone rang with a picture of her face on it.

"Are you OK?" As my best friend, we could skip over things like 'hello' and 'sure is cold this time of year'. But we couldn't skip over the truth, and as I stared at my bed, the sharply angled ceiling sloping above it, I tried to answer honestly.

"Not really."

I rolled off the bed and walked two feet past my couch and into the small kitchenette. Though I had a full-sized fridge, I did not have an oven, a stovetop range, or a dishwasher. There were, however, two coffee pots and I refilled my mug from the multi-cup carafe that had finished brewing while I consumed the cup provided by the single-serve dispenser.

Technology at its most useful.

"Do you want to talk about it?" Mo's side of the line had the peaceful quiet that meant she was at home and not in her shop.

I shrugged, though I knew she couldn't see. Talking about things had its place, and though I wasn't ashamed to have feelings, I didn't know what having them and sharing them would do besides burden other people. It also might break the dam I had built around my emotions, and I wasn't sure I could rebuild it before the reading.

"Just wishing I'd gone out there more to check in on him."

The coffee maker beeped, and I refilled my cup. Staring into the swirls along the surface, I waited for the inky blackness to hold an answer or the keys to my future. When nothing appeared, I added creamer and started drinking.

"Was he sick... or?" She let the question hang there and I didn't have an answer. After talking with May, I'd researched the trial he was sitting on the jury for. Despite hours clicking on articles hoping for anything related to his death, I came up with only grainy news stream footage and speculation about what the verdict would be.

"I need to see the death certificate, I think. Do they put cause of death on those?" I drank my coffee and stared at the dogs. Trigger had been missing both index fingers and a few other extremities, sacrifices to the American people to keep the government's secrets. We'd both been hospitalized, injured by the same people who'd hurt Ruger, and I'd seen his medical record. The man was healthier than I was, medically speaking. There weren't a lot of maladies that can appear and kill you in the course of a few months, but I hadn't asked. Her muffled voice came through the line followed by a deep masculine reply.

"Chris isn't sure, his patients don't usually die but he can ask. Do you want me to come with you?"

I pictured my red-headed best friend, freshly returned from her lover's retreat. She was probably sitting in her vegetation covered house with the volunteer firefighter man she was in love with. Mo was flighty, chaotic, and could come off as unintelligent, but she was a solid human that would drop everything for the people she loved. Unfortunately, I always seemed to need her at the cost of her happiness or time with someone else.

"I think I'll be OK," I lied. "But thanks. Maybe I can bring the new dynamic duo by for your special pup-cakes later."

"Are you sure?" She asked as I refilled my coffee mug and ambled over to the metal rod I used as a closet and stared at my wardrobe.

"Yeah... We'll survive. Now... what am I supposed to wear?"

Lawyer's offices are never what I imagine.

In my head, they look like *Legally Blonde* conference rooms with heavy wooden tables and wall to wall bookshelves of leather tomes filled with legal text. When that seems out of place for a cityscape high-rise, my brain conjures glass-topped desks and leather armchairs with at least one wall of obligatory books.

Even in the golden age of technology, I still firmly believe lawyers' offices should be filled with books.

What they should not be filled with are back issues of Sports Illustrated, Styrofoam busts wearing wigs, and an angry Korean dry cleaner worried about my fur-children getting hair on the clothes.

Patterson's law office was in a strip mall off the main freeway, headed out past Dayton. He had a single door opening into a shared lobby space with Kayla's Beauty Supplier and Kim's Dry Cleaner, and the section allotted as his office was roughly the size of the Fonz's toilet stall in *Happy Days*, with a similar smell, color scheme, and vibe.

"Thank you all for coming!" The senior Patterson beckoned me in, his grandiose gesture nearly toppling an ornate desk lamp. While he righted it, I noticed his back faced the window looking out on the parking lot, giving him a clear view of the lobby and anyone else who entered. Based on the maximum occupancy, we were the last to arrive.

"Would anyone like anything to drink?" The lawyer bounced on the balls of his feet, hands folded in front him.

May was seated in one of the two carpeted office chairs that faced his desk. The dogs and I took up residence behind her and the remaining chair held a man in a cheap suit who possibly worked for the government based on his attire, haircut, and look of eternal suffering. Blue eyes flashed my direction, a disarming smile beneath a close crop of dark blonde hair, and I looked away from the suit.

A single sheet of paper sat on the desktop. Beneath it was an over-sized calendar blotter with the ends hanging just past the edge of the desk, two flat screen monitors that were over five years old, a wireless keyboard that might have been fished from a dumpster based on staining and cracked keys, and a mouse. To the right beside a bookcase of memorabilia and an inadequate number of books, sat a wire basket filled with a stack of mail featuring angry red "Final Notice" stamps emblazoned on the front.

We all remained silent, staring as he switched from bouncing to rocking.

"We have coffee, water, soda..." He shifted from foot to foot, a few beads of sweat clinging to his hairline, and I clocked him at around forty. Mr. Patterson lacked both height and musculature, his slender frame bordering on emaciated, while the suit and jewelry he sported contradicted his lack of income. Depending on what he owed and to whom, he could probably make a decent dent in that past due stack if he hocked both.

"We're fine," I spoke for my collective, incapable of watching anyone struggle in an awkward silence I didn't create. May and The Suit shook their heads, and the lawyer let out a pleased guffaw before settling into his seat.

"Alright then, we'll get right down to brass tacks then." He cleared his throat and picked up the sheet of paper in front of him. Through the plate-glass window behind him, I could see the reflection of a handwritten letter scrawled over the top half of the page, the bottom stamped and signed twice. Best guess was Trigger and a notary, assuming the letter itself was his will and the length was a reflection of the attitudes and opinions of the author.

The man didn't behave as though he owned much and if he did, he wasn't really one to hem and haw over parsing it out.

"Now, let's see here..." The lawyer fidgeted, and I caught him checking the clock.

"For the love of dog, dude. If you are stretching this out for billable hours, I have to warn you I have a short attention span and a penchant for petty vengeance, the likes of which you have never seen. This room is tiny, it has too many people in it, and the longer I stand here, the more likely I am to start plotting your demise." Winnie perked up at the mention of petty vengeance because she was also a fan of chaos. "And while it's usually non-violent, I'm not inherently opposed to actions that cause non-lasting physical harm."

"No, no, Ms. Sharp. That will not be necessary." He cleared his throat again and started reading. "The last will and testament of Clyde 'Trigger' Sampson, being of sound mind and body, dictate the following--"

"Before you continue," May interrupted, shifting in her seat to look at me. "Who is that guy?"

The Suit looked at her and then up at me.

"Griffin Allen, I'm a financial officer with NFCU, Mr. Sampson's financial institution as well as his estate executor for any charitable allocations. My job is to coordinate asset transfer between the estate and beneficiaries and any remaining payments--within reason." He offered a pointed look to the attorney. "To the executors of the will and any other outstanding debts."

May looked at me again, and I shrugged.

This was my first human death and my first time being named in a will. The man could have claimed to be our CO, and I'd have offered him a "sir" and a salute before carrying on with my day.

"What's eight cubed?" I asked him and he blinked at me.

"Eight times eight is 64 and 64 times 8 is... thirty-two, carry the three... 512?" He answered and I looked at May who shrugged back. Neither of us was a numbers person nor had I actually expected him to perform math on the spot like a trained monkey.

"Sounds right. I accept his money man declaration."

"You don't want to confirm with a calculator, Ms. Sharp?" He gave me a look far too familiar for someone I was meeting for the first time, eyes soft at the corners and with a small uptick at the corners of his mouth. The blue of his eyes and the soft pink of his lips were alarmingly appealing in a face worn by sun exposure and time and I forced myself to look away.

"Nope. Do you?" I asked and he laughed, shaking his head.

"Right then... sound body... dictate the following," Patterson continued. "My sole surviving family member, Ruger, is to live with Cynthia Sharp, former Army Specialist and her canine, Sgt. Winnifred Pupperson. Half my personal assets are to remain in a brokerage account for his care and upkeep while he is with her, and she is required to take him to the shooting range once a week in my memory. She will shoot at least 100 rounds every time she goes."

With a dog on either side of me, I dropped my hands to pet them, needing the comfort.

"I leave my business, Shots Fired, under the management of Helena May. All records of finances and associated rights transfer to her. Due to the nature of the business, she is empowered to hire anyone necessary to manage in-person functions."

May reached behind her to pet a dog.

"My house is donated to the VA for use as part of their veteran's outreach and rehabilitation program to assist with reducing the crisis. Don't screw it up."

We turned to look at the financial adviser, who we associated with the VA.

"I'll make sure they get the message. Now..." He pulled out a tablet and opened several documents, as did the lawyer. "It's time for signatures."

They both set their devices in front of us, and we stared at the screens. Patterson's was simple, an acknowledgement that he'd read the will and, in my case, that I had taken custody of Ruger, who the State of Ohio considered property.

We both signed.

The second device had multi-page documents about money, assets, transfer of title and routing numbers for transfers or fund withdrawals, as well as an audit process for charges. There was a contact name of Griffin Allen for all advance requests and he was also the listed point of contact for receipts and reconciliations.

"Jesus..." May breathed, and I nodded behind her.

"Can I skip the money part and just take the dog? I promise to take him to the range, but I don't want or really need any money... that I know of." I looked between both men, who shook their heads in unison. "What happens if I don't sign, don't accept the money, grab my dog leashes and run?"

"You can't run away from this." Griffin the Suit offered me another soft smile. "Even if you don't sign, the account is in your name, and it becomes a legal cluster for you to not have access to or information about the account. The IRS most of all will take great exception to you not reporting it as part of your holdings."

"But I won't be holding it. I'm just holding dogs." I gestured to the dogs on either side of me and decided to pet them. "Dogs and... coffee usually."

"And snacks," May added. I jerked my head her direction in agreement.

"Holdings is a term for assets in your name that you are required to report to the IRS. It is considered property you own, real or otherwise, that you must be taxed on." Suit Man's voice went up a tick in volume, like talking about assets and taxes gave him a minor woody.

"Oh, must I?" I switched to an English accent, because it felt very "taxation without representation"-y to me. "But I don't want it. I bequeath it away! Be gone money!"

"Not with how the account is set up. It's technically Ruger's." Griffin did not use an accent, because apparently he takes his job and death seriously.

"So why doesn't he pay taxes on it?" I crossed my arms, hiding my tablet signing hands from sight.

"Because he doesn't have a social security number... or thumbs." Griffin pointed at the thumbless paws in question, then back at the tablet. "You could try to get him the first one, but without the second... you'd still have to sign."

"Damn tax fluffers." I released my thumbs from my armpits and slouched against the nearest wall. May went first, wading into the many pages of legalese. I stewed for a minute, pissed that I was inheriting money. I never wanted money; I just wanted a dog... Technically, I wanted my friend to still be alive and now that he wasn't, I just wanted to be in charge of his descendent like a non-wicked stepmother. Or mildly wicked, but not to my children.

Now I had to find someone to manage my kid's money.

Like a pimp, but the parts of my body being sold would only be the ones used for canine care. My brain started to drift to Trigger. His quick shots with only a few remaining fingers, the steady way he could move between his chair and other surfaces, and the absolute authority he held over his domain.

"Do you have a copy of Trigger's death certificate and manner of death?" I scrunched up my face unsure which man to ask. Griffin and the lawyer both looked at me, and May paused to hear the answer.

"What do you want that for?" Patterson shifted between butt cheeks, his smile not meeting his eyes that darted around under his drawn eyebrows. The laced together fingers on his desktop went white and my hackles went up, as did Ruger's beside me.

"Because I have questions." I narrowed my eyes and puffed out my chest, mirroring gorillas in the jungle. "Don't people, death associated people, have to... send something to start the whole... Will process?" My intimidation lost some of its effectiveness when I didn't know the name of any occupations associated with the death process. A quick glance around the room and I noted that Finance Man was also taking notice of the twitchy lawyer, bolstering some of my lost momentum. "I mean... it's not like you get a list of daily deaths, right? How do you learn your clients died to start this whole process moving?"

Everyone was now watching the lawyer, hands stilled and paperwork halted.

"Well... In this case, he had my business card with him and the medical staff contacted me when they couldn't resuscitate him."

I was pretty sure the "whole will process" was called execution of the estate, and his lack of correction made me suspicious. Lawyers loved reminding people how much more they knew than the average person. They also loved correct terminology and legal definitions.

Was this man even a lawyer?

"So... he died in a hospital?" I lowered my eyes, studying him with my arms crossed.

"No, no. He died in a hotel room." Patrick inched the chair farther away from me, looking everywhere but at us.

"A hotel room? Why was he in a hotel room and not taken to a hospital for treatment?" May launched to her feet, fists balled on the desk getting into his face. The lawyer licked his lips, catching drips of sweat with his tongue. "Are you saying no one looked at him or tried to save him?"

"Well, he was serving on a grand jury case near Columbus, and they were sequestered there. The whole jury was... sequestered there." He paused, searching under his desk. When he found a bottle of water, the plastic crinkling in his shaky grip as May and I closed in on our side of the desk. Taking a small sip, he swallowed hard and tried again. "So anyway, when the paramedics got there, he was dead."

Patterson wiped at his brow with the back of his hand and May looked between me, Griffin, and the attorney. I watched her make the same connections and come to the same questions I did, but it was Suit Man who spoke first.

"Keep signing, you two. The will is real, there was a copy in Mr. Sampson's portfolio, and you are still Ruger's guardian. May, you still are tasked with running Shots Fired. I'll make some calls and see what the cause of death is. And who signed off on it." Griffin stood, taking his phone out of the inside breast pocket of his blazer.

"That's really not..." Mr. Patterson was wearing a light blue button down and despite missing the top few buttons, his hands were working the collar like it were strangling him alive. Beneath his arms, large pools of sweat were darkening the shirt.

"Winnie," I started, and she looked at me. My eyes remained trained on the lawyer, and she let out a soft growl, turning his way. Her paw took a single step forward, and he screamed.

"No! Please! I didn't do anything, I swear!"

I didn't call her back, allowing her to take another step closer. Sadly, that's when the lawyer fainted.

Chapter Three: Under Oath

Winnie cocked her head to the side, and she glanced at me over her shoulder.

"Yeah, I don't know what the hell he thought you were going to do from over here either." I leaned forward on my palms and glanced at the heap on the floor. Ruger let out a soft whimper and I scratched his head. "It's OK, baby, no one's mad at you."

"Do you think we should call a medic?" May was back in her chair, arms crossed, eyes on the books beside her. "Or maybe we can just pronounce him dead and serve his will to the listed beneficiaries."

Winnie flopped over and was licking her lady town, completely unconcerned that she'd caused a man to pass out in fear by taking two itty bitty steps. If I wanted to make a man pass out, I had to punch him in the face. Now if I punched him in the face, it would just be... hitting a man when he's down.

"I doubt he's dead." No one made a move toward the man on the floor. "Come on!"

Everyone looked at me, including Winnie. My shoulders hunched, I sighed and slouched around the desk to look at the lawyer.

Patrick was lying on his side, the dense cloud of sweat forming a solid cloud of humidity in his airspace. In addition to being wet, it was also hot and had at least two or three levels of odor above a high school boy's locker room. I gagged, switching from nose breathing to clenched-teeth mouth breathing in an impersonation of Darth Vader.

"Oof, dude did not believe in deodorant." Crouching beside him, I took hold of his chin, tilting his face toward the light coming in from the windows, and parting his jaw. "Or toothpaste, jeez. No blood or bumps, he didn't hit his head on the way down. Tongue appears intact, no bite down injuries..." I pushed his mouth closed again and palpated the hinge point. The two were still properly nested and nothing creaked or crumbled.

Based on my extensive past injuries, this is usually the part medics apply pressure up and down my limbs to check for breaks or lumps. But every inch of the man in front of me was moist, a word as unappealing as its definition. The thought of touching him made my skin crawl and I decided checking his head was due diligence enough.

Hauling myself back up, I looked down at the short man's domain and eyed the finance man. His eyes were fixed on me with an intensity I usually reserved for describing Winnie in the throws of a cheese pursuit. "Are you a narc?"

"You want to rifle through the papers on his desk?" Griffin countered and I smiled. "You were in PD, this counts as plain sight."

He winked, and I rolled my eyes, but grabbed for the stack of mail first. May reached for the tablet she'd just signed on and opened it back up. I glanced over to see her quickly enter the passcode she must have memorized from his first pass. Griffin scooted in beside me and wiggled the desktop mouse. The ancient CPU hummed to life beneath the desk, displaying a screensaver that quickly faded into a password entry screen with a large cluster of dead pixels in the upper corner.

"Baseball bat?" I wondered aloud, looking between the tech and the notices.

"Think someone was sending him a message?" Griffin looked at the monitor case, tracing a crack in the black plastic frame.

"Only one way to find out. Unlock it." I went back to scanning return addresses while he stared at the password box.

"What was the iPad passcode?" He inclined his head toward May who was working her way through what appeared to be his downloads folder. I scanned return addresses on the past due bills. One from a leasing company for this ridiculous space, a furniture rental company, technology rental, student loans and an alimony payment.

If this technology was rented, he wasn't getting his deposit back.

"1234," she answered, and I rolled my eyes a second time at the sheer basic-ness of this man. Griffin hesitated and then put the four-digit pin in. The computer denied him access and he looked at me.

"Enter 'password' capital P." After a long load time, the device came to life with a nudie pic of a bikini-clad model as the monitor wallpaper. "While you're in there, reset his password to 'dick pic' one word, capital D as punishment for that poor woman who probably deserves better. And maybe make his background an actual dick pic."

"She's probably fake, if you count the fingers." Griffin chuckled, and I followed his line of sight to an eight-fingered hand.

"Then give him an AI peen too." I went back to my stack of mail. At the very bottom was a hand-addressed envelope with no return address and no postage. The writing was in all caps, perfectly spaced, on a generic non-security white envelope.

Patterson groaned at our feet, and I whistled for Ruger.

"Sit on him," I ordered the dog. Lumbering over with a minor limp, the large pit bull mix stretched back and then flopped over on the man's chest. "Winnie, get the legs." My ninety-pound shepherd Malinois mix took up her post as cement shoes.

I flipped over the envelope, careful not to make unnecessary contact with the leftover tape on the flap. Inside was a typed letter printed on generic paper with an offer, no name at the top, no name at the bottom, and nothing to indicate it was the only one written.

In incomplete sentences, the letter outlined a proposition: Read a will, a legitimate one, and receive payment from both the deceased's estate and a third-party. All documents and contact info would be provided, authenticated, and straightforward. If accepted, the lawyer was to put a green square in the window. No digital communications, no questions, and no one would get hurt.

Failure to follow instructions, and his debts would come to collect.

"Crap." I read through it a second time. Griffin leaned over my shoulder, scanning the text while his clean scent surrounded me.

"Dummy didn't listen, look." He nodded to the monitor, more of the clean woodsy scent displacing the BO wafting up from the unconscious lawyer. I glanced at the open browser history and found the man had been googling Trigger, his shooting range, estimated property value, death related stories... it looked a lot like my search history until you got to the porn.

"Could have lived forever without seeing the rest of that browser history." I shuddered and Griffin chuckled with a casual shoulder bump.

"Anything you want to see the results of, let me know. I'll turn on incognito mode."

His eyebrows suggested a wink without his eyelids getting involved. I jerked back, looking at him with a curled lip.

"Look at this," May said, breaking my gaze away from the baby blues, staring at me with mirth.

Almost like... was he flirting with me?

I took the tablet from May and looked at a series of scans in a PDF. Images of a crappy hotel room with a queen bed and a roll-in shower were followed by a typed report summarizing a series of calls for service, a trial delay, and finally a "check the well" that concluded with the locating of the deceased in his hotel room. Head trauma, likely fall, hair and blood on the edge of a white stone dresser / desk combo unit.

"What the hell?"

We glanced down at the voice rising up from the floor. The lawyer was awake, weighed down by two dogs who might not weigh more than him individually, but together were immovable. His body wriggled beneath them, but it was as unproductive as telling a lawyer not to research a dead guy. Dog weights were more efficient than tying someone up, and less likely to be considered illegal, so long as I pretended they were impossible to move and deaf in both ears.

"That's my question for you." I turned the tablet around and held it near his face. "What the hell?"

"You can't look at that! It's private property!"

"We can, you unlocked it and handed it to us." It was a partial truth, since the iPad went to sleep, and we unlocked it with his stupid simple 1234 password. "Why do you have these reports, Patrick?"

"It's none of your business! I'm calling the cops!"

"Great! When they get here, you can tell them how you murdered a dear friend of mine and accidentally stabbed yourself when you passed out in your office like a little bitch." I grabbed for his letter opener, looking for the least fatal soft spot. Before I could reach it, my body was forcibly moved to the other side of the room by Griffin's arms wrapped around me. Despite his occupation and suit, the man was stronger and more capable than I'd originally given him credit for.

"You can't stab him." The finance guy warned, though he didn't sound particularly sure of himself.

"I can if you get out of my way," I insisted, fighting to get around him only to come up short when I made eye contact with May. She was back to searching through the iPad and cross-referencing the desktop computer. With certainty, she walked around the desk to a file cabinet and pulled open the metal drawer.

"Get out of there! That's confidential!" The lawyer was starting to wheeze from where he was captive under the dogs. "I'm calling..."

"Maybe you should relocate one of them, so he doesn't suffocate." Griffin's lips brushed my ear, sending goose bumps prickling up and down my arms. My eyes drifted from May to the man who was now just holding me in his arms. It wasn't the most intimate position I'd been in with a virtual stranger, but I wasn't sure it was all that appropriate given I was no longer threatening to stab anyone.

"Ruger, off." I watched the large black dog struggle off the lawyer's chest to lumber over. I reached into my cargo pocket and passed him a treat, tossing Winnie one to reward her for not leaving her post of human paperweight. "Happy?"

Griffin's laugh rumbled through me and I felt him nod.

"Who brought you this will?" May asked, holding up a faded piece of printer paper. It was the type of faded that came from being in a pocket or wallet, but the paper itself was still a crisp white.

"The guy, OK?" Patrick Patterson spoke from the vicinity of Winnie's tail, and I regretted slightly that I hadn't let her have cheese recently. A fart to the face would be almost as good as a letter opener to the aorta.

"What guy?" Griffin and I asked at the same time, and I resisted an eye roll.

"The guy!" Patterson needed a new vocabulary. "He was wearing a black suit–white guy, mid-twenties. He came in here with the will and said they'd pay me ten grand to read and execute the will. Plus, I could collect from the estate as the attorney of record if I just... said I was the attorney. He knew about the bills, my gambling debt, that I was going to lose my practice, and my wife is cheating but I needed proof and the PI I hired turned around and sold the photos to her. She took me to the cleaners... not this one. My son..."

"Cry me a damn river Patterson, I don't give a fluff. Tell me more about the mid-twenties guy in a black suit with a will. You sit with your back to a plate-glass window, what kind of car did he drive? What direction did he come from? Brown hair? Blonde? Tall? Short? Heavy-set? Skeletal? Paint me a damn picture!" I lunged forward. Once again, Griffin's arms were securely around me, keeping me flush against him when my feet had started back toward the man on the floor.

"There's a picture on my phone! You're crazy, lady!" The lawyer tried to scoot backward but Winnie held him in place.

May grabbed the phone and passed it to me, her eyes lingering where Griffin held me against him. We exchanged a look, but her half shrug suggested she thought it was probably a good idea to leave me there.

I switched to looking at the phone in my hand. Waking it up I winced at the repeat of a bikini clad woman screensaver. The phone had a four-digit passcode, and I assumed the man was as dumb as he looked and repeated everything everywhere.

"The code is... what the hell! How are you in my phone? That password is secure!"

I rolled my eyes, opening the photo app and immediately regretted it. "What the hell is wrong with you!"

There was at least one whole page of dick pics. His dick next to a ruler, a stapler, a summer sausage... it was like he'd read a how-to guide for establishing a frame of reference and applied it to his one-eyed snake to the horror of all who trespassed here. "This is your real security measure. Freaking sick!"

Griffin slid the phone out of my hand and scrolled up for a full twenty seconds while I took a vested interest in the fur on top of Ruger's head.

"Dude." He judged the lawyer while handing the phone back, a single image enlarged to fill the screen. "Don't exit out of that, though."

As advertised, the man in the picture was wearing a black suit. He was probably thirty, with sandy brown hair in a buzz cut and a smattering of freckles across a sharply angled nose that could shade an anthill. His eyes were hidden by the reflection off black framed glasses, the type issued by the military. The glasses went with the rigid posture and high-shine shoes that most soldiers kept alongside their military IDs.

The image was taken through the window, and the man was walking toward a black sedan. It was newish with a tint that was probably illegal in some states. Zooming in, I studied the out of state plate but couldn't place it with the glare through the window. My only certainty was that it wasn't an Ohio plate.

"Looks like a marine. Maybe former, with the spare tire in the middle." Griffin zoomed into the center of the man's body, and I saw a slight lump. It could have been a little extra weight, or he could have been smuggling something into or out of the lawyer's office. I glanced at him from over my shoulder. His hands were still wrapped around my waist, looser now than they'd been but it still felt like we were cuddling.

"You could let me go, you know."

"No!" Patrick and May disagreed. I glared at both while the man against me rumbled in amusement.

"Whatever." I handed the phone back to the money man. "Was anything missing when he left?"

"Like what?" Patrick glared around Winnie's tail.

"I don't know... Files, clothing... anything?" He shook his head, and I blew out a breath. I glanced at Griffin, redirecting my attention toward him. "Search the other pictures, see if there are more. May, is there anything else in that folder?"

"Not really." She sighed, dropping heavily into the chair. "Just news articles about the trial, some stuff about the explosion at Trigger's place... nothing super damning. Also... this is for you."

She handed me a thick folder with the Kirby's Critter Care logo on the front and Larry's business card stapled inside. It had to be Ruger's medical record... Something about the size made my stomach flip.

"That's because I don't know anything! I didn't kill the man! He fell! I was doing due diligence so I wouldn't be accused of shit like this and now you're here, treating me like a criminal anyway!"

May and I looked at each other.

"He is a criminal." I stared at my shoes, deflating into my breath. "Not sure his crimes are Trigger related."

"Do you think it's possible?" She picked at her thumb cuticle. We weren't talking about the lawyer anymore.

I looked into Ruger's golden eyes. I felt the adrenaline of a righteous investigation fade. In its place was just a weary sadness that sank into my bones, and I deflated. Ruger let out a soft whimper, the doggy equivalent of a sigh.

"I don't know..." I shrugged Griffin's arms off of me and moved over to May. Taking the chair beside her, I leaned forward onto my elbows and looked at my clasped hands. "Have you ever known him to fall?"

"Not sober..."

I scrubbed my hands over my face, staring into a corner of the room. In my mind, I saw him pulling out a handgun and shooting the bull's eye from fifty yards with his middle finger. Trigger had run the range from his chair with fewer fingers and fewer problems than most business owners. Something about him falling out of his chair, hitting his head and dying while in a hotel room, serving on a sequestered jury. It didn't sit right, but it also wasn't impossible.

"Who was on trial again?"

"Marius Howser, he was the campaign manager to Tommy Stump, that Governor who won but then didn't but then did."

I nodded but couldn't put a face to either name.

"Any service history for either of them?"

May paused and I lifted my face out of my hands to look at her.

"Not the campaign manager... I think Stump bought his way out with daddy's money. But... the attorney who was going to be charged with them... I think he served." She worried her lip between her teeth, her hand trembling slightly. "If he didn't fall on his own... I mean... They buried him already, Cyn. Do you really want to walk down this road?"

"Do you think there was an autopsy first?"

She shrugged and looked out the window, far off memories fleeting across her mind she wasn't ready to share. "Even if there was. Who do we go to? What justice is there in death that he never got in life?"

Ruger came over, resting his oversized head on my leg. Stroking his fur, I looked into his eyes and tried to find an answer. Nothing about this made sense, but did I really want to kick a hornet's nest over on a hunch? Did I know anyone who would exhume a body if there hadn't been an autopsy?

It's not going to bring him back.

"I don't know." Rising to my feet, I decided that if the lawyer and the banker wanted my signature, they could request it virtually through one of the apps like a normal person. The only way

I was making it through the rest of today was by leaving now. "Winnie, come."

The German shepherd mix shook herself, jingling her collar before appearing around the edge of the desk with a big stretch. We walked toward the door, raising a brow at the man blocking our exit. His suit was as rumpled as it had been before, but his baby blue eyes shined with concern and something that tugged at my belly. Despite barely meeting a half hour ago, he looked at me like an old friend.

"You're not really known for letting things go, Sharp." He moved one step out of the way. The move still put him within touching distance of our exit, but there wasn't a lot of space to work with. I stepped out into the lobby, looking at the dry cleaner wrappers and the beauty supply logos.

"People change, Mr. Allen." I opened the exterior door and let the dogs lead the way out while Mr. Patterson sputtered protests about signatures, decorum and protocol. The fall chill burst in and cooled the remaining sweat that still clung to my body. Sticky and defeated, I was ready to fall into bed and let the day end in a vat of Bailey's spiked coffee. "People change."

"People might, but I doubt you do. I'll be seeing you." He tucked a paper into my cargo pocket.

Chapter Four: Near Miss

After I angled my Jeep into the parking spot just past the drive through, I turned in my seat holding the pup cups. Winnie's face was in the white and green cup so fast, I was grateful I never painted my nails, lest she get confused and eat my hand. Whipped cream splattered all over the skin of my thumb and fingers as she worked deeper and deeper into the two inch tall cup.

Ruger was not as enthusiastic.

He sniffed at the cup, eyes downcast to the floorboard somewhere beneath the pet hammock I'd re-installed. Since we'd left the lawyer's office, his already subdued mannerisms had wilted into an almost catatonic state. My own mood was mirrored in his, so I pulled into the nearest coffee chain for the largest, pumpkin-est, least reasonable beverage they'd serve me and two pup cups. But as he lay there, refusing the whipped cream, I wondered if not even coffee and sugar could fix this.

"Come on, baby boy, it's good?" I encouraged while using my other arm to keep Winnie away from him. The black dog barely lifted his head before he angled away curled into a void ball. Withdrawing my arm, I put the full cup in the cupholder and picked up my own. Taking a long drink, I waited for the caffeine and sugar to somehow solve all my life's problems like it usually did.

Fall had started to hit as October soldiered on. Beside the roadway, leaves were changing into a rainbow of red, orange, and brown above a light blanket of fallen friends already spilled on the ground. The cooling weather meant we were nearly back into hoodie season, and I'd been home from the Army for a year. Soon the tumultuous pace of autumn into winter and the holiday season would give way to the gloomy new year, and we'd be... right where we are now.

Missing a force for good that had been snuffed out for reasons we didn't know.

"This sucks." I put my coffee back in the holder and backed out of the parking space. We had a thirty-minute ride back to Sweet Pea and the entire rest of our day to fill with... probably more coffee. Baileys if I had any, but I think I drank all of that the day I got the news, and my gastrointestinal system refused to allow me to purchase more. Somehow, my liver agreed, and we ended up leaving the grocery store yesterday with just a mountain of cheese and edible cookie dough.

Coffee and unbaked cookies would have to do.

My phone rang over the car's Bluetooth, and I stabbed the answer call button without looking.

"Hello?"

"Hey, Cyn," Larry said through my car's speakers, and I flinched. Though talking to people had the potential to be a decent distraction, talking to Larry these days usually ended in either an argument or me throwing something. Our break-up wasn't all that messy, at least not the second time... or the first time... or the third.

How many times did we break up? I should probably start naming them, but they all came down to "that time your mother was an ass" or "you didn't respect my boundaries and autonomy". None of which he refused to listen to as he insisted that we get back together and I was reminded why I hadn't wanted to date him in the first place.

"I wanted to see if you were bringing Ruger in. He's done with his follow-ups from the injury, but... I heard he was in the room when the body was found, and I want to make sure he's OK." His words ran all together, like he thought I'd hang up if he took a breath. It was the most to the point he'd ever been in a phone conversation, and it halted my brain mid train of thought.

Larry held his breath over the line, waiting for a verdict.

"Probably should." I glanced at a sign that said I was still twenty-five miles from Sweet Pea while Larry remained silent on the other end of the line. When a quarter mile passed without a peep, I checked the screen to see if the call was still connected. The numbers continued upward, and I hesitated to fill the silence. "Are you... free today?"

I cleared my throat, trying not to sound like anything other than a normal patient.

"I have some time."

His vague answer grated but I bit back my usual snark. We were no longer sex friends, or even regular friends, so perhaps this was how exes conversed. It was not an experience I was familiar with since I didn't really date before him, nail and bail being a miliary artform for men and women, but if it was, I'd respect the custom.

"We'll be back in the area in half an hour. Do you have an opening we can be scheduled for... sometime after that?" My fingers tightened on the wheel until each knuckle was white, and my forearms throbbed. Formality and professionalism were painful, and that was before the conversation was with someone I'd seen naked.

"Yeah. Just come by the clinic whenever you get back into town," he replied, and I nodded.

"Cool. Thanks." I started trying to slowly pry my fingers from the steering wheel to end the call, when he cleared his throat. "Yeah?"

The silence stretched on, and I considered ending the call and claiming it was an accident when questioned later. Nothing good comes when the man hesitates to speak but...

"I bought out the Carter's share in my practice." He exhaled like the words weighed the same as my Jeep and I bobbed awkwardly.

"That's... cool. So, you won't have to work at Eggplants anymore?" I tried not to shudder at all the squirrel food visuals I'd gotten in the male strip club. So many of my PI "cases" had ended up with me there, looking at a man's nuts, and never for a reason that made sense. Larry had been working there as a bartender when I first met Levi and though his junk was covered, I was secretly grateful the opportunity to show it off for more money would never be granted to him.

"I won't be... but there's something you should know about the money." My phone beeped with call waiting and I glanced at the display.

"My ma's calling. I'll see you in a bit, yeah?" I clicked off before he could go on, answering my mom. She wasn't exactly high on my list of casual conversationalists, but on The Awkward Scale, she blew Larry clean out of the water.

"Hi, ma," I answered.

"Cynthia!" she shouted into the line, and I turned the volume down on my speakers. Hopefully there was no permanent damage to the subwoofer, because my hearing would never recover.

"Yeah, ma. You don't need to yell."

"Where are you?" She was still shouting, but neither of the dogs in the back was disturbed by her voice. Growing up, I couldn't remember her shouting keeping me awake either, so perhaps it was an acquired trait for self-preservation.

"Driving back from the will reading. What's up?" I winced when I remembered I hadn't told her about the will reading, or Trigger's death... or Ruger. She would not be happy to learn she was the last to find out about a new grandchild. Or that these two canines in my car would probably be it for grandchildren when it came to my loins.

"What will reading? Who died? Was it that old bat, Mrs. Margot's sister?"

Touched a nerve there...

Mrs. Margot's sister was like the uncensored version of my mom... which was saying something because my mom's bathrobe had never been tied.

"No ma, it was Trigger. I um... he left me Ruger. His dog. I'll bring him by after the vet checks him out. What do you have against the other Margot?" I tried to gloss over my visit to Larry so she wouldn't get her hopes up. Much like Mo, my mom was deeply invested in me being happily... kept in orgasms.

She didn't actually care who they came from or if we were in a serious or stable relationship.

Contrary to Midwest mother stereotypes, she was also not concerned with whether or not I procreated or if those orgasms came from a man. Two out of three of my older siblings had provided enough progeny to satisfy that genetic need, and my lesbian sister and I were off the hook.

Sadly, we were still expected to lead fulfilling sex lives... and take copious notes. While my sister obliged, my notes generally contained the words "mind your own business".

"Trigger? That man who owns the shooting range?" Her voice had kicked up another decibel and Winnie shook out her massive ears in the back seat. "Wasn't he on that jury?"

"Yeah. Wait, how do you know about that?" I asked, then instantly regretted the question. My mom knew about everything.

Between her job as a professor for the local community college, her position as a town council elder, and her salacious social life with the other seniors in town, there was no one my mom didn't know the business of. Being on top of a federal case tried in our state was child's play compared to keeping track of who was currently boinking who and whether or not they were up to date on vaccinations and venereal disease testing.

"Cynthia, that case is national news. Why wouldn't I know about it? I'm not an out of touch, old lady! I read!" She huffed into the phone line, and I itched the spot between my shoulder blades against the back of my seat.

"I know, ma. I'm not questioning your knowledge of true crime, just who was serving on the jury... Wasn't it a sequestered, anonymous deal?" I rubbed my back harder, anxiety making me itchier. My mom was like a living speakerphone and coming out of my car was like having a PA system of judgement.

"You know, nothing that includes a single member of this town or a neighboring one is a secret." She scoffed at the audacity of such a thought, and I silently agreed. Not even our town's dispatcher was required to keep anything she heard confidential. Jenny had refused to sign the confidentiality clause and no one else wanted the job, leaving the old chief between a gossip and a ringing phone.

So much worse than a rock and a hard place, since both involved the sound of someone annoying.

"Fair. So, what's up?" I tapped my finger on the steering wheel, anxiety crawling in as the signs for Sweet Pea started declaring I was less than ten minutes away. It was not every day one had to go see their ex with a new dog and suspicions his owner was murdered.

"I need you to come to dinner," my mom proclaimed. The thrumming fingers on the steering wheel stuttered while I tried to parse out the words.

"You what?"

"You need to come to dinner. Tonight, no excuses. I know you don't have work and Seth mentioned that his coworker you've been dating has to work late, so I know that you're free."

My mouth worked like a hooked fish, but no words came out. "But..."

"It's not negotiable. I'll see you at seven," she concluded and hung up.

Two sets of ears poked up from the back seat.

"Well, that was rude," I muttered, turning into the dirt parking lot for Kirby's Critter Care. "She could have at least said goodbye."

I pulled my Jeep into the lot beside Larry's pickup. Brianna's car wasn't present, and I wondered if he'd hired another vet tech or if I was walking into a "spend time alone with Larry" situation.

"Maybe we should wait until someone else comes to the clinic..." I said to the dogs, Winnie's hot doggy breath right against my neck. Condensation formed and drool dripped along my spine. "Ick! Ok! OK! Geez!"

Wiping the slime off my neck with the sleeve of my shirt, I opened the car door and hauled myself out. Winnie clambered over the front seat and raced to the clinic door at top speed while

Ruger waited patiently for me to shut my door and open his. Then he held still while I lifted him down from the too-high seat and placed him on all four paws in the lot. His energy was still low, but his nose was damp, which I took for a good sign.

"Ow! Damnit, Winnie! I've had my prostate checked!"

I whipped around at the male exclamations of distress to see a folded over Larry and a pleased Winnie with her nose in his junk. The man's pained expression gave me an un-ladylike amount of glee that was probably both petty and totally justified as Ruger lumbered over at a more respectable pace. They were all congregated in the doorway to the clinic, Larry's lean, muscular frame clothed in scrubs while his dark brown hair looked mussed above wire-framed glasses.

After surgery paperwork day, I concluded. A true testament to how well and how long we'd known each other. Scrubs, plus glasses, and no other staff meant he'd spent the day saving furry lives.

"Did you tell her to do that?" He wheezed up at me and I just shook my head. A smirk playing at the corners of my mouth.

"No one needs to tell her to do such things. She just does them, this is the way."

"I'm sure you are *super* on top of telling her not to, too." He held open the door for us to go inside, muttering quietly about lucky they're cute. Ruger paused on his way past for an ear scrunch which Larry fulfilled, before we were all standing in the poorly furnished waiting room. Dr. Lawrence Kirby, DVM, was technically a commercial vet. Until the town's only other vet went on a sapphic romance cruise that never ended, he hadn't needed a waiting room, and this space had been a library with no exterior access. When she left, he became the sole caregiver for all the animals, both commercial, domestic and wild, for the whole town.

Forcing him to put in a public access door and a waiting area.

"Where is everyone?" I asked, glancing at the reception desk. I wasn't completely sure who staffed it. The techs had taken turns while he tried to find a receptionist, but a layer of dust said the answer was currently nobody.

Larry's hand went to the back of his head, rubbing behind his neck and showing a sliver of abs that stole all the moisture from my mouth.

"They're gone for the day. We're actually only doing surgery on Thursdays and then everyone heads home so I can get paperwork done."

A buzzing replaced his words in my ears as I just stared at the exposed bit of skin I'd definitely bit before... Even confirmation I was right couldn't bring me back to this planet.

"Cyn?"

"Yeah?"

Silence took over the clinic. Fluorescents hummed overhead, and I was painfully aware of a faucet dripping somewhere in the back while outside traffic streamed by at a rate of two cars per four heartbeats. Winnie's head butted against my hand, forcing me to look away from him and down to her.

"Hi, girl." Ruger sat on my foot, and I scratched under his chin. "Hey handsome."

Larry cleared his throat, and I made eye contact with him, strategically avoiding a visual route that would take me past any part of him I might want to put in my mouth.

"Do you have his records?"

"Yeah, they're in the car. I'll go grab them." I glanced down at the anchor on my foot. "Excuse me."

With a long, tortured sigh, Ruger lay down and cleared a path off of my foot. Chuckling, I turned toward the door and opened it to a white Ford Taurus pulling into the lot.

"Looks like you have a-" The window rolled down to reveal the barrel of a gun and I flung myself back inside as the shots peppered the side of the building and glass cascaded around us.

Chapter Five:
Un-Closed Case

"Why aren't you shooting back?" Larry shouted, the shots ending as quickly as they started. My body was hovered protectively around Winnie and Ruger while my foot was jammed against the door. My leg braced for impact that never came.

"I don't have my gun."

The silence continued, gravel crunching outside and I chanced it. Crawling to the window, I crawled up the adjoining wall and peered out in time to see the car turning left onto the highway with the tires squealing.

No rear plate.

"Why don't you have your gun? You're always armed! You love shooting things and people." He was pressed against the floor.

I searched my pockets for my phone. When I came up empty, I went over to the vet who'd flipped a table and taken cover. He'd corralled both dogs with him behind it and I tried not to be too soft inside that he'd taken care to secure them.

It was probably part of being a vet.

"I don't love shooting people. I love punching assholes in the face. Shooting people is messy. And no one has been shooting at me, so I didn't think I needed to take a gun to a will reading, OK?" I saw the outline of his phone in his pants pocket and stuck my hand in there to grab it.

"People are shooting at you now!"

"No, really? Is that where bullets come from? Thank dog you're here, Larry. I'd be lost without you." I unlocked his phone and called emergency, preparing to shout at Jenny until she connected me with Carla only to luck out.

"Sweet Pea Emergency," Carla said, annoyance evident in her voice.

"Carla! Someone shot at me, and through the front window of Kirby's Critter Care. White, Ford Taurus, probably a 2000s model with no rear plate. They went west on the highway about a minute ago. No injuries here."

"Did you tag the car? Any external damage you made that I could tell the staties in the BOLO? Bullet holes and leaking fluids are easier to spot than a generic car." She asked, full cop mode activated.

"I didn't return fire. Aside from the lack of plate, the shots came from the passenger-"

"Why didn't you return fire?" She interrupted, and I huffed out a breath. Keeping below the window, I worked to the front door of the office and slid the deadbolt into place before moving back toward Larry and the canines beside the upturned waiting room coffee table.

"Because I don't have my gun. It was a long barrel, probably a ri-"

"But you're always armed!"

"No one's shot at me recently!"

When she remained silent, I considered just hanging up and tracking down the shooter myself, but I heard furious typing on the other end of the call that let me know she was working. I picked at a stain on the coffee table, keeping everyone low to the ground.

"OK, people have been alerted, and Daniel is on his way over. Stay away from windows and anything with a clear line of sight. Do you want me to call you back on this phone number or yours when Daniel gets there?"

"Does it have to be Daniel? Why aren't you coming?" I asked, seeing Larry raise an eyebrow out of the corner of my eye. His brother may have once been hot, but he'd never been competent or intelligent. Family loyalty aside, I'd rather she dispatched Judy Hopps from Zootopia than Deputy Kirby and that was a fictional cartoon rabbit.

"Because I'm dispatching and not out in the field for a while. This phone?"

"Yeah, Larry can talk to his own brother." I huffed out a breath and could nearly hear laughter on her end. "Any reason Larry can't give Ruger his check-up since we're here? I guess I can't get his records from outside until Deputy Dumb Dum arrives, but after?"

"That's between you and the doctor. I have to go." Something caught in her voice and I could barely hear the sound of her feet running before she dropped the phone call.

"We need to stay away from windows. Can we go to an exam room and start the physical until your brother gets here and then I'll get the file?" I kept an eye and an ear toward the lot, and it was quiet out there. Larry shrugged and started to stand. "Hey! Staying away from windows means you stay low!"

"Are you kidding? I have to crawl on the floor?"

"Do you want to get shot?" I countered, crouching low and doing a bear crawl up the lobby until I reached the mouth of the hallway. There were no windows in this section, allowing me to rise to my full height while Larry followed behind. Winnie and Ruger watched us, Winnie's eyebrows dancing in thought while the large black dog was just staring, his large head resting on crossed paws.

"Come on," I hissed at the dogs, waving them over. "But stay low!"

Both rose to normal height and trotted over with no regard for my warning.

Their general lack of height was not necessarily an excuse to walk normally.

"Looks like your new dog listens as well as your other one does." Dr. Kirby snickered, opening the door to an exam room with a number 3 beside the door. There was a metal table inside that rose and lowered, a counter with a small computer, drawers, and a few glass jars with vet office essentials sitting on the top.

"Shut up, Larry." I scooped Ruger into my arms and placed him on the exam table. The dog wasn't as heavy as Winnie, but he somehow felt denser. Like despite his stature, he'd packed on significantly more volume and could double as a battering ram if I needed to break and enter somewhere. "What do you need me to do?"

The doctor wiggled his eyebrows, and I flipped him a middle finger.

"Hold him steady for me." Larry switched modes into a professional doctor. He took a plastic sleeve and a thermometer from a drawer and put the two together. With a little lube, he checked Ruger's temperature and then moved on to listening with his stethoscope, followed by gentle palpitations of his dog shape, noting a bit of pain reactivity when pressure was applied to his rear leg where he sustained a knife wound protecting Trigger.

"How many times a day is he doing the stairs in your apartment?"

"I don't know… morning bathroom, after breakfast bathroom, return from work, after dinner. I guess four-ish?"

"Shit, Cyn. That's a lot for his leg, especially the stairs in that apartment."

"I thought it was healed!" I hugged Ruger close, apologizing with kisses.

"He's still not equipped to do stairs that often."

"Are you saying I should move or carry him? Or build a ramp?"

"I wouldn't dare give you life advice. I'm just saying he'll reinjure himself trying to do those steep stairs that often. Do you think he'd let me draw blood?"

Ruger and I exchanged a look. I personally thought if he took a thermometer in his backside, a needle in the paw was no big deal, but maybe he had different thoughts. I was still reeling from all the accusations about how I'd failed him after only being his guardian for a week.

The dog gently licked my hand, and I nodded back at him.

"Yeah, I think you can go for it," I advised and tried not to look at the needle Larry prepared.

"I don't have a vet tech; can you shave this region?" He pointed to an area about four fingers above the articulation point between the paw and leg. I looked at the razor and Ruger's tan dog sock. He looked as enthusiastic about this whole experience as I did when I was forced to be in the hospital after one of my "incidents". Taking his paw, I pet the region a few times and when he didn't withdraw it, I shaved it, so the skin was visible and the ridge of veins more obvious.

Larry moved in, swiping it with an alcohol wipe, inserting the needle and filling a tube with anti-coagulant so efficiently I nearly missed it. He pressed a four-by-four gauze pad against the spot and pointed toward a stretch bandage roll. I handed it over and he wrapped the gauze pad to the dog's paw, tearing off the roll and setting it aside while Ruger continued to lay there in a partially lethargic state.

"Has he been eating?" Larry grabbed a treat from the jar on his doctor side of the exam table. "Drinking water and eliminating normal? How have his bowel movements been?"

Ruger declined the treat and let out a long huff, placing his large head on his paws.

"Some. They gave me a bag of food for him, but it was in a Ziplock, and the sketchy lawyer's assistant couldn't tell me what it was or what was in it, so I started weaning him off it onto what Winnie eats. Today I found out that the lawyer is being blackmailed and has cash problems, so that's going straight in the trash when I get home—liquid poop be damned. His water consumption has been mostly normal, but he only eats some of the food. I expected some poop troubles with the sudden change, but they've been squishy not liquid…"

"There's some initial tests I can do here, but a lot of the tests are done off-site and I won't have answers immediately, but maybe do the bland diet for awhile? Boiled chicken and rice?"

A loud pounding shook the office at the same time Larry's cell started ringing.

He answered while I opened his cabinets, searching for knives.

"I'm stuck outside! You better not be hooking up while I'm standing out here!" Daniel's voice exploded from the phone, and I rolled my eyes. Stomping toward the front, I summoned Winnie and had her scent the air above the window.

She made a "gross" face, confirming only Daniel was here.

I unlocked and opened the door while remaining behind it for cover. Daniel strutted in without checking and Winnie shoved her head into his junk, sending the man doubling over in pain.

"Damnit, dog!"

"You should know better than to walk into a place without checking, Deputy." I shut and locked the door with a hefty dose of sarcasm while staying clear of the vacant window frame. "It's a poor officer that blames the attacker for his own failures."

"Ugh." He rose, trembling slightly, and stood in direct view of the broken window.

How is this idiot not dead?

"I wanted to get your statement and confirm what caliber you were shooting before I started checking for casings and embedded rounds. Need to make sure I knew which were the shooter's and which were yours." He winced, face red as he ambled awkwardly and spoke in a high pitched murmur.

"They should all be the attackers unless Larry takes potshots at cars on his lunch break." I moved farther from the window, taking shelter closer to the coffee table. Daniel standing in plain sight was honestly too tempting a target for most people. Not just shooters, but water balloons, paintballs, and flaming bags of poop.

I'd rather be shot for something I did than caught in the crossfire of revenge against Daniel.

"What about when you returned fire?" Daniel was standing with his hands on his hips, surveying the broken glass and the coffee table we tipped for cover.

"I didn't return fire."

"Why not?"

"I don't have my gun. But the shooter was in the passenger seat-"

"Why don't you have your gun? You're always armed!"

"For the love of dog! No one has been shooting at me recently! I didn't think I needed to be armed to go to the reading of a will. I'll be sure henceforth and furthermore to take a gun with me everywhere. Pooping, screwing, pants, no pants, I'll make sure my under-boob has space to hold my weapon, OK?" I slammed the table back upright and pointed to a hole in the wall. "That's where the bullet is stuck if you want it. There's probably one or two in the exterior façade. I heard three shots total. Now excuse me while I see if they make sweat absorbing under boob holsters and if not, find a craft store to sell me supplies to sew one."

Winnie followed me down the hall away from Daniel. I didn't have a destination in mind besides away from him and ended up in Larry's office. Ruger was already there, stretched out on a dog bed in the corner with all four of his paws in the air and his front toofers showing like a vampire bat. Winnie walked over and flopped down beside him, head resting on his neck while I stole Larry's desk chair and spun in quarter circles facing his ceiling.

Who the hell was shooting at me now?

I rotated side to side, thinking about this past month. The only "cases" I'd investigated were petty theft and neighbor disputes. A few would-be hauntings if the homeowners weren't Mr. Magoo level blind, and one missing pet case that wasn't actually missing but taking a nap at the neighbor's house because children are loud and annoying.

"Cyn?" Larry knocked on his own door frame. I lifted my head to look at his scrunched expression and the few sheets of paper clutched in his grip. He was viewing them and eyeing the dog, something not adding up in his doctor brain.

"Sup?"

"Has Ruger gotten into anything at your apartment or at the farm?"

"No. He mostly just lays places. I think he's depressed, which... I guess we all are? His human died." I stared at the large black dog as well and Winnie nudged him with her nose. He let out another sigh and his stomach audibly burbled.

"I think..." Larry looked at his papers, back to Ruger before finally meeting my gaze. "I think he was being poisoned."

"What? What do you mean? Why would someone poison him?" I asked, flinging myself gracelessly to the floor to hug him tight. "Will he be OK?"

"I think so. We should give him an IV with some electrolytes to flush his system. And we might definitely switch him to the bland diet. Throw away anything they gave you with him, food, treats... anything he can put in his mouth."

"Even his toys?" I asked, looking at the dog. It may have been personification, but I had a feeling the toys held memories of his person.

"If you can't wash them, or they are filled somehow, yeah. I'm sorry, but..."

Daniel walked up, looking between me and the two dogs.

"Huh..."

"What now?" I demanded, trying not to cry for Ruger. He was a good dog; he did not deserve to be poisoned. I was going to throw out every kibble of dog food in my apartment and replace all of it with new, clean kibble and take all the toys I could to my parent's dishwasher. It's possible it was left over from whatever they'd used on Trigger, but if he was being poisoned...

"You knee anyone in the junk recently so they might want to kneecap you?"

"What? No. Why?" I looked around the room with renewed confusion. If he was threatening me, I was pretty sure I could find something to make him regret it. "Is that an invitation to hit you in the nuts with a baseball bat?"

He backed up and clutched at his bits.

"No, because all of bullets were aimed about two and half feet off the ground, based on where they were lodged. I assume someone was trying to kneecap you as revenge for their junk."

"No, I've left every man's junk alone... at least recently. Are you sure they weren't just a really bad shot?" I asked, still searching the room for a weapon to protect myself from Daniel. He was probably not a threat, but it was good practice to always have something to hit him with in hand.

"The groupings were all downward. A bad shot gets the angle right at least once or twice."

"There were only 3 shots, Daniel! How can you determine a pattern? That's like calling someone who kills two people a serial killer, but those two people were in the same room, and one was the spouse, and the other was the dude they were cheating on them with." I picked up a leather-bound textbook and tested the weight. Seemed like a solid blunt force option, but did I really want to do that to a book?

"First of all, your choice of analogical comparisons is disturbing and I'm glad you aren't marrying into my family." Larry huffed out a breath in the corner and I resisted the urge to roll my eyes. This conversation and relationship were old news. "Second, when all three shots hit within a few inches of each other, I think it's safe to declare it a grouping and a general location."

Daniel extended his phone, and I paused my search to stare at the three bullet holes. One in the door trim, and two in the far wall almost perfectly in line with it.

"How did the window break?" I asked and Daniel swiped to a picture of a rock. "Sure... Why waste bullets when there's rocks. So, if no one wanted to kneecap me, what else do you think they could have been targeting?"

I was still holding the large book, but I was now looking at my lower body for offensive, shootable, parts.

"Well, if they weren't trying to shoot you," Daniel began, his eyes flicking to the corner of the room, and I followed his line of sight. "Then they were trying to shoot one of your dogs."

I dropped the book.

Chapter Six: Breaking News

Every finger was wrinkled and slightly singed, but the dog toys were still not clean.

All of the durable chew ones were in a box to take to my parent's house, their dishwasher a better bet than my scrubbing skills at getting into the tooth grooves and cleaning the dishes that might have touched poisoned food and water. On the way home, I'd stopped at the grocery store for chicken and rice, then the pet store and bought all-new food, dog dishes, and dog dish mats. Every kibble of dog food in my house was tossed in the dumpster out back with a silent prayer that the raccoons would be smart enough not to eat it.

Then, for the past hour, I'd been scrubbing everything.

The new dishes were cleaned and sanitized, water supplied in new stainless steel bowls on all new absorbent mats in new dish holders. Ruger was asleep on his back in the new collar I bought until I could wash his old one, while the open windows attempted to dilute the scent of bleach from the floor, counter, and fridge scrubbing I'd conducted.

Pulling out the last green tennis ball, I dropped it onto the towel with its other heavily scrubbed brethren and pulled the plug of my sink. My heartbeat was still too high, the fitness tracker on my left wrist buzzing that I needed to relax was fighting a losing battle with the anxiety twisting my guts.

"No one can hurt you guys," I mumbled, as the fire door at the bottom of my stairs opened unannounced. I picked up the black semi-auto pistol from my counter and leveled it at the opening of the stairwell leading into the apartment. "Whoever is there, you better announce yourself or I will shoot you!"

"Cyn?" Levi called, and I set the gun back on the counter. "It's Levi."

"Hey, you can come up," I shouted back.

Footsteps continued up the staircase. Levi's floppy light brown hair and wire-rimmed glasses came into view, then his square jaw, long sleeve henley, jeans and work boots. He was still gorgeous, and there were abs under that shirt that were positively sinful, but I noticed a complete lack of interest in my belly at the sight of him.

No butterflies.

No excitement.

We hadn't connected in a week and instead of wanting to jump his bones, I just wanted to jump into bed and take a nap. It could have been the depression, or my general overwhelm, but I had a feeling we really just weren't that into each other.

"Hey. I thought you had to work?" I asked, walking around the counter to give him a hug. He held on extra tight but didn't go in for the kiss. It was confirmation of what I'd suspected, and I knew everything I needed in that moment. Letting go, I took a step back and inclined my head toward the couch. He nodded and we sat down while I kept an eye on the chicken and rice in the instant pot.

"I did, but I left a little early. Can we talk?"

"About how you don't think this is working out and maybe we should see other people?" I decided to just get the stupid conversation over with by filling in the end game. He reached behind his head to scratch the back of his neck, raising his shirt to show me some of the glorious abs that had sucked me in and I ogled them... Despite the lack of chemistry and common interests, I was going to miss those abs.

"So, you feel it too?" Levi was still a little bamboozled. His light brown eyes looked between the two dogs, and I remembered again how horrified he was the first time he spent the night, sober, and woke up with a Winnie tail in his face. "You aren't going to like, tell your mom I broke your heart, and she should lock me in her sex dungeon?"

"Nah, dude. Also, gross. If I were going to throw you any-where, it would be in that freight container your uncle locked us in, but I'm too tired to be vengeful." I patted him on the shoulder awkwardly while his face paled at the memory. His uncle had tried to kill me, and his aunt, and had successfully killed at least two other people, so it was a pretty safe assumption this relationship had always been a little doomed. Levi was fun while he lasted, but he was more or less wallpaper, nice to look at, interesting to touch, but overall, just a nice aesthetic whose time had passed.

"I'm... sorry about that." He swallowed and started eyeing the exit.

"It happens." I shrugged and he turned to stare at me. "What?"

"Shouldn't you be... more concerned?"

"I ran out of norepinephrine about ten minutes ago, so my fight or flight is offline. I'll jumpstart it if a living threat appears."

Standing, I moved toward the kitchen to grab the giant bag of dog toys, my laundry bag, and my car keys. The instant pot beeped, and I disconnected the cord to bring that along as well. Taking his cue from me, Levi also stood up and patted his pockets. He hadn't taken anything out of them when he arrived, but it was a nervous tick to make sure he didn't drop anything that would force him to return.

"Do you need help with all that?" he asked, and I shook my head.

"I've got it, but thanks. Have a good night." I watched his backside as he left for the last time.

Seth and Heidi's cars were already in the driveway when I pulled up to my parent's house. Heidi lived a little over an hour away, so if she made the trip in, I could expect my sister Molly would be joining us via Skype with her wife.

Yes, most people used Zoom now, but my parents were using Skype until it was officially eliminated, and they were forced to use different technology. There was a rumor the end of life and shut down was upon us, and I was not prepared for the phone calls begging for tech support but some things in life were just inevitable.

"Alright kids," I said to the two canines in my backseat. "There are probably a lot of children on the other side of that door. Heidi's two kids, two teenagers and Seth's two... well, one kid and one Satan-possessed miniature war crime in progress. You need to stay close, stay alert and know when to hide."

Winnie sneezed in a way that suggested this was not a war zone, but Ruger gave me side eye at that. The tip of his tail wiggled softly and I reached around to pat his head.

"It's not going to be the worst thing to happen to us today, but it might be the loudest."

Two quick raps sounded on my window and I jumped, reaching for the gun in my center console before seeing Carla on the other side. Blowing out my breath, I opened the door and climbed out, stuffing the weapon in my cargo pocket and visually clearing the street before letting the dogs out through the back door. Winnie took her usually flying leap while I helped Ruger down more gently.

"Good to see you're taking this threat seriously." She watched my dogs while I circled the car and unloaded my bag of human and dog washings as well as the locked and hot instant pot. "Were you trying to give yourself a pep talk?"

"Warning Ruger what horrors await him inside." I trudged across the front yard and up the two step front stoop to the blue front door. Though I'd grown up in this house, I was never really prepared for what awaited me on the other side of the door since returning from the Army. Could be another broken arm, pot brownies, a sex toy sales event, or just a normal family dinner with all of my siblings and their offspring.

"What level of violence has Sylvie chosen today?" I asked, knowing that going in blind was often a safer choice, but I didn't actually want to go inside yet.

A scream cut through the house before me and my shoulders crawled up to protect my neck.

"Yeah... she's in a mood."

Carla let out a breath, her hands on her abdomen.

Her slightly distended and pouchy abdomen.

"Oh shit, are you..." I swallowed as another scream cut through the house and Ruger flattened his ears. Slinking low, he tried to hide behind me.

"Yeah... and she's pissed." Carla squirmed. I wanted to hug her, but my hands were full, and I was terrified if I hugged too hard the baby would pop out like it was on a flume ride. Having watched dozens of animals be born had not dissuaded me of the notion that you could accidentally push a baby out.

"Congratulations!" I tried to look excited for her, and she laughed. "I guess this is why you aren't in the field?"

"Thanks. Yeah, it's an adjustment. We didn't do it on purpose... We just got a little carried away-"

"Nope!" I interrupted her, throwing open the front door. Winnie stormed in, locating Sylvie like a heat-seeking missile. Together, they could bring the world to its knees.

Ruger flattened himself on the concrete and refused to enter.

"I know, baby." I crouched low to stroke his head, giving him kisses. Carla went inside to see if she could do anything about the untold horrors within, though I doubted she'd have any sort of luck if her pregnancy was the trigger. "I know it's scary. But we have to go inside. You can hide out in the basement, or the backyard, but in order to get there, we have to get through here."

Winnie reappeared in the doorway; the telltale orange flecks of artificial cheese substance stuck to her muzzle.

"Damn that kid," I grumbled, but the dog lowered her head and licked Ruger. He raised one eyebrow, black nose working rapidly before his tail started thumping gently in excitement. Ruger looked to me, eyebrows alternating in question before I let out a small sigh. "Yeah, go get some damn cheese. Fair is fair."

He wiggled a little faster and inched forward a little farther, the low crawl of the optimistically terrified. Despite the excitement and the promise of snacks, he still wasn't sure. I walked in first, hauling my load, and dropped the laundry nearest the door to the basement. With a free hand I turned back to my new charge and motioned him in.

Ruger entered the house and I smiled. His nose started going again and he followed it toward the kitchen. Grabbing my sack of dishwasher goods and their dinner, I let him lead me. Just before we entered, I called out. "Dad, are you wearing pants?"

Silence came from the kitchen with the sizzle of cooking noises.

"Dad?"

Someone was humming and I peeked around the corner to see my dad in his usual jeans and a sweater with elbow patches. His outfit was covered by a pink apron, and his ears protected from the chaos with headphones the same size and shape as I wore to the shooting range.

Standing beside him in a matching set of headphones was Seth's son, Erich, who was humming. Ruger walked cautiously up to the boy and bumped his stirring elbow with the short snoot. Erich startled slightly, then turned to pet the dog, looking up at me with a smile.

Hi, I mouthed at him.

Erich stole a zucchini from my dad's cutting board and offered it to Ruger who happily chomped the veggie. Deciding this was his favorite person, Ruger sat on Erich's foot and accepted pets while the boy continued stirring with his other hand. Smiling, I walked all the way into the kitchen and opened the dishwasher, grateful to find it empty.

"What are you doing?"

I jumped out of my skin and clutched my chest.

"Geez, Ma! Volume," I croaked, waiting for my heartrate to return below stroke level. "I know it's loud in here, but you don't need to be a foghorn."

"What are you putting in my dishwasher?" She said again, only slightly quieter. I continued to add dog toys onto the top rack. At least two looked like dildos, so I guess her confusion was warranted, if not her indignation. If I were putting dildos in here, they would not be the first to grace this dishwasher and the number of users would be limited to just me.

"Dog toys. And dog dishes. I also need to wash a bunch of dog bedding and collars downstairs. And my underwear, but that's pretty normal…"

A surly teenager with teal streaks in her blonde hair and a clip-on nose ring slouched into the room. I knew by age it was my sister Heidi's kid, but I had no idea what her name was. Heidi had moved away initially, and the first two kids were born on the west coast somewhere, and by the time she moved back pregnant with kid number four, I was in college. When I got home from the Army, the first two were well into being teenagers and I avoided her house and them.

Teenagers scared the living shit out of me.

When my sister came over, she was usually solo and helping my mom with some manner of eighteen plus behavior that children resulted from. The one time her husband was also here, I hadn't thought to ask who had custody of her offspring. Looking at this one, I suspected it might have fallen to her and wasn't that a kick in the pants.

Like the rest of the Sharp women, her figure was full and accentuated by the teenage clothing of high waisted jeans and crop tees. If I had to guess, it probably wasn't a pleasant experience for her in school. Her ears had white wireless headphones inserted into the opening, music drifting over occasionally with a heavy beat, and I guessed that like Erich, she had sensory processing issues.

Unlike Erich, I doubted she had ever been formally diagnosed or acknowledged.

"Why do you need to put them in my dishwasher?" My mother was indignant.

"Ma, there have been..." I dropped my voice. "Far less appropriate items in here."

"But these have been in dog mouths!"

"Some of those have been in people's... lower orifices," I hissed back and she clamped her lips shut going slightly pink. "Look, you know I scrub everything at home. But someone was poisoning Ruger. They also shot at him today. I just want to get everything extra clean, no chances. Just this once, can you..."

"Someone shot at you?" The teenager in the corner shouted and I swear it was like a record scratch. Dozens of faces appeared in the doorway. All of them sporting the Sharp build of tall, blonde and nosey, ranging in age from Sylvie's 8 to Heidi's freshly 50 and... however old her husband is.

"Technically, this time, it wasn't actually at me." I hedged, adding dish soap to the dishwasher and turning it on extra hot. "They were aiming for Ruger who happened to be near to me...

Well, him or Winnie… but based on the poison…I'd say Ruger was the target."

I looked at the German shepherd who was now standing beside my dad receiving vegetables alongside Ruger.

"Who would shoot at a dog?" One of the kids asked and I shrugged, the answer another question that had been gnawing at my insides for a while. It made as much sense as killing a juror and making it look like an accident. If the goal was a mistrial, wouldn't they want to make headlines?

"In Winnie's case… a lot of people. She's got enemies." The shepherd's eyebrows danced, and I nearly laughed. "Really, anyone whose been near her farts or on the receiving end of her prostate exams."

"Did you shoot back? Did you kill anyone? Was there blood?" Sylvie fired off excitedly and I watched Seth carry a laptop into the room with my sister Molly's face on it.

"No, I didn't have my gun. There was no blood."

"What? Why didn't you have your gun? Aren't you supposed to always be armed?" Molly said from the great Skype beyond.

"Aren't you supposed to be a pacifist?" I stuck out a hip and fisted my hand on it.

"What did Levi say? He said he was going to stop by and see you." Seth set my sister on the kitchen table while subtly corralling Sylvie toward a seat away from the sharp objects. The rest of the Sharp clan took seats along the benches, a few chairs appearing from the formal dining room.

"He said he wasn't that into me and we should date other people." I paraphrased, not ready to get into it. "I need to start some laundry. I'll be right back."

"Hang on." My mom touched my dad's arm. He took off his headphones and motioned for Erich to do the same. All around the table, my family quieted. "We have an announcement we'd like to make before you all start branching off and Molly has to go."

"Ma, I already know about Carla," I whispered, but she shook her head.

"No, it's about your father and I." She swallowed and he took her hand, the pair of them presenting a united front that brought me back to a few too many trips to the principal's office.

A bead of sweat dripped down my spine.

"As you know, we have been professors for a number of years. First at the university level, and then at the community college level, exploring the inter-relationships between society, sexuality, and community. It's been decades of discovery and learning, and we've stayed in the area to be near all of you despite numerous offers to guest instruct abroad."

My palms got damp, and I tried to swipe them down my cargo pants.

"With everything going on in this country, after decades of fighting and protesting, to end up right back here... It's just bullshit. We're ready for a break and we've decided to accept an offer to study in France. We'll be leaving at the end of the month."

Stunned silence filled the room and Seth cleared his throat.

"I guess we should also add..." He swallowed and looked at Carla. "That with the new baby coming, I've accepted a new position with better pay. Carla was offered a ranked admin position, so we'll also be moving... to Oregon the second week of November."

"Y-you're leaving?" I asked, looking between Carla and my parents. "You're both leaving?"

"Actually..." Heidi started, and I shook my head. "Cyn, we need to go back to—"

"No. Just... this can't... Just, no!" I shouted. I walked quickly to the entry way, grabbed the laundry sack, hauled it to the basement and when both dogs followed me, locked myself inside.

In one day, I'd managed to be dumped by the guy I was dating, my parents, and my siblings. My dog was being poisoned, and someone shot at us. I glanced at the bed and said a silent plea to whoever listened to atheists that I could fall asleep and wake up to the news this was all a dream.

Chapter Seven: Jury's Out

Coffee aromas greeted my nose just before the bed beside me dipped and my mom's vanilla coconut lotion filled the air.

"Rise and shine, Cyn."

It was a weird thing for her to say, and I squinted into the basement darkness to see if it was her or a pod person. The short blonde hair looked like hers, as did the short, round, Midwest frame with skin that would never tan. Her shabby pink bathrobe was still too long in the sleeves and too short in the middle, but none of that was impossible for a body snatcher to fake.

"Did you hit your head after I locked myself in the basement?" Scooting up in bed, I propped my back against the wall. On the floor were two stainless steel dishes, freshly cleaned of chicken and rice, and a bowl of clean water. "How did you get into the basement?"

"This place isn't Fort Knox, Cynthia. You can pop the lock with a screwdriver. After your siblings left, I came down and you were asleep, so I let the dogs out, gave them some food, and moved the laundry over. You slept like the dead."

She extended the coffee out to me, and I accepted. It was another odd gesture on her part. Normally, if I behaved poorly at family dinner, I could expect stern glances, to pour my own coffee and a whole lot of judgement. For some reason, this tantrum was being treated with kid gloves, and I was being forced to admit to myself that I had a tantrum.

"It's been a rough week, and I haven't been sleeping well. I'll call Seth and Heidi and apologize for being dramatic. Sorry to you as well. I know it's none of my business what you decide to do with your retirement." I took a long drink of the coffee, surprised when the sweetened drink made the bitter admission go down easier. "You are all doing what's best for yourselves and your families and that's what's important."

"And you?" She looked at me with her X-ray mom vision. "What's best for you? Do you need us here?"

I closed my eyes and took a few more sips of my coffee.

"Ma, you and dad were ready to be done with the whole parent thing before I came along, and you didn't really interfere a lot when I was growing up. I'm pretty self-sufficient and have learned to get by on my own. It's just this past year, I've gotten used to you, Carla and... OK, not so much Heidi, but I've gotten used to you guys being around. Helping out... It's hard to imagine this town without all of you." I spoke into the coffee mug, wondering if creamer was like tea leaves and my future could be found swirling inside.

"Are you going to stick around here?"

I swirled the coffee like a glass magic eight ball made with playing cards.

"Uncertain… I need to buy a house. Or rent a house. Some place without a bunch of stairs Ruger needs to tackle every time he wants to use the potty, and I have a job here. Buying or renting, the people with houses do not let you have the houses if you don't have a job." I took another drink and then stared up at the ceiling. "You said you were following the trial Trigger was on. Do you know what's happening?"

"They recessed for a week. But it's supposed to pick back up Monday. You can watch the recap videos." She pulled her phone out of her pocket and scooted up beside me. Side by side against the wall, her legs barely came to my knees while her head sat at my shoulders. It was a little too much perspective on how creepy Taylor Swift must have felt standing next to Sebrina Carpenter. "There's a bunch of clips online from the major news outlets, but there's a lot of people livestreaming from the galley. Governor Tommy Stump is a well-loathed narcissist, and people are waiting for him to be outed in open court."

"Isn't that illegal? I thought they took your phones before they let you into the courthouse?" I watched my mom type 'Marius Howser Trial' onto the video site and dozens of grainy courtroom video feeds filled the screen. Ruger was nestled beside me and Winnie shifted so that her back was spread lengthwise up my leg. It was sad commentary on my research skills that I never considered searching a video sharing site for clips.

"No, what did they teach you at that school?" She tutted and I rolled my eyes, looking at a clip from the day before Trigger died. The title was "Courtroom Chaos" and had over a million views.

"Can you click that one?" I asked and my mom obliged. The video started with regular proceedings, the backside of a man's head at the defense table hung in defeat. In the jury box, there were fourteen people, presumably the twelve regular jurors and two alternates, at least half of which were shifting. Their eyes kept darting toward the galley, the prosecution table, and something beyond what was shown in the video.

On the witness stand, a woman who resembled a praying mantis was being questioned by the defense lawyer. The questions were muffled but the answers were more emphatically no, over and over again until she shot up and flung out her arm... and her hand.

Which detached and landed in the jury box. Several of the jurors shouted, jumping up and running away. The courtroom erupted in sound, and Ruger growled.

I glanced beside me at the dog, his hackles up, growling at my mom's phone.

"Rewind it." I heard the video stop and go back to a question about gripping or grabbing and... the shouts started, his hackles went up and a low growl reverberated. "Pause it on a shot of the jury box."

I looked back at my mom who was holding out her phone and I scanned the box. In the upper corner, Trigger remained steadfast in his chair. Instead of looking at the hand, or the woman who had lost it, his eyes were firmly fixed on something behind the defense table.

So were the defendants.

"Damn…" I let out a breath and looked between the dog, the phone and an image of thirteen anonymous strangers in a public courtroom… full of suspects. "Mom, can you ask the town elders if they'll meet with me and maybe send them a picture of the jury?"

My mom looked between me and my new dog.

"You think one of them killed Trigger?"

"I think someone did. He doesn't fall down, he doesn't startle, and he doesn't go down without being pushed there. I was going to let it go, but the asshole poisoned my dog." I pulled the business card from my pocket and stared at the suit man's name. "Let's hope Griffin Allen can get me a meeting with a disgraced former campaign manager."

"I knew you'd call," Griffin smirked. We were standing outside the federal pen, my Jeep full of dogs next to his obnoxiously sized pick-up. The bed was filled with bales of hay and lengths of rope, the man himself looking like something out of a dirty novel in half-buttoned flannel shirt and tight in all the right places jeans.

Based on his clothes, he probably actually needed the truck for non-finance labor, but it was Friday.

Numbers man should have been working on numbers.

"What's with the getup? Posing for a fake farmer's only dating site?" We were walking up to the guard gate, a man who looked like Santa Clause sitting there watching CCTV with tired eyes and a clipboard.

"I own a farm near the dairy. We have horses and its feed day. The numbers, happily, continue to multiply with little effort on my part despite my continued salary." He smirked and Santa Claus gave us a partial acknowledgement with a flick of his eyes.

"Name?" He monotoned.

"Cynthia Sharp."

Security man nodded and paused with his pen above the paper, flashing his eyes at the man behind me.

"Griffin Allen."

Another nod.

"IDs?"

We both pulled out ID Cards. Mine issued by the State of Ohio; Griffins issued by... the Department of Defense?

"I thought you were a finance bro?" I hissed at him. The guard had checked our IDs and handed them back without much interest. "What the hell do you need D.O.D. clearance for?"

"I told you I work for the Navy Federal Credit Union, and I served in the Navy, special forces. How do you think I knew so much about you?" He chuckled and reached around me to open the door, his body brushing against mine with a zip of awareness. "Aside from what I've seen from my own farm."

"YouTube? Like everyone else," I grumbled. We were now facing a younger black woman with a clipboard and a metal detector. "Also don't watch people from your farm like a creeper. It makes you look... creepy."

"I'd have said hi, but you were usually knee-deep in catastrophe, and I was too far away to help."

I couldn't fault his reasoning, and it irked me.

"Gun check is over there, phones stay with me, and the prisoner will be waiting in Interview C."

I handed her my phone and started toward the metal detector.

"Don't you need to hand over your gun?" Griffin asked and I gave him my best death glare.

"I don't have a gun."

"Why not? Aren't PIs always supposed to be armed?"

"My gun is at home, OK?" I grumbled. "Where's your gun?"

He waggled his eyebrows instead of answering and I rolled my eyes.

"Shut up."

"I didn't say a word," he countered, passing through the metal detectors behind me and invading my personal space bubble. Two more buttons had come undone on his flannel, giving peek-a-boo glimpses of his smooth chest that were somehow not as appealing as his easy-going nature and general willingness to join me on stupid missions.

"Your face did, and it was rude."

"You don't like my face?" He flashed a dimple with his next smile. While I waited for the guard to pat me down, a man in scrubs passed by us toward the door labeled infirmary. The lower half of his face was covered with a paper mask, hands in gloves, but his buzz cut was on full display. Taking hold of the handle, he pushed open the door and I glimpsed an office behind it. A large metal desk with a coat rack just barely visible held a wool coat and a rumpled plastic dry cleaning bag with a paper hanger, bent and mangled like someone had stuffed it in a suitcase.

"Cyn?" Griffin handed me back a package of cookies that had fallen out of my pockets.

"Hmm?" The door shut on the office, and I tuned back into security who were staring, arms crossed and feet tapping, pointing to a bank of rooms in the opposite hall.

"We're meeting him in Interview C."

I shook off the weird sense of lost memory and followed them down the hall, prepared to meet the fall guy of an attempted murder.

Chapter Eight: Marius Howser

"I was wondering when you'd finally show up."

"You don't call, you don't write..." I did in my best impersonation of an Italian grandmother. When he snarled at me, I dropped the accent. "How the hell was I supposed to know you wanted me to come here? I don't know you."

Orange was not Marius's color. That was the first thought that popped into my head when I walked into the room. The man would have been better suited to the old time-y black and white stripes than the neon orange of modern days.

His once bronzed skin was now pale and yellow. Faded bruises marked his cheeks and knuckles, thick calluses taking shape on the inside of his palm. His shoulders still sagged in defeat, but the light in his eyes said he'd take this victory.

My second thought was that if he was winning that many prison fights, he might have attempted to murder someone.

"Woulda thought the second your friend turned up dead, you'd be itching to talk to the criminal on trial when he died." He sniffed indignantly, as if it was the most obvious next step.

"No offense, but you have a solid alibi for his time of death, so a personalized invitation would have helped." I sat across from him. Instead of taking the second chair, Griffin decided to hold up the wall under the video camera like a specter who couldn't be filmed.

In movies, interview rooms were little concrete boxes with a metal table that had loopholes for handcuffs and a few metal chairs. The suspect's chair was usually bolted to the ground, as was the table and one of the walls had a giant one-way glass mirror for people to observe. At Sweet Pea, it was just a giant wooden table in a portable trailer attached to the breakroom.

At the federal level, it was a stainless-steel table in the center of a concrete room, handcuff loops on the table and chair, weird tiles on the floor that were either yellow on purpose, or yellow from the days when smoking was treated as healthy, and a video camera in the corner.

Based on the smell of bleach that lingered in the air, it was also possibly the room they murdered people in.

"Who's that putz?" Marius jerked his head toward the cowboy in the corner. I spared a quick glance at Mr. Allen.

"My hairdresser, Clayton. Isn't he fabulous? I love the shaved chest look." I jokingly dragged the back of my fingers down my own sternum with my head thrown back. Both men looked down at Griffin's exposed chest, surprise and embarrassment turning the Navy man's cheeks pink. He quickly buttoned the top four buttons and sniffed, wiping under his nose to cover his face.

"Sorry. Didn't notice."

The former campaign manager scoffed and shook his head, leaning back to study us side by side.

"Compared to the others, I'm a little disappointed. I was hoping you'd be back with the Latin fellow. I heard he made it home from his mission, figured you two would get back together since you have another dog to train." His smooth, cultured voice cracked slightly from some sort of sustained damage that hadn't healed.

"Don't know who you're talking about," I lied. My stomach flipped and I felt slightly sick. If Cruz was back, I was happy for him. It would have been nice of him to relieve me of my guilt over thinking I'd gotten him killed, but whatever.

"Yeah, you do. And it looks like he wasn't interested in re-connecting. Pity, you're kinda cute in the right light." Marius did the slow once over and bile crawled up my throat. I wasn't interested in being ogled by pervs in federal prison, whether they'd been framed for their crime or not. He'd worked for, and alongside, a criminal. He'd known enough to be framed, and hadn't batted an eye until far too late for plausible deniability. So clearly, we were not working with a Zest-fully clean wrongful conviction candidate. At best, he was tried for the wrong thing before they found the right one to charge him with. "You could stand to drop a few pounds though if you ever want someone to bang you with the lights on."

Griffin snarled and kicked the metal table. The man chained to it jerked suddenly and smacked his head against the stainless-steel surface, releasing a small trickle of blood from his nose.

"What the hell, man? Chill!" I warned the once-Navy accountant. I was taken aback by his sudden fury, jaw and body clenched in anger while his back was straight enough to double as a flag pole. If I weren't in the middle of a major life crisis, I'd think he had a thing for me. "Do you need to step outside?"

"No," he growled, and I tried not to think too hard about the wicked things the sound did to my lady parts. "Just... get this over with."

"That's what she said." The prisoner snickered, and I considered throwing a punch of my own. Biting the inside of my cheek, I counted to ten and decided if that didn't calm me down, I'd wait until I drew blood. "You two are such snowflakes. Tommy would easily have gotten his zealots to eat you alive. Can't believe that idiot is governor."

"You put me on the list, you expected me to show up... how did you know about the dogs? Did you kill Trigger, or did you bribe the idiot lawyer to read the will?"

"Neither, Sharp. I know everything about you... and your deceased friend."

"Then you know I don't have any interest in your games, Howser. How do you know about the dogs?"

"Patience, Sharp. You'll never get anywhere without patience. Maybe that's why you go through men. You can't give them time to warm up to your personality before throwing it at them full blast."

His comment punched me in the gut, and I lashed out so he wouldn't see the bullseye he scored.

"Have you always been an obnoxious slime bucket, or is that a recent development from getting your ass kicked in prison?" I snapped, forgetting for a moment that he was either completely unhinged or working on that insanity plea. I knew I was a lot, and so did the men I dated. All they had to do was watch the freaking internet. If they were surprised by my life, it was their fault, not mine. "Maybe I should call your ex-wife and ask her."

"Is that really an appropriate question, given the circumstances? Clock's ticking Miss Sharp." His toothy smile bordered on manic, eyes bouncing back and forth. I drew back from the table, trying to get a clearer view. "Tick tock, tick tock. My days are numbered."

"What do you mean, your days are numbered'? The trial resumes on Monday and there's a ton of witnesses. If we find out that Trigger was murdered, it's an easy mistrial, they have to start over with a new jury." I scooted back in my chair, just in case his lunacy was contagious.

Or he thought biting off part of my face would sell the whole crazy plea.

"Do they? Are you sure about that?"

I blinked at him and then looked at the numbers guy in the corner.

"No, not really. Look, just tell me why you wanted me to come here so I can ask my questions. Or leave. Because I think you have something to say and I'm tired of waiting for you to come out with it. All the other jibber jabber is just really freaking annoying."

"Someone's lost her sense of whimsy. Is it because Cruz is back, and he didn't call you or because someone killed your friend and left you a dog?"

"So, you agree he was killed, and it wasn't an accident?" I asked, wishing I had my phone to get his words on record. "Do you know who did it? And how? Was it you?"

"Of course he was killed. Anyone with eyes could see he wasn't going to fall in line and Stump needed a very specific outcome from that jury. As did Milton Geissinger. And Trigger wasn't going to give it to either of them, nor was he going to let anyone else in that room do it. As far as how, I heard he hit his head. If he fell, he was helped. One way or another. And I've been here, so the only thing I've helped is myself."

He made a stroking motion in the air and winked.

I gagged and wished Winnie was here to bite his nuts and take away his recreational activities.

Scrubbing my hands over my face, I tried to read between the crazy. What he was suggesting was either an altercation where Trigger got shoved out of his chair and hit his head, or... Ruger's face swam in front of my mind's eye.

Or poison.

If it was poison, was someone there to administer it? Or was all of this just the conjecture of a guilty man? Marius had been in custody for nearly a year, juror selection taking almost eight months to complete between constant new recruitments due to conflict of interest or the ability to be impartial. Though my mom had filled me in on a lot of the drama, juror selection wasn't part of the public record, and I wasn't sure how they got away with dismissing so many considering each side was only supposed to get four… I think?

I'd taken exactly one law class and thought it was a bunch of crap.

"Look, I'm not a lawyer, a cop, or anyone else bound by confidentiality. If you want to tell me what really happened, everyone's going to know it. If you're hoping to get confessional leverage, I have no authority. If you're hoping to piss me off so I murder you, not gonna happen."

"Everyone already knows, Miss Sharp. I was in charge of the Stump campaign, and it was going great. Divisive politics, weaponizing the cycle of abuse behaviors against populations most often associated with committing it, we couldn't lose. Do you know who doesn't see manipulation, isolation, distrust, and forced dependency coming? People who use those tactics on those they consider weak. Then Tommy went off the rails, stopped following the program and started stuffing ballot boxes. He was paying second-class criminals to pilfer mail-in ballots, old ladies to complain on air that the other side had done it… it was so unnecessary. We'd basically already won, and he was ruining it with obvious cheats."

"So you bludgeoned his opponent?" I guessed, because I could now picture the candidate they were talking about, and I was deeply disappointed this hadn't gone the other way. Stump had used hate and fear of change to rouse a racist sub-population and spurn them into life.

Once someone waves that flag, you can't put that kind of knowledge back in its box.

He showed the people of Ohio that some of our community members were willing to slaughter others based on skin color, gender, and identity.

Then applauded them for it.

It isolated neighbors, made women take the long way home, knives in their pockets, and refugees fear being murdered in a country that promised to protect the tired, poor and huddled masses yearning to be free. My mom's words from the night before bounced around in my head, and I understood her need to leave.

But this wasn't what I'd fought for, and it wasn't what I could leave behind.

"No. I didn't do shit to Charrish. She'd already lost, but what he did called it all into question, and I was done taking heat for an asshole who couldn't follow directions. I walked the hell away. Next thing I know, there's a bloody bat in Milton's car, it's got my fingerprints on it, and the lawyer's walking off scot-free while I'm sitting through a sham of a trial, waiting to die."

"I don't think Ohio uses its death penalty..." I muttered. "I mean Charrish is alive, though she withdrew her candidacy and that piece of shit won by default, I don't think you get the death penalty for fixing an election and battery."

You probably should though.

My hand shook on the tabletop, and I moved it to my lap. Anger mixed with disgust and something more volatile. Coming here was a mistake, I knew that, but I also couldn't connect this man's awful existence with Trigger's death yet and I needed it to be his fault so I could sleep easier.

"You aren't getting it, lady!"

"Then clue me in, turd nugget!" I snapped at him. "Because right now you're telling me that you're a shitty person who collected a bunch of other shitty people, rewarded them for being crap humans, and then threw a tantrum and quit when the candidate took it a step further. Did you really think that level of dumb could be contained? And what does any of this have to do with Trigger and Ruger?"

"Whether the trial ends in guilty, innocent, or dismissed, I'm a dead man. They're going to arrange for my death, in here or out there, I'm a liability as long as I'm breathing. But Trigger wasn't going to let Milton and Tommy off the hook. He was pushing for the evidence they buried to come out and he was insisting that they get added to the charges. No matter what any of the other jurors said, did or offered, he wasn't going to offer a vote unless they agreed to keep the investigation open. And at least one of the officers was going to do it."

"Which officer?"

"Something for you to figure out, he's in Columbus though."

"OK, why would the other jurors care whether or not Trigger was forcing the issue? It's not like they would be jurors on all the trials." I was losing patience with this man. Partly because I didn't actually care if he got killed, in jail or out of it, and partly because

I felt guilty for not caring. Mostly, though, I just wanted to go hug the dogs and tell them I was sorry that this meeting hadn't turned into a magical 'he's alive!' moment.

"Because most, if not all, of them are being blackmailed. Stump and his lawyer rigged the whole thing. Everyone on the jury is one of his puppets." He shook his head like I'm the idiot. "If he or his lawyer didn't off your friend, one of the jurors did."

Marius started coughing. The coughing got louder, more wet, and blood splattered on the table in front of him.

"Shit!" Griffin ran over and pounded on the door. "Help!"

The door opened and two guards rushed in, helping the man get back upright as he hacked, wheezed and gasped.

"Get the nurse!" One of the guards shouted, tilting Marius's head back and trying to clear his airway. "Lay him flat? What do we do?"

With one last cough, the prisoner went silent.

No wheezing.

No coughing.

I looked at the guards and then at the still form of the man in the jumpsuit.

"Is he... dead?"

Chapter Nine: The Senior's Swinger Society

It was a coin toss who I wanted to call less. Either my boss and tell him I couldn't come to work because I was being held for questioning in a federal prison after watching a man die, or my mother who would be super disappointed I didn't have the incident on camera. The woman for sure a voyeur, but more importantly, she hated when stories lacked adequate endings. Being deeply invested in this court case, she wasn't going to believe it was over if his death happened off-screen.

"Who are we calling, Sharp?" the warden asked, my cell phone in her hand. Though I wasn't suspected of murder, I was still only allowed to make one phone call so the prison could 'control the narrative'.

That was PR Speak for find a way to make it look like my fault.

"Larry Kirby. Also, you need to bring me the dogs from my car and their water dish or I'm calling a lawyer for unlawful detention and animal endangerment." Sadly, I didn't know any lawyers, but I was certain I could find one.

"Fine." She pressed the contact in my phone and set it on the table on speaker. It rang twice before Larry answered.

"Cyn?"

"Hey, Larry. I have an angry warden glaring at me and I need your help."

"A warden? Please tell me you mean a game warden because Winnie accidentally hunted something and you don't have a license," he begged, and I wished I could pat him on the head.

"No, federal prison warden. I need you to call Joseph and tell him I'm going to be late to work. Someone died in front me and now they want me to answer a bunch of questions."

"Shit, Cyn-"

"Not done. You said Ruger was being poisoned. Do you know with what and how?"

"High levels of trazodone laced with fentanyl." Larry sounded like he was reading from the dog's chart. "The trazodone is normal to be there, he has a prescription from the stab injury. The fact that it was laced with fentanyl says someone was trying to poison him and make it look like an accident."

I nodded even though he couldn't see me, triggering something the dead campaign manager had said about Trigger.

"Who do you know in the human medical field who owes you a favor? You or me?" I tried to keep my eyes focused on the phone and not on the four penitentiary workers who were staring at me. The camera had mysteriously stopped working the moment we walked into that room. Howser had been at the infirmary before he was brought in, and the doctor escorting him had left for the day.

He was also not actually a registered employee of the prison but had impersonated someone who was. All cameras with his entry and exit had also mysteriously gone dark around the time I'd come in. When I asked about the dry cleaning bag on the coat rack in the infirmary office, I was told to stop talking and make a phone call.

"What about the hot dog judge's husband and Nurse Pluto at the VA?"

"Perfect. Get them to dig into Trigger's death records. I need to know if he had any active and filled prescriptions, whether the medical examiner or the VA did any testing on his remains. And if they did, I need to know if blood was sampled."

"You think... I thought he hit his head?" I could hear Larry rubbing his facial scruff through the line and I knew he was just as overwhelmed as I was.

"You can pass this on to Carla and let her run with it. It's not your job, I just knew you had Ruger's records and Carla won't call Joseph for me anymore." I drew small concentric circles on the tabletop. Soon, Carla wouldn't be the police chief or part of my life at all. She and my brother, my niece and nephew and the unborn bean would be across the country. I tried to shove that down before a tear could slip out. "Just... she's pregnant so try not to stress her too much."

"I can handle Joseph. I'll let her call the VA folks since she's more familiar. Where are the dogs?"

"They're in the parking lot. But they should be on the way in here if this prison doesn't want to be sued and also find out whether or not the Godzilla rampage jokes were a gross over-statement." I gave a dark meaningful look at the warden who immediately talked into her radio. Larry was quiet, listening.

"I'll get you a lawyer. Should I tell your mom?"

"Yup. She probably knows a lawyer who practices naked. Really spice up this unlawful detainment." I gave a half-heart-ed laugh and Larry joined me. He confirmed, disconnected and I faced the now slightly pale prison staff.

"Who wants to get started before someone who helped write the de-pants-apation proclamation arrives? And some-one go look in that infirmary office for the dry cleaning sleeve."

I pulled up to the farm with five minutes to spare before my shift began. There was a small crowd gathered at the ice cream parlor, and the barn was buzzing with activity. Larry's truck was in the lot, as was Joseph's, the farm manager and owner. Glancing back at my two canine partners, I tried to get a vibe check.

"What do you think? Should we pretend we're still in prison?" Winnie's eyebrows danced while Ruger twitched just the tip of his tail. Both scented the air and neither made sounds of anger or distress. "Probably safe?"

Ruger's tail wagged slightly harder and Winnie shoved her proboscis-like snoot into my face.

"Right then."

Outside my window, the farm stretched for at least ten hectares. It had goats, sheep, horses, cows, and miles of open space for all of them. Facing the roadway was an ice cream parlor and gift shop, the wide front porch home of Winnie's photo spot and the interior home to fresh ice cream. The collection of tables inside were perpetually sticky, the color indiscernible beneath layers of caked on ice cream that never came off. A painting of the farm's fake owners, an old couple hired by Joseph to make the place quaint, smiled down on everyone in loving creeper style.

The marketing explanation was as convoluted as the man's explanation for drinking a case of beer a week in the ten by ten shed he used as an office. It sat halfway between the barn and the ice cream parlor with a single window and a single door. I'd once slept on its floor to avoid a potential killer and it was far more comfortable than it looked.

Finally, there was the barn with a deep gouge in the side from when Winnie caused a bull to escape and he got his horns stuck in the side on his rampage to... somewhere.

Reaching over to the floorboard, I grabbed my backpack with a spare hat, sunscreen, human snacks, dog treats, water bottles, collapsible dog dishes, headache medicine, my eReader, pepper spray, a knife, emergency freeze dried coffee, a single burner camp stove, fuel, waterproof matches, and a collapsible tea kettle. Some people prepared for disaster with bullets and jerky, but I prepared with snacks, coffee, water and dog supplies.

Personally, I thought my odds of survival were better.

Also, my odds of encountering disaster.

Adding extra snacks, treats and water to my cargo pockets, I exited my Jeep and opened the door for my furry children to exit. Winnie easily leapt out and I paused Ruger. Placing one hand under his butt and back leg curve, the other under his chest, I lifted him out of the vehicle and set him down beside his new sister.

He sneezed in disgust.

"I'm sorry! Larry said I was letting you do too much. Yell at him."

Ruger sneezed again and I got the feeling he would not in fact go yell at Larry. Sighing, I tugged my ball cap on and walked toward the big red barn. As I got closer, a cacophony of voices filtered through the open doors mingled with the smells of Bengay and VapoRub.

"You're a disgrace to this barn in those boots, boy," a raspy voice cracked, followed by the thud of something solid connecting with flesh and a masculine grunt of discontent. "In my day, if you owned a farm, your boots looked like you knew how to shovel manure."

We rounded the corner, and my heart stopped.

Milling around was just under two dozen seniors, well past sexagenarians in age alone, in various states of dressed. A man in assless trousers was sitting on a straw bale, two women were feeding the horses topless with breasts that were not defying gravity. Another couple were kissing aggressively, pressed against a stall door, and the person who'd whacked Joseph was Mrs. Zuber, my Kindergarten teacher with a drinking problem who happened to also be wearing nothing more than strategically placed tassels and go-go boots.

"What the hell is happening?" I asked, while Winnie trotted over to one of the men who produced a treat for her. Ruger glanced at me, and I shrugged. "Not all of them have pockets. Exercise caution."

Larry peeked out of a stall and heaved a sigh of relief I heard from forty yards off.

"She's here," he announced, and everyone turned in my direction like a molasses monster army.

"Dude!"

"Sorry, but..." He disappeared back inside a stall, and I can only assume the end of his thought was 'I'm a giant ass man-baby who's scared of naked old people'.

"Cyn!" Mrs. Zuber called, and I waved, moving closer with a flat-eared big black dog who realized he might be on the wrong team.

"You can go hide with Larry if you want," I offered him, and he showed me the whites of his eyes. "It's OK."

He scampered, multi-color tail waving majestically in his wake. "What's up, guys and gals? Lose your pants?"

"Your mom sent us! She said you needed our help with identifying some people and maybe an alibi for suspected murder?"

Mrs. Zuber cracked her knuckles, eyes shining dangerously while the smirk lurking just out of sight promised my alibi would be horrifying. "We just finished an orgy you can say you were at."

A single cough choked out, my chest constricting and the world getting fuzzy at the edges. "Please, dog, no. The first one, identifying people, yes. The alibi, not so much. Turns out threatening a prison warden with a naked lawyer ends questioning super quick. Did she send you the picture?" I stopped a respectable distance from the group, not the least of which was for the preservation of my sanity and continued vision. Despite being rumored to attend their orgies, I had never actually seen some of their cracks and crevices. This point of pride would remain mine until I died.

The over-sized red barn had a series of stalls along both walls, facing a milking station in the center, with a large arena on the other end. Most of the livestock gave birth in the arena and were allowed to spend time with the calf there. It was also where school children were ushered to watch milking displays, horses were brought after injury to slowly work up their gait, and various other activities that were better off conducted in an indoor enclosure.

With the positioning of the seniors, most of the major pathways were obstructed. If there was an emergency, they would be both a liability to the evacuation process and an impediment to the safe movement of animals. If Larry was behind them, he could manage the stalls. Being over here meant I could cover the arena.

Keeping me from seeing naked grandpa butts was just a fringe benefit.

"Did you really see Marius die?" One of the topless women walked over and I kept unwavering eye contact to not inspect whether or not her nipples pointed at the ground or forward. If I wasn't mistaken, this woman was Allison, and she was one of my mom's closest friends. "Was there blood? Foam at his mouth? What I wouldn't give to have seen him castrated, but I'd settle for a violent end."

"Yup." I popped the p. It made me fairly uncomfortable that I had watched a man die and felt absolutely nothing. Death used to bother me... didn't it? "Did you two have... grievances?"

"You could say that." She spat on the floor and my lip curled. The fact that I couldn't remember if death bothered me was pretty messed up but spitting on the floor was just disgusting. "So, was it violent?"

My hand waggled, unwilling to commit to a characterization of his death. It wasn't the worst death I'd seen in the past twelve months. Despite serving in a war zone, all of my combat training and sharpshooter skills hadn't been of any use until I'd come home to US soil. Then I seemed to see people die almost monthly. "Do you know if anyone has had a chance to look at the picture? Discreetly..."

"Why? I'm sure you know his death means they've concluded the trial." One of the lip-locked couples had broken apart and the person imparting that wisdom was wearing linen pants and a T-Shirt that declared her the 'World's Greatest Grandma'. "So, they won't be all in one place, but it'll be easier for you to talk with everyone since they won't be sequestered but it'll make tracking them down a bit trickier, especially with federal courts being able to draw from large sections of the state."

I bit my lip to avoid rolling my eyes at the obvious. The ending of the trial hadn't immediately clicked, but I did know juries were released once a trial ended and that federal juries had larger pools. Instead, I nodded and looked at my boots. They were covered in dust, mud, and what was probably poop of some kind. If my family owned a zoo, we could have fondue night and play *It's Feces but What Species?* like in that romance book series I'd binged.

Instead, I got to play *Will My Boobs Be Down There One Day?* Poop games would be better.

"So, you have names for me?" I toed some dirt, trying to unearth pants and a top for half the assembled group while also hoping there was a typed list with pictures, occupations, home addresses and a dossier worth of information. Not that I wasn't willing to put in work, but it would be nice for someone else to give me a jump start.

"Well, we have the first one," Mrs. Zuber said. She pulled her phone out from somewhere, followed by her glasses, and then spent a solid minute adjusting the position of the device relative to her face. "Madison Lockward, twenty-seven. Looks like she works for a small Columbus news station as a meteorologist. Overqualified, cute, and probably in need of a haircut."

Mrs. Zuber turned her phone around and showed me a side-by-side photo of a woman in the jury box with a short brown bob and her headshot on the station's website. The profile listed her as the behind-the-scenes scientist for... "Chris Summers? Sounds like a weather man. What's his legal name?"

"Does it matter? We weren't looking into him." She gave me a heaping helping of side eye, and I nodded, gesturing for her to continue. "He's a gorgeous dumb dum. His newscasts have been crap recently, can't predict the rain when it's already coming down, but that's how we found her. I've been watching his newscasts for a decade and I can't stop just because he's hit a bit of a prediction rough patch, you know?"

I did not in fact know, because I just checked the weather app on my phone, but I nodded along to avoid a lecture. Millennials ruining the world with their apps and gadgets, no human touch, blah blah... I would not be touching any of these humans unless they washed their hands in front of me and made zero detours on the way to a handshake.

Since I'd also just been dumped, I probably wouldn't be touching any other humans either unless Mo showed up and forced hugs on me.

"Cool, can you send me that? I'll go see her after work."

"Or you could go now," Joseph declared, and I cocked my head to the side.

"You look like this is really important to you. So, you should round up your pals and head out to Columbus!" He looked so hopeful, while all the seniors looked lost and confused. "With pay! I insist, least I could do for all your hard work."

"No, we don't want to go with her. But I do think it's time for ice cream," a bald man declared without any teeth. The seniors all agreed, and they rose, a slow-moving tide toward the ice cream parlor while Joseph sweated and attempted to leapfrog through the mass.

"There's children in there," he whimpered, jogging ahead of them. Laughing, I walked over to the station with clipboards and the day's current checks.

"Cyn?" Larry asked, and I turned to look at him. He was still wearing his lab coat, stethoscope around his neck, and Ruger on his heels. My newest child was carrying a chew stick, Winnie appearing beside him with sad eyes because she probably devoured hers whole and now wanted to eat his too.

Damn, my kids were as predictable as Seth's.

"Sup, doc?" I said in a Bug's Bunny voice to the chilling first screams of a Lululemon Mommy in the ice cream parlor confronted with the future effects of gravity. My smile got impossibly bigger. After confirming which tanks still needed to be checked, I grabbed gloves, a thermometer and a mask, to head toward the milking station.

"I was able to get the information you asked for. Well, Carla did." He leaned against the counter beside the box of gloves. My smile withered to dust and floated away on a cow fart breeze as I turned around and did the same. "Trigger had no active prescriptions, but you were right. No one had tested his blood that they could find, someone wiped the ME's computer, but there were swabbed samples from Trigger's impact point taken by the crime scene techs. The blood contained high levels of trazodone laced with fentanyl, which would account for instability, but there's no confirmation it's his blood or an official investigation. They can't claim he didn't fall over from that alone or that he didn't take it willingly without more. Also heard from the prison, that's what killed Marius."

I nodded, wondering if the fake doctor had brought it in or the prison had it on-site.

"Also, there's two naked guys behind you." Larry gave me a two-finger salute and scampered away with my children.

Chapter Ten: The Best Defense

"Guy's kinda a weenie, isn't he?" The voice behind me was somewhere at elbow level. Hands on my hips, I contemplated my choices. Running away was definitely at the top. At the bottom was turning around and talking to him, sitting in the middle of the goat enclosure topless without sunscreen, and getting a root canal. "We aren't actually naked."

Relief flooded me and I turned around.

Then slapped my hands over my eyes.

"You filthy liar!" I hissed at the short, round, white man with a bald patch surrounded by a white hair crown. Beside him was a thin black man with lean build, softer in the center, and small dusting of hair on his chest and head. "You dirty old man liar, may you suffer the curse of a thousand pharaohs!"

"I'm not a liar! Look!" The air moved near my calf and I glanced down, hands cupped in front of my eyes like horse blinders. Covered in dust were two sets of leather loafers, the smaller of the two with one aloft in my general vicinity. "You owe us an apology."

"Technicality! What are you, a lawyer?" I snickered, turning away to get a clipboard to start my actual job. The day off was probably rescinded when I did successfully convince the naked seniors to leave the premises.

"Actually, yes." The deeper voice startled me into looking, deep brown eyes drawing me in. If I focused on the taller man, I was likely not to encounter any one-eyed snake heads, but like a trainwreck, my brain kept wanting to look. "We were under the impression that you may need an attorney but more that you'd likely need to speak with us?"

A shout came from the ice cream parlor, and I spared a glance toward the athleisure mommy crowd, belittling Joseph while the senior's slurped and gummed their frozen treats. "Any chance you'd talk with me..." I glanced to the far end of the milking line. "Over there?"

Before they could respond, I started walking and hoped the men would follow.

Preferably with pants that appeared out of nowhere, but the universe didn't like me that much.

I stopped at the first collection tank, pulled on the gloves from my pocket, and crouched by the metal cylinder with my clipboard and thermometer. Footsteps scraped through the dirt behind me, and I realized the position I placed myself in. "You have to stay behind me. I will not be eye level with strange men's junk."

"Your mom might have a point about you being a prude." The footsteps halted, and I guessed it was the shorter of the two. "I'm George Truman, this is my partner Percival White."

The names pinged something in my grey matter and I scribbled the temp reading on my clipboard, shutting and locking the tank. With care, I stood up with the clipboard angled to block the lower view and studied the worn and weary faces in front of me. Deep lines set between both of their eyebrows, their skin the type of sallow that came with too much time indoors, but I couldn't place the names or the faces.

"We were the prosecuting attorneys on the Marius Howser trial." The tall man extended his hand, and I followed suit. "Percival."

We shook and I did the same with the shorter man.

"George."

My hand returned to the clipboard, knuckles turning white to keep it from drooping in the slightest. Percival's chest had the marine corps logo tattooed on the left breast, the lines faded with age and slightly obscured by hair. I tilted my head. "You served?"

He nodded but didn't expand on his time in the service. Given his estimated age and skin color, I could only guess what he endured. Still, his eyes held a softness that betrayed a kindness no amount of evil could steal away.

"You can call me Percy."

My gaze shifted to the shorter George, who immediately shook his head.

"Nah. Just your regular 'parents worked in government, became a lawyer, worked in government' person. Also, I was too short for the Globetrotters." Mr. Truman laughed at his own joke and my head fell to my shoulder. "It's a basketball joke."

"Was it though?" Percival let out a bark of laughter while I walked to a nearby stand and grabbed a roll of shop towels and saline vinegar rinse. "It just sounded bitter."

Wiping off the thermometer, I opened the next cylinder. After taking the readings, I locked up the cylinder and cleaned the metal rod while I considered what to ask them. "Were you guys assigned the case before or after the jury selection?"

"Before. This case was ours to prosecute from the moment the ink dried on the arrest warrant. When the homicide detectives come to you confidentially and say they think it's too easy, something's off but there's no evidence to explain the niggling feeling, you know something's wrong. But all the way through pretrial depos, we worked with Detective's Lilith and Kim. Nothing came of any of it, not a single lead on how to proceed. Not that Marius was innocent, mind you, but this case was off from the beginning."

"Marius said Trigger was gunning to get Stump and Geissinger investigated, planning to refuse a vote without it, had you guys heard this? Do you know the officer's name?"

"Why? What do you need his name for?" Percy's voice was laced with accusation.

I stood and turned involuntarily. George was pensive, reflecting on his own opening statement while Percival stood waiting. It was an interesting dynamic the pair shared, predator waiting to strike while the seemingly meek prey laid the groundwork. It was clearly a technique they perfected, but not one that made sense in the moment. Unless...

"You know I didn't kill him, right? I don't have access to, nor inclination to kill with, drugs. If I take someone out, it will be by shooting them, blowing them up, or punching them in the face without realizing there's traffic behind them, so they fall in front of a semi and get squashed like an insect." A dark blue suit with a bleach blonde hair piece came to mind and a sinister smile tingled in my jawbone. Some people needed to be punched in the face and hit by a truck. "But sneaking lethal doses of narcotics into a federal prison is a little too *premeditated* for me, ya know?"

The pair looked briefly horrified and I saw George reach for his junk reflexively. "I retract my prude comment. You're terrifying."

I shot him finger guns. "Things to remember."

"We don't know who he was working with to get it investigated. Or how the hell Howser would be in the know unless someone was spoon feeding him intel." George shook his head, eyeing my clipboard like he wished he had something to write on.

"So, what were you setting me up for?" I redirected us away from Howser's ramblings. They were likely chaos and misdirection on purpose.

The two men exchanged glances and a whole conversation flowed in the literal blink of an eye.

"How much do you know about this case?" Percy adjusted his stance to a reverse parade rest- hands discreetly placed in front of his man parts. My eyes finally went wherever they wanted and found that there wasn't anything of interest besides their faces. "For example, what he was charged with, how long the process took, the backstory?"

"Nope," I replied, turning to the next drum. "May told me he was the campaign manager of Stump, who's the... governor?" They nodded. "Originally, the candidate accused his opposition of election fraud and then was found to have committed that fraud, confirmed by his campaign manager who caters to abusers and sadistic pricks, but then that opposition was found bludgeoned, and the evidence pointed to the lawyer but only the campaign manager was arrested. Attempted murder?"

Three more drums had been inspected while I summarized my understanding, and still I wasn't sure where they were going. If all of this was common knowledge, why was I being forced to look at their naked chests? "So, what does all that have to do with juror selection and case assignment?"

"When the evidence started coming in, we thought someone was feeding it to the cops. Just small believable bites that a person with investigative knowledge and timing could orchestrate. The two men were arrested; the baseball bat that's used for the bludgeoning is found in the lawyer's car. The day Geissinger agrees to talk, video footage is located showing Howser driving Geissinger's car alone time and date stamped the day of the attack. It's from a previously invisible camera, time and date stamped from within a few minutes and an eighth of a mile of where Charrish was found bloodied and beaten. Another video, again from who knows where because we looked, surfaces. This one has Geissinger out drinking with his Air Force buddies, time stamped at the time of attack." George wipes at the sweat on his face, a few flies circling the shining scalp of his head. Outside, it was only sixty, but inside the barn it was much warmer. "We let him go, and like smoke, he's gone."

"Do you think he's dead?" I gave up on my cylinders and leaned against the metal railing between two Jersey cows. "Or do you think someone is helping him hide? Someone with military connections and investigative skills who... oh." I swiped my own brow and shook my head. "Not me. No amount of service family vows would allow me to shield someone who gets in bed with a Nazi. What was his MOS? Do you think he fed the evidence to Law Enforcement?"

The two shared another loaded look and went back to covering their junk.

"We couldn't find out. It just said intelligence." Mr. White bit the bullet to answer, and I didn't fault them. Intelligence encompassed such a broad spectrum, it might as well be sunscreen for secrets. If the government wanted to do something sneaky or illegal, they called it intelligence and hoped no one noticed how dumb that was. "But if he did, it was with help. He was in custody the whole time with zero unmonitored communication."

My brain set that aside for the moment. Despite not wanting a person who bludgeons a woman into hospitalization on the street, I had other priorities.

"Ever heard of a lawyer called Patrick Patterson? Works in a strip mall that shares a lobby with a dry-cleaner and a beauty supply?" George shook his head, but Percy let out a burst of laughter.

"Ambulance chaser, skirt chaser, and gambling addict. He was the defense attorney for a low-level drug dealer a few years ago and I personally thought he deserved the time more than his client. Who's he to you?"

"A blackmailed executor of the estate. Talk to me about jury selection. I heard it took eight months?" I left out the part that I'd heard it from a dead sociopath. Again, silence passed between them with a million words, and I started to wonder if this relationship was more than professional. The only humans I'd shared that level of closeness with were... Well, Winnie.

So, not a single human.

"This was another area where it felt like we were being spoon fed. Jurors were 'accidentally' dismissed from the hold room so that when someone was found ineligible, we had to send out another summons. On the third go around, suddenly everyone who walks in is available, has no conflicts, and is a reasonable choice? Except for your friend... The defense attorney was being leaned on heavily by a man in a suit to get him dismissed. Eventually the bailiff ejected him from the court, but she wouldn't say who he was or why he felt entitled to do that. Elsa, the bailiff, she's a force to reckon with and I think he's the reason the media came down hard on her." I tried to picture the bailiff George was talking about, but nothing came to mind. When I got home, I'd have to look up pictures of her.

"Did you talk to someone in the clerk's office? Find out if something was up or weird with this batch of summons?" The lawyers nodded but didn't look like the information would be worth sharing. "OK, so someone either messed with their system and arranged for these folks, or someone is lying. Different problem. Any weird rules or... something? Something that screams someone inside the court was in on... whatever this is?"

It was a stretch, one that I couldn't explain trying to make. The whole courtroom in the videos hadn't looked legitimate. If I streamed two thousand episodes of Law and Order, all of them would have looked less staged than the scenes being live streamed.

"There was one. Your friend was the one who suggested it." Percy rubbed his chin, connecting a new constellation in his mind. "We don't normally police the audience or other courtroom members, but he stated that he had a severe allergy and asked that no nuts or analgesics be brought into the box. The judge took it a step further and had jurors disclose anything they needed with them in the courtroom, including medications and related conditions. Guy next to him panicked, said he should carry an EpiPen." Percival mopped his own brow, and I passed them both a clean shop towel. It wasn't soft, and the blue color might leave a residue, but without sleeves they needed something.

The squeegee effect was not working for them.

"I remember that." George took over the story and I regretted my decision to provide towels when I saw their hands no longer concealed the past-prime squirrel food between their legs. "That man insisted that if he had so many issues, he should be dismissed and replaced. He was offered a new seat, and offered the opportunity to leave, but then he got real quiet. Like he needed someone else to pull the string on his back. I think the judge kept Trigger because of his requests... he didn't trust it either."

"You said next to Trigger. Next to him which way? Left, right, in front?"

This caused them a great deal of wrinkles as I watched Winnie appear around the stalls in the center of the barn. She pranced toward us with Ruger plodding along on her heels.

"Shoot, left? No, right? We renumbered them so many times because of complaints and requests." They patted their brows, and I opened the picture on my phone. Percival pointed to the suited man to Trigger's right. "That guy. It's funny, he was also the most upset when we kicked out that guy coaching Abramian. When he showed back up, it was like a direct challenge to Elsa and when she tried to quietly remove him, that artificial hand flew into the jury box."

"Wait, what?" I looked away from the dogs and focused on the men. "The guy you kicked out of the courtroom reappeared the day before Trigger died? And when he was about to get kicked out again, a witness causes a distraction?"

"Well, now that you mention it..." Winnie shoved her cold wet nose into George's butt and he screeched out loud, leaning back and giving me a full frontal that would scar me forever. "What the hell?"

"Amateur proctologist," I explained, petting Ruger and making a mental note to give Winnie a bath, and another to search for another angle of the courtroom chaos footage. Percy let out his own screech and I peered around his back. "She's an equal opportunity inspector. I need the name of that suspect with the false hand."

Chapter Eleven:
A Courtroom of Suspects

After a late shift at the dairy, I'd usually open Sharp Investigations later in the day. But with the pinging of my cell phone on the new to me Senior Swinger's Chat, I gave up at six in the morning and started the day. To save Ruger extra trips upstairs, I'd carried the food downstairs on my first trip so that after outdoor potties, we could eat and caffeinate in the office. Against my better judgement, I also sent off an email to the VA Loan people to see what, if anything, I might qualify for as well as a real estate agent to show me listings of houses for rent or sale with the stipulation that I had no idea what I could afford or was qualified for.

I didn't think they'd be calling me back.

With two freshly fed dogs and two cups of coffee pumping through my veins, I approached the freestanding dry erase board armed with printouts, tape, markers, a notebook full of data and coffee number three. After an hour of scouring the internet, there wasn't another angle of the Courtroom Chaos video. It was the only date and time with guaranteed footage of the defense hassler, and I had no line of sight.

"Ugh, I never wanted to make another conspiracy board," I sighed. Setting the tape dispenser and markers in the trey, I started arranging the pictures on the board. Taped at the top was Judge Aurelius Benson, a black man who'd presided over a large number of cases in his seventy years of life, but this was the first one where the defendant turned up dead. For his sake, I also hoped it was his last.

To the right of his image, I placed the still screen grab of all twelve jurors my mom had pulled from the internet feed. Beside it, I wrote the numbers one through fourteen, with Madison's name by juror number six and Trigger's name by juror number ten. With a deep sense of sadness, I drew a line through his name but left his picture untouched.

He would be remembered as the only juror who looked ready to mess people up.

Left of the juror box I placed the prosecution, two senior prosecutors with more years of experience than I had lived on this planet. Studying them fully clothed, Percival White and George Truman were opposites in height, weight and hair present on top of their head. But the two had made a good team when interviewing witnesses and didn't look nearly as convinced of the case they were trying as the news media had made it seem. Watching them on the videos posted online, I got the impression that both lawyers were under someone's thumb to keep going. After speaking with them, I couldn't discount the possibility that the thumb wasn't just the pressure of case closures placed on attorneys. I jotted down the notes about the murder weapon, discovery, and juror selection hellscape, but they were reading like a dead end.

A pity because if you have to see old man penis, it should at least solve your friend's murder.

Not that I had all that much confidence in penises of any age.

Across the imaginary aisle I put a picture of Marius Howser and his attorney, Jackie Abramian. A younger woman in her late thirties with a pert nose, flawless hair bun and expression that said her client was guilty of a lot of things, but not this one. Writing their names underneath them, I drew a line through Marius's name but still listed facts about him beneath his name with bullet points: campaign manager, amoral major bag of dicks, dead, fixed the election.

Most of that was conjecture based on meeting him, but I really wasn't too upset he was dead. Only that it wasn't more bloody, violent and dismember-y.

"Stella would say I need to go back to therapy," I said to Ruger, who was lying at my feet. Winnie was on her dog bed behind my desk with all her paws in the air. "She's probably right, but I'm tired of hearing the line 'all life has value'. Every day I'm reminded that people like that, his candidate that's now our governor, and the president with his asshole posse get to go around existing and being celebrated. Not all life has value. Some of it actively takes away from the value and safety of everyone else's life and if we viewed the planet as a whole system, they'd be the equivalent of a cancer cell that evaded apoptosis and needed to be excised."

Ruger sighed and set his head down on the brown paws crossed in front of him, tail tip wagging.

"You get it."

"I get it, but it's dark." I spun toward the back door where the man spoke, gun drawn. Griffin stood in the doorway from my stairwell into the office space. His hands raised slightly; an eyebrow cocked at the gun in my hand, but otherwise nothing in his posture gave an indication he was concerned or experiencing a threat to his life. The good-natured lilt to his mouth and unbothered ease with which he walked were the skills of a spy in a sitcom. "I come in peace?"

"Why aren't you scared?" I lowered my gun but kept the safety off. "Do you often have guns pointed at you?"

"Not recently... but I guess because I don't actually believe you'll shoot me."

"You sure? It's starting to creep me out how often you just appear." I flipped the safety on and tucked my gun back into its inner pants holster. "I get that banking is probably boring as fluff, but I don't think you should be ditching your work to stalk me."

"It's Saturday. Credit Union financial management arm is closed." He walked up beside me and leaned against my desk. Together, we studied my conspiracy board, him with the casual interest of someone invited, though if he were a vampire his ass would still be outside. Pretending he wasn't there, I wrote down what little I knew about Jackie Abramian. She was a recent graduate of University of Cincinnati Law School, passed the bar on her first try, didn't have any family in the area, undergrad poli-sci minor somewhere out of state, second career for her.

"Probably why she wanted this case," I said to Ruger, taking a drink of my coffee. The dog waved his tail majestically in agreement. In front of the defense table, I taped a picture of the court reporter. She looked like the job had been hers since it fell into one of the six occupations women were permitted to have. I wrote her name, Ethel Beavers, beneath the picture.

With nowhere else to put them, I stuck the bailiff and the known reporters on site in the center of the room. Elsa Woodruff, the bailiff, was new to the gig but an imposing presence and I understood why it was dangerous to re-enter her court room. Jennifer Jessups from Fox news, had spent the whole time waffling between her devotion to the party and the cowardice of a man who'd turn on it no matter what they did. CNN and ABC were a constant rotation, but the staffers were generally young interns, NPR had sent a dude who looked like AC Slater from *Saved by the Bell* and dressed like a comic book reporter. His reports were factual with little exposition, and I wondered if that was part of his mild-mannered alter ego, or if he really didn't want to put himself into the story. Patrick Patterson's picture of the man who'd delivered the will in an upper corner beside the printed image of my false-handed suspect with a question mark. Her name listed on the deposition as Jennifer Doe, and legally non-existent.

When I found the man in the suit, I imagined I'd also find Jennifer.

Next to her I drew the silhouette of a man with a face mask and stethoscope. Beside his name, I wrote fake doctor, stole prison doctor's dry cleaning, left it in the office, came and went in scrubs, face covered, no cameras. Since they were being threatened with a lawsuit, I was given a picture of the dry-cleaning bag, Kim's Dry Cleaning, and I had an asterisk to look up where those were located. I'd shown the guards my pictures from the jury box and of the man in the parking lot, but no one could tell me if any of them had been the faux doctor due to the mask and gloves.

Finally, I pinned up pictures of Tommy Stump and Milton Geissinger, though I couldn't tell for certain if either of them had stepped a single foot in the court room. They were as entrenched in this madness as anyone else. Stepping back from the board, I studied my recreated scene and then looked into my empty coffee cup.

When I turned to get more, I nearly jumped out of my skin at the sight of Griffin still leaning against my desk. His eyes locked onto my board with equal parts interest and indifference, like he cared despite himself and didn't want anyone to know.

"Fluff, I forgot you were there." I walked past him to the coffee pot and poured the rest in my cup. While I drank it, I dumped the old grounds and put a new filter and fresh grounds into the maker. Shuffling to the sink, I got water and added it, a subtle hiss letting me know the pot was still warm and I might be overworking the poor appliance. When I turned around, Griffin was studying my conspiracy board with a trained investigator's eye. "Anything popping out at you?"

He snickered, a saucy smirk letting me know he had in fact served in the navy and retired with the same humor as the rest of us.

"Hardy har har." I hid my smile behind my next drink of coffee. The accountant was growing on me, and I didn't have room in my life for anything or anyone that would add complications. Friends were just people I disappointed with my absenteeism and new romantic partners were out of the question. Levi had taught me that new people did not appreciate the life I lead, and old ones were booted from the job for a reason.

"Well, my first thought is that you should work on your penmanship." He looked at the pictures, studying Madison's face and the information I'd scribbled beside her, namely her home and work addresses, occupation, and social media mined degree in geology and geography. "What is a rock and map person doing providing weather science for a small news channel?"

It was on my list of questions to ask her, but he hadn't asked like he expected an answer, so I decided to scroll through the past hundred messages in the Senior Swingers Investigator's chat. Aside from a lot of lewd innuendo, snark, and suggestions about creative places to insert objects without a flared base, there was a fair amount of investigative skill and tracking down a cousin's neighbor from two houses ago.

"Juror number 4 is Noah Anderson, owns a pet store off the interstate called... are you kidding me?" I switched to a browser and searched for the business name with the city as a modifier.

The business profile popped up, along with the website and a catchy tagline that made my skin crawl.

"What?" Griffin walked up beside me and looked down at my phone. "Noah's Ark?"

"'We have two of everything', bleh. It's biblically creepy. But the face matches blondie. Looks like he's a transplant from Utah, LDS, and the business is closed on Sunday." My stank face was getting worse so I switched back to the horny senior's chat while Griffin went to write the info on the board. His penmanship was worse than mine, but I kept the comment to myself since my hand was cramping, and I still had to text.

Naked old people made me less uncomfortable than overly devout religious people. As I saw another jpeg of someone's butt cheeks, I reminded myself that the chat was still better than my browser. Millions had been slaughtered in the name of God between The Hundred Years War, the Romans, the Sunnis and Shiites, and World War 2.

No one had been killed by naked grandma butts... probably.

"Please tell me that isn't all on the website?"

"Only if you like being lied to." I kept scrolling through and found another one.

"Juror number eleven, Olivia Hartley. She does ghost tours, and history walks in old town Columbus." The website link they sent was both eerie and cheerful, perfectly matching the dyed, straightened black hair and black pinafore Wednesday Adams vibe of the juror in the picture on the screen. "She has a BA in Architectural History from University of Columbus, years don't align with Jackie, but we should do a vibe check if they know each other. She was a city planner, quit when… she punched the director for groping a coworker in front of her. Kind of think I want us to be BFFs."

I used the search feature in the chat to filter by the word "juror" and saw a few leads on juror two and the foreman, but nothing concrete for the board. When the coffee maker beeped, I was out of coffee and ready for a road trip. Grabbing a travel cup, I filled it with all the coffee that would fit along with some oat milk creamer and put the lid on. Crossing to the window, I checked the sidewalk and saw no one making a mad dash toward the investigative office allowing me to safely flip the sign, draw the curtain, and lock the door.

"Alright, moneyman, you don't have to go home, but you can't stay here," I slung my backpack onto my shoulder and leashed up both dogs.

"Where are you going?" He followed me to the back door, loping along with the energetic gait of a puppy. I pulled it closed and locked it, double checking that the latch caught before starting down the alley to where my Jeep was parked on a side street.

"To a tiny news studio in Columbus."

"Explain to me again how you talked me into bringing you with me?" I asked Griffin as we stared at a squat block building in the middle of an industrial park. On one side of it was a garage spitting sparks and the metal clink of wrenches and bolts, the other a nondescript doorway that had a red light over it declaring "Filming in Progress". Based on who I'd seen walk in, they were either filming porn or NFL Cheerleader auditions.

Neither would surprise me.

One would be harder to conduct a news broadcast next to than the other.

The on-air light was off above the news studio door, a collection of cars in the lot joining a breaking news van with a large antenna. It featured an MNPP logo on the side that matched the business name on the broadcasting channel license and network. If they followed the normal news schedule, which I'd been forced to search the internet for and when that failed, asked the seniors about, the station would be gearing up for the afternoon news cycle.

"Because I was holding your coffee and a dog leash while you unlocked your car and refused to give them back unless you let me come with you as back up." He didn't even try to lie to me as he drank from the franchise branded paper cup we'd stopped for shortly before arriving in the city when I ran out of coffee and patience with the constant buzzing of my phone. "Your phone is dying."

"I know. It's not used to getting this many messages." I blew out a breath and glanced at the red bar blinking at the top. "Maybe I can leave the chat and just ask someone to only send me the highlights."

"Based on the number of them who want you to be aware of how hard it was to find out whatever it is they learned, I doubt you'll get that kind of agreement out of them. But I could type it out and let you know how it goes? They have four more names for you."

"Great. Any of them 'Murderer McPoison Face'? Cuz that would be super helpful right now."

My own pumpkin coffee was already gone, as were both pup cups I'd ordered. Ruger had happily licked his cup clean, and I had to feign allergies when a tear slipped out at the sight. Knowing he was doing better was the best news I could get after weeks of having my heart ripped out.

"No. They all have normal, non-incriminating names. Imagine if people had to be named after their inevitable profession and personality traits?" He gave me a broad smile. "You'd be Explosions LaDog Lady."

"You'd be 'Annoying Numbers Guy'," I countered, but it came out with a laugh, and he smiled at me wide enough to show dimples.

"What's the plan?" He asked, eyeing the building.

I looked at him aghast.

"I thought you would have researched us before forcing yourself along! We don't do plans! I was just going to go in and ask to talk to Madison."

"That's a terrible plan!"

"I'm not really known for my plans," I grabbed my trash and opened the car door. Turning to my furry compatriots, I made eye contact with each one in turn. "You will stay here. You will not jump out after hamburger patties, hot dogs, doughnuts, cheese, squirrels, skateboards, or purse snatching criminals. Do you understand?"

My eyes stayed trained on Winnie, the real reason we had to have this talk.

She huffed out a breath and flopped onto the seat.

"Thank you."

I shut the door and walked toward the door, tossing the empty cup.

"This is a terrible idea!" Griffin appeared beside me, breath tickling my ear. I swatted in his direction to clear the tickle.

"All my ideas are terrible ideas! No one is making you come with me." I reached for the metal door. Before I could grab the handle, it flew open and slammed against the brick wall behind it, spitting out a fast-moving woman on a mission carting a paper box.

"I told you I'm done!" she shouted.

A muscular man in a suit scurried after her. He wore veneers and a wavy side part, a clear weather man look, but not one I'd consider hot. His leather shoes slapped the ground, tassels bouncing on the tips of his toes.

"But if you leave, they'll shut down the station!"

"Madison?" I called, catching up to her short legs in a couple of quick strides.

"What?" She turned, ready to yell at me and going completely pale. "Shit. I'm so sorry. I never meant for him to die."

Chapter Twelve: The Madison Movement

The coffee shop across the way served a decent drip dark roast and allowed dogs on their patio. The inside boasted exposed brick and creepy artwork of personified coffee beans, but outside it was just regular city weird.

Which meant Jazzy Java also had a delightful view of a man dropping his pants to run his naked ass along a wall. Two currier bikes narrowly avoided death by rapid van, and at least two pieces of nearby litter could double as murder weapons.

Once Madison had purchased everyone a coffee, the three of us settled into a metal table with the dogs leaning heavily on each of my legs for comfort. Ruger recognized Madison and gave her a headbutt, a pretty decent sign she wasn't the reason he'd reacted to the courtroom video my mom showed me.

And a point for Griffin who'd once again restrained me from attacking someone I suspected of harming one of the few people on this planet I cared about.

Before I could choke the short woman, Griffin had interceded and asked for clarification, one that required relocation because it involved *whisper* blackmail. Chris had been easily distracted with a mirror and one of the actresses who exited the neighboring studio, and our whole crew had hoofed it out of the industrial park to the street frontage café.

But now that I was sitting here, looking at one of the last people to see Trigger alive, I wasn't sure what we were doing. I knew that she could provide context for his life during the trial and maybe pare down the twenty-ish people in the courtroom to a more reasonable number, but then what?

Did I really trust the justice system anymore?

"Tell us about the blackmail." Griffin started the ball rolling while I stared absently at my coffee. Both of my hands were occupied stroking dog fur, so I was relying on a plastic straw to convey caffeination to my face.

"Right…" She stirred her drink with a wooden stick; empty sugar wrappers tucked under the edge of her cup to prevent them blowing away. Instead of manicured nails, Madison's fingers had torn cuticles and ragged edges from chewing them off. Her clothing was well-worn wool skirts and oversized sweaters, nothing attention grabbing or newer than three years. "It's my fault."

She put the lid back on her coffee and took a drink. If she was waiting for someone to disagree, she wasn't facing the correct audience. While I wasn't above coddling, I didn't know her that well. If she wanted to keep taking the blame, I was going to let her until I had definitive proof to the contrary.

"What was your fault?" I clarified, since she'd sworn she hadn't actually killed him.

"The blackmail. I deserved to be blackmailed. I mean, you can't be blackmailed if you don't actually do something that's blackmail-able..." She used coffee to stop the onslaught of words, a moment to collect them into a coherent sentence that I would have appreciated if she wasn't wasting my damn time. So far, all she'd done was piss me off and confirm, tangentially, what the prosecutors alluded to—some people were being blackmailed into service.

Winnie could see that, and she was licking her lady parts.

"My friend was poisoned and so was my dog, could you get to the point?" I snapped and she startled herself into speech.

"I never wanted to be a meteorologist. My passion was always geology, specifically earth formation and movements and their impacts on the resulting landmass and microclimates." Madison paused for a drink of coffee and Griffin looked thoroughly confused beside me. If I wasn't angry, sad and tired, I might explain science to him, but since I didn't ask him to be here, he could work the internet and figure it out himself. "It's how I ended up learning enough to work in meteorology when academia didn't pan out., though I never lost hope in research assignments."

Pushing her glasses up her nose, the woman looked wistfully off into the horizon, and I read between the lines.

"Why didn't academia pan out?" Griffin asked and we both turned to him, her expression more guarded but subdued than my blatant declaration of his idiocy.

"Because she's a female and nothing has changed in that institution since its inception. Women are considered inferior, dismissed and oftentimes either assaulted or overlooked in the process of trying to make it." I looked at her clothes again. The complete absence of visible feminine attributes and secondary sex characteristics. "Did you report him?"

Madison shook her head and looked back down into her coffee.

"I thought he loved me." I nodded and tried not to offer unsolicited psychotherapy. Winnie got up and went over to Madison, placing her head on her lap and offering silent comfort and solidarity in place of my reflexive offer to provide violence on someone's behalf. Once her hands tangled into Winnie's fur, she appeared to move forward in time to the moment.

I felt slightly bad about wanting to choke her.

"I promised not to let another man manipulate me. When I took this job, I never stopped looking for what I actually wanted. The station manager claimed to understand when I told him it was temporary, that I would help out until I was able to find an actual project that required my expertise." She paused for another drink of coffee, pushing up her glasses again. "Then a research project came up that I'd always dreamed of. One of my old graduate teaching assistants reached out about a last-minute opportunity to go abroad where they discovered topographical features that mirror shifts in tectonic plate movements, matching both documented and pre-documented seismic activity."

Her whole face came to life while Griffin's had glazed over. I was a biology person, but I knew enough to discern they were interested in studying land mass movements relative to earthquakes.

"Is the goal to see if you can predict future earthquakes by trying to graph times and patterns?" I asked, using my newly free hand to drink my slightly chilled coffee. A burning in my stomach reminded me that seven-ish cups of coffee without food wasn't a great idea. After this, I'd need to find something to help my stomach lining not dissolve prematurely.

"No, we were hoping to measure the movement and directionality then reverse engineer it to see what the world looked like before." Her smile was radiant, and I shook my head.

"You want to prove Pangea?"

"Yes! Wouldn't that be amazing?" Madison was practically bouncing in her seat, and I chuckled, her easy joy contagious. If time were more than a human construct, her passion had transported her back to when she'd last felt hope and excitement. Envy and awe fought for top billing in my gut, but acid reflux won, and I let out a burp.

"It's pretty cool."

"What's Pangea?" Griffin asked.

We ignored him.

"So... What happened?"

Her face immediately crumbled.

"The station manager threatened me. He said if I tried to leave, he'd call the project lead and tell him I had stolen equipment. But I didn't steal it! The meteorological equipment is mine, I purchased it myself when I was studying the long-term effects of extreme weather on land mass shifts. I have the receipt, but he said no one would believe me because who would believe that a news studio didn't own their own weather kit?"

Her eyes were starting to mist, but now that she was talking, she must have needed to get it out.

"So, I started giving Chris bad information. I made him look like an idiot, predicting rain in the middle of an August heatwave, sunshine in a rainstorm... I called in false tips, made up reports and forged informants. Mr. Tate is a terrible man, so I decided that if he could try to ruin my future, I would have his station shut down. There's only four of us, and Chris, Jasmin, and Sam can all get jobs in other places. But I didn't know someone was keeping track, until I got summoned for jury duty."

Madison's hands were shaking now, and I tried not to hold my breath alongside her.

"At first, I thought it was weird that I would be asked to serve on a federal jury proceeding, but I was also kind of glad because maybe by the time the trial ended, the station would have gone under? Except the notice looked weird, and when I showed up for the summons, it wasn't at the courthouse. These two guys in black suits were waiting for me at the community center in a back conference room they'd rented out. They didn't give me their names, but they looked like brothers from what I could see, though one of them kept out of sight wearing a paper mask. They said they knew what I'd been doing and that if I didn't want to go to jail, I'd do what they said."

Griffin sucked in air beside me, and I rolled my eyes at him. He was the worst person to take on interviews, reacting to every statement like a movie theatre patron.

"What did they ask you to do?"

"They handed me a jury summons that had been modified to my name and address. It was a really crap job, like something done with scotch tape and markers? He said I'd show up for the notice and not to worry about it. I said they have a record of who gets summoned, and the man insisted it would match. I didn't believe him, how could I?"

"No one would believe that."

"Unless they knew someone... or had access. But these guys didn't look like they'd have access, so I made a back-up plan." Madison pressed her palms into the table and spread them wide, unrolling her metaphorical plan.

Griffin's leg bounced beside me. Either he was really into this story and second-hand anxious or he forgot to pee before we left the house.

"I told them it looked really fake and would raise all kinds of red flags, but they swore it would work."

"What did you do?" I asked, since she'd clearly been on a real jury in a real trial and somehow everything had worked.

"They were right. I went in ready to tell the woman at the counter that I'd been fired, and this trial was estimated to be really long, and I needed the paycheck, but I didn't need to. My letter, name and social all matched and I was placed in the room for selection." She shrugged, still baffled that she'd served on a federal jury and not ended up in prison.

"Is that how everyone got on the jury?"

"I don't know. We weren't allowed to talk to each other, but I think at least a few people were legitimate random selections. Like this one guy, total golden retriever sitting next to this goth girl and a soccer mom from Springfield. I only know that Trigger made a lot of waves by sending notes to the foreman for the judge and the attorneys. Every time he passed a note, juror nine got so angry and two, three, four, seven and eleven would get shifty. But I was too stressed to pinpoint if it was ONLY when he passed notes or if they were always shifty." Bringing her thumb to her mouth, she started chewing on the skin around the nail bed, thinking and worrying. "We were supposed to get everyone to deliver a guilty vote if it came to that."

"What do you mean 'if it came to that'?" I tried not to wince when the skin broke and blood pooled around her fingernail. Surprised, she pulled it out and wrapped a napkin around the finger, still looking confused and a little lost.

"I feel like you know what it means... you were there when he died." The macabre undertones in her statement sent chills down my spine. "When I heard he was dead, I decided it didn't matter. The research trip starts in a few days, and I'd already accepted it. They were holding my place for the trial, but even if I'd missed the trip, I wouldn't stay with the news station. I left the kit I bought, just gave it to them. It's not worth my life. When you spend time near people like that, people like Stump," her voice dropped to a whisper. "One wrong move, one comment on their behavior ends with your death."

"Not always, though?" Griffin asked, trying to bring a little cheer into the conversation. It was like he researched 'reasons to be cheerful' and then tried to infuse them into everyday life. It was obnoxious.

And a little sweet.

Like I could wrap him in a blanket and keep him safe from the harsh realities of life.

Madison patted him on the hand, offering me a sideways look of confusion. "Maybe in your world. In mine, 'if it comes to that' means he was always going to be found dead, one way or another."

I shrugged at her. "He's a rescue, they tend to see the silver lining."

"You're really stacking them up." She motioned to the dogs at my feet.

"No joke. The grocery bill is gonna suck. Did you see anyone with pills, drugs or... I don't know... who looked like they used?"

Madison was shaking her head before I even finished the question.

"They searched us for contraband before we came into the courtroom. Only people with documented medical conditions were able to bring anything in. There was a guy with a nut allergy who had an epi pen, another guy with asthma who got to keep his inhaler, and I think a third one had something for seizures? Maybe..."

I pulled the picture of the jury out of my cargo pocket and showed it to her.

"Who had what?"

"That was the guy with the EpiPen," she pointed to juror number nine, the only person wearing a suit and looking as stern as Trigger. If memory serves, he was the same man who'd gotten belligerent when Trigger was allowed to stay, and over the rules limiting bringing in medications. Maybe he was concerned over his own EpiPen getting taken away? "I remember thinking he was a dick. This guy had the inhaler." She directed us to juror five, a man with bleach blonde hair and an upside-down visor. "And this is the maybe seizure dude." Juror number twelve, a young guy with curly blonde hair and a dopey smile.

"Thank you, Madison. Really. I'm sorry things went the way they did."

"I've gotta go pack for my trip. For what it's worth..." She glanced between me and Ruger, standing up as she did. "Trigger was the best among us and possibly the only one who cared about right and wrong."

She offered Winnie one final pet. "They say everything happens for a reason, and I'm willing to accept that for me. But some shit's just wrong. I hope you find them. Not sure I care if it's alive or dead."

"Me too," I agreed, and she squeezed my hand on the table before turning away.

We watched her walk across the lot toward an older Nissan and slide in behind the wheel. Tears stung at my eyes, and I let a few of them fall for the man we'd all lost. A dedicated soldier who'd been burned by his country but never lost his sense of justice.

"Let's get you some food." Griffin stood up and offered me his hand. Winnie and Ruger both wagged their tails in agreement, forcing me to nod and accept the offered limb. He pulled me up and into a tight hug that felt too familiar for someone I'd just met. But I sank into it, letting his arms hold me together when it felt like everything was falling apart. If only for a moment, I needed the illusion that everything would be okay.

"And maybe while we eat," he whispered in my ear, sending shivers down my spine. A reminder of other ways to use men in times of crisis if one were so inclined. "You can tell me what Pangea is... or take me somewhere I can order it?"

I collapsed against him, laughing.

"Never change, puppy."

Chapter Thirteen: Feed the Birds

"So, this is Pangea?" Griffin looked at the pink sweet bread next to his massive wet burrito covered in red sauce and cheese. He took a knife and fork to cut into his burrito, and I could smell the chili that immediately caused his eyes to water. The banker was in trouble and I was in for lunch and a show.

"No, that's pan dulce. Pangea is a geological concept that all land masses were originally one and seismic or other planetary disturbances caused them to shift and separate." I took a bite of my street taco, starting with the carne asada. After living in Texas for canine training, I was pretty sure Ohio Mexican food would always disappoint, but this hole in the wall space had the authentic vibe and clientele that suggested it was worth a shot. Based on the bright red face, watery eyes and empty water glass in front of Griffin after two bites of burrito, I knew I had made the right call. "You OK there, puppy?"

"Yup." He wheezed, reaching for a tortilla chip. "Never better."

I laughed and let him dig his own grave. The dogs were in the Jeep outside, autumn keeping the temps in the comfortable sixties for them. Thanksgiving was just over a month away and my family wouldn't be here for it. Last year, my parents had made a small feast, my broken arm and invisible eyebrows making the meal more entertaining than it should have been. Seth and his kids had been there, but this year...

"You OK over there?" Griffin asked and I glanced at him. Sweat dripped down his hairline, but over half the burrito was gone.

"Yeah, just thinking."

"About that guy you're dating? Think he'll be mad we're getting lunch?" Griffin asked, stealing my water.

"So freaking creepy. No, Levi broke up with me for being... constantly in harm's way." I pushed some rice around my plate.

"What about that pet doctor? Seems like he wouldn't mind another spin on the old teacups." Griffin wiggled his eyebrows, and I held up a butter knife in warning.

"Call my teacups old again, and I will poke out your eyes, pal."

"Well, at least we're pals." He smiled and blew out another desperate breath. "You sure you're good?"

"Yeah. You? Need me to call the fire department?"

"Ha ha." He swiped snot from under his nose with the sleeve of his shirt. Sugar skull Dia de Los Muertos decoration seemed to mock him with me in equal measure, a reminder that both Halloween and Day of the Dead still loomed on the horizon and soon children would take to the streets for candy and mischief. "So, if it's not that we're both hopelessly single and should go on a date, what were you thinking about?"

"That you're lucky you live in Ohio, gringo." I mocked him, and he gave me the finger. "I also don't think we should go on a date."

"Maybe that's just me then. What do you think about our case?"

"Our case? Since when do we work together?" I asked, biting into my second taco.

"Since we both watched a man die in front of us and got locked in separate rooms for separate questioning. I think that means we're in this together, don't you?"

I ate a chip piled high with salsa and crunched it loudly in thought. While I didn't need a second human, it might be nice to have someone to talk at when I needed to work through ideas. Griffin's hopeless optimism and knowledge of finances might be helpful if this turned into a money thing.

"He's not the first man to die in front of me, I'm not sure that makes you special." I dumped salsa onto my taco, chewing slowly to savor the flavors. "What did you do in the Navy?"

"Not sure that's something to brag about, but ok. I was in special forces." He panted after scooping some salsa on a chip for himself. "How are you eating this?"

"You said special forces earlier, what did you do? Eye in the sky? Admin stuff? Recon? Drop and shoot?" I ignored his question about the salsa because honestly, it wasn't that hot. "Eat crayons with the marines and pretend they taste good?"

"Field intelligence operations."

I read between the lines on that one.

"You were a spy…" I crunched another chip. Watching Griffin, I noticed the way he sat, relaxed and carefree, the way he radiated hopeful ignorance talking to Madison. Being a spy made it possible that all of it was an act. Even now, I took notice of how beneath the beads of sweat, he still maintained proper awareness, baby blues sweeping the room at all times. "How do you go from spy to money guy, Mr. Allen?"

"Pissed off the wrong politician with the right connections." He shrugged and took another bite. Between watching him and keeping an eye on the dogs, I'd nearly forgotten the overly active Senior's Chat wreaking havoc on my phone. Griffin had created a notes app with the names he'd gleaned from the discourse, and as I scrolled through the incoming stream, it seemed like more and more were clocking out for an afternoon nap.

I glanced up at the man across from me, noting his silence after a vague answer.

"And?"

"And what?" He asked, looking out the window.

"And… what did you do? How did that lead to accounting? And Sweet Pea of all places?"

The man didn't answer, just stared at a brown sedan entering the parking lot at a slow crawl with jerking movements. Every few feet, the driver would stomp on the brake, then release, gas it, lurch forward, and repeat. Dropping two twenties on the table,

Griffin stood and walked to the door, forcing me to follow for the safety of my parking lot canines while I stuffed the last taco in my mouth whole.

Once outside, we moved to stand behind the Jeep like bumper sentries.

As the car got closer, I could see the driver was a teenage boy with slicked back hair and acne. Beside him was a man in a tie dye shirt with a ponytail, glasses and... a steering wheel that he kept redirecting away from other cars.

"Why does that car have two steering wheels?"

It lurched to a stop in front of an office two doors up, and the man exited with the cool air of a man convinced his life was not in jeopardy. The teenager got out, looking green around the gills and suspiciously damp in the trouser region. Standing, he had the long gangly appearance of a high schooler who didn't do sports. Black skinny jeans, a black band tee, and I put him more in line with the goth kids but didn't rule out the drama club.

"You're getting better, Steven," the man said, not a hint of sarcasm in his voice. If my testicles were real, they'd have shriveled at the knowledge this kid's driving had once been worse.

"This is so dumb. I don't see why I have to drive anyway, the planet's dying and it's not like I have a car." He huffed, and I put him in the emo drama club with a minor in pretending to care.

"I'll see you next week nevertheless." Ponytail pressed his palms together and bowed his head. "Namaste."

"Whatever."

Shoulders hunched, the kid slid his phone out and went to work as he slouched over to a waiting minivan. The woman behind the wheel was a bottle blonde with an inch of roots, her mouth moving in a near constant stream of invisible dialogue that was either part of a Bluetooth phone call, or she was rehearsing her Oscar monologue. Beside the brown car, ponytail stood perfectly still in the center of the sidewalk, staring up at the sky.

His long brown hair and scruffy beard looking familiar in the late morning light. Behind him, the storefront featured a bird urging her chicks toward the edge of the nest with the name: *I Believe You Can Fly Driving School.*

Talk about weighted messaging.

The man's head tilted, and I saw it.

"That's the foreman." Pulling up the chat and Griffin's notes. "Brant Harris–owns a driving school in Columbus..."

My phone died and I looked between the blank screen and the building, double checking the business name and address.

"What do you remember the seniors saying about him?" I asked Griffin over my shoulder. He was bent over, sweating. A loud gurgle came from his lower abdomen followed by an audible fart. "Never mind. You should... find a toilet."

I started moving closer. Brant continued to stand there, watching the sky with all the attention and focus Winnie reserves for someone holding a snack. He didn't blink, barely breathed, and if not for the slow rise and fall of the hairs below his nostrils, I'd think he was a powered down robot.

"There's a bad omen on the horizon," he said when I was a foot away and I jumped.

"Brant Harris? Foreman from the Marius Howser case?" I asked, deciding to give back another foot and stand a respectable two feet from the man.

"That's what it says on my documents. But those are certainly not without flaws, and anyone can write anything, you know?" I took a half step farther away from him and sniffed slightly. There was no smell of the Devil's Lettuce, ethanol, or... I had no idea what LSD smelled like, so that remained a potential explanation. "Who we are is not defined by what we put on paper, but by what we put in the universe and right now, what's in the universe is not being well-received..."

I followed his line of sight to a group of small black starlings. They circled above in a mass, not quite circular, but an erratic dance against the grey clouds that echoed with their cries across the concrete strip mall of suburbia.

"Sure... murder tends to do that. Did you ever talk to Trigger?"

The swarm grew in chaos, and I resisted the urge to cover my head. Being pooped on by a bird wouldn't be outside my range of luck, but it would be really gross. As I'd already seen Winnie eat something questionable off the ground by the coffee shop, there were already really gross things in my future, and I didn't want to add to the list.

"His death angers the birds."

"Does it anger you?"

He puffed out a breath and looked at me for the first time. His eyes tracked to the Jeep behind me and I saw two sets of ears poking out of the window.

"You are the guardian. Come to seek justice and safety, the birds brought you to me, but I don't know how I can help." His face crinkled and I mentally re-evaluated his age. I'd placed him in his forties initially, but he may have been closer to sixty. The timeline would have better lent itself to experiences in the summer of love, and permanent chemical imbalance.

"Marius Howser said most of the jury was blackmailed. Were you one of the people being blackmailed?"

"Should you be using the word blackmailed?" His response was directed at the sky.

"I... why should I not?"

"Why should you not, what?" He swayed gently in the overcast light.

"Use the word blackmailed?"

"Who said you shouldn't?" A cloud briefly drifted away from the sun and bathed him in light. Silver strands glittered in his hair.

"You just did!"

"Did I?" He gazed pensively into the sun as the cloud returned to conceal its light. "Perhaps the birds told me. Language is fraught with historical injustice."

Groaning, I pulled out my phone to search what LSD smells like, and the history of the word blackmail, only to discover the device was still dead.

"OK, well, assuming we can use the word, and you are not higher than the empire state, were you blackmailed?"

"I can see that you don't think I'm rational, but I assure you the birds know a great deal. When the men in suits came, attempting to remove me from jury duty, they told me not to allow it. All of the threats and leverage they believed they had, the conviction I had better things to do and would gladly be relieved of my duty, were for naught."

I tried not to point out that he didn't *see* anything, I flat out told him. But at least we were getting somewhere.

"Is that how they did it, then? Blackmailing people they wanted to control into sitting on the jury and attempting to bully those legitimately called on to pass the summons along?" It begged the question how they could possibly know who received a summons, and how they found their would-be targets for blackmail. "How did you end up the foreman?"

"I believe that is how it happened. Can't know for sure without a complete inventory of all parties and I'm afraid not everyone was inclined to speak with me, your friend included. He found me... spacey..." Brant glanced over at Ruger and gave him a small smile. "His dog did not share similar burdens. The birds told me to turn down the men in suits, and I'm glad I did, but they did not tell me death would befall my jury mates."

I stared at the starlings and then saw a crow land on top of the brown car. Its head shifted, one amber eye inspecting us with a too-knowing look.

"What would you have done differently if you'd known?" I asked, not sure the question was relevant, but I was curious anyway. The man was clearly orbiting the rings of Saturn, and somehow it gave the illusion of perspective.

If I knew someone would die, I'd probably try to stop it.

Then end up setting something on fire. Breaking something. Maybe getting shot at.

"I'm not certain. If death is forecasted, it's near impossible to stop." A second crow landed beside the first and Brant tensed. "Though I still would have upheld my civic duty, I may have been less inclined to allow some of the slights I witnessed pass me by. The media, the lawyers, the bailiff, they all seemed to know something and those who tried to speak up were silenced. Such as it is, the crows acknowledge the attempted murder."

Griffin moaned and I looked over at him, he was now squatting, clutching his guts, and sweating. I couldn't smell or hear anything, but I guessed there was about two minutes between this and his ass being on fire.

"Is he unwell?"

"He's too white for real Mexican food," I replied, watching realization hit him before he ran back inside to the nearest bathroom. "My guess is diarrhea."

A third crow landed, and Brant looked at me, fear etched into his paler face.

"What? He'll be fine, everyone poops a lot occasionally, it's not..."

A gnarled finger pointed at the birds. "A murder. A murder is going to happen right in front of you! Please, leave me!"

He darted inside his office space, and I stared at the three crows, all of them watching me.

"I know it's a raven in the story, but if any of you say 'nevermore' I will shoot you." I walked back to the car to wait out Griffin's stomach problems with a dead cell phone and a new sense of dread. Stroking Winnie's ears, I met Ruger's eyes and pretended the crows weren't still watching me.

"That man's just crazy. No one's going to get murdered in front of me. If they do, I'll eat a pound of dog fur."

But if they did, it wouldn't be the first time... for the murder or the eating of dog fur.

Chapter Fourteen: Real Estate Royalty

By the time I got back to my apartment, my phone had been dead for three hours and I was scared to plug it in. Griffin had politely requested I leave him at his vehicle with directions to anywhere with a public restroom that would allow him to absolutely wreck it and promised I was done with field work for the afternoon.

I directed him to Amber's Shoe Ambrosia and said I was more or less out of motivation to track down jurors this late in the day. I'd attempted to call the attorney, Patrick Patterson, with follow-up questions only for a recording to say the line was disconnected.

"Do you think the Seniors will be mad at me?" I asked Winnie. Her eyebrows danced, the little indentions over her amber eyes moving in a wave that suggested I knew the answer. Ruger was flopped on his side, eyeing me from the corners like I should know better than to leave the house without a charger.

"I don't own a car charger," I told him, and he huffed out a long breath, rolled on his back and then flopped to the other side, facing away from me. "Wow, judgey much?"

Winnie's response was to fart, loudly, and then fan it my direction with her tail.

"That's chemical warfare, lady!" I waved a hand in front of my face, gasping for air. I turned on the oscillating fan and let it cleanse the air in my office while the phone got some juice, and I made some more coffee. My whiteboard was still in the middle of my room, and I knew where I needed to go next, but I really didn't want to find out about "God's plan for the animals".

"Knock, knock!" A cheery voice called in to my back door and Winnie jumped up. Before she could take two steps, a dark-skinned man with a big blonde wig, press on nails, and a killer pink suit walked in on pink snakeskin stilettos. "I heard you need a home?"

"Umm..." I stared at him, his handbag the correct size for a small dog... or an army of gnomes. "Yes?"

"Great! I'm Princess Liana, reigning queen of Rentals That Aren't a Drag, and I am here to show you what's in our inventory and see if we can get you and your little babies into a new place. How does that sound?" Liana finished, striking a pose in the middle of the room and a terrier popped its head out of her bag, barking like Meowth after Team Rocket delivered their monologue. "And this is Fluffy."

"Do you breathe air?" I asked, stunned at how many words she'd said in so little time. "Also, coffee?" I gestured toward the machine that just beeped. Maybe I couldn't walk in heels, coordinate a pose with dogs, match an ensemble, or look that good in pink, but apparently coffee makers obeyed my caffeine needs.

Between that and being a dog mother of two, I was really going places.

Mostly outside and to places with potential murderers, but those counted as a places.

"Thank you darling, coffee would be divine. I take it black, like my men and my ass." I swallowed my request that we refrain from oversharing in the future. If my choices were Liana or some Tom Nichols in a polo on wife number two mansplaining the market to me, I'd take the drag queen.

"I'm cool with the last two, but black coffee is disgusting, and you should rethink your life choices." I gestured to the assortment of options before me. Princess Liana floated to the chair in front of my desk and draped her lithe frame into the seat with the precision of a marksman. "Like seriously, you can expand your horizons right here, free of charge and judgement."

"Look at you, vanilla latte, judging me for coffee. I've been hated on for skin color, drag, and being gay, but your line in the sand is drinking plain coffee?" She questioned as I put coffee in two mugs that nearly killed the pot. Small coffee mugs were for the weak and the lame.

Shrugging, I nodded as I doctored mine into a delightful off brown.

"Two out of the first three aren't optional, and drag looks hella fun, but how can you be all that." I gestured up and down. "And drink the bitter liquid of sadness? No one that fabulous should do anything boring and this is boring."

I dropped the cup off in front of her, sad and black beside the most glamorous existence to grace this room. I dropped into my chair and stared at the phone having seizures on my desktop. My body quivered, shoulders hunched to my ears, while I wondered how many notifications it would take to kill the vibrate motor.

"Someone's popular," Princess Liana commented, sipping the bitter liquid.

"Murder's popular, I'm just an excuse to be nosey." I gestured to the board. I'd added the four names Griffin had pulled from the chat before the phone's death. Juror number eight, Meggie Elliott, a soccer mom from Springfield. Brant Harris, the Foreman, who taught driver's ed out of a strip mall in Columbus and believed the birds spoke to him. Deanna Schafer worked for an assisted living facility in Cincinnati, juror number seven and my top suspect based on her proximity to drugs. Then Oliver Hartley, juror eleven, whose name was remarkably similar to Olivia, but he looked like a mop-headed enthusiast from the suburbs. He worked in IT for some corporation, completely remote, and lived next door to Olivia.

Something told me one of them was meant to be there and the other one was an accident.

"That's some whacked out shit up there, hun." Princess Liana interjected her opinion into my thoughts, and I startled back into the room without disagreement. "You look like a nut job with that board."

"That's... not an inaccurate assessment. What brings you by? I just filled out the interest form and half of it was blank?" I took another long drink of coffee as the phone finally stilled on my desk. Two hundred and eleven text messages.

I didn't even know the notification numbers could go that high.

"Well, I saw your app and thought I'd come in and get started working with you before the vultures turned up. There's not a lot of people looking to move into this town that aren't moving into the senior's apartments, so stiff competition and I was up anyway. Now..." She pulled a tablet out of her bag, the terrier wearing pink bows panting politely with her paws on the rim. Winnie and Ruger had both lifted their heads at her bark, but neither cared enough to even come over and sniff. I'm not saying we discriminate against small dogs as a family, but you wouldn't find one in my house unless it wandered in by mistake and I confused it with a house slipper. "It says you're looking for a house. No stairs, reasonably sized yard, kitchen... preferably with an oven?"

She glanced up at that and I shrugged.

"I don't have one. I used to use my mom's but... Let's change preferably to definitely. Also, coffee maker outlets and... a shower and a toilet?"

"In the kitchen?" Liana pressed a manicured hand to her chest.

"No, in the house. Although in the kitchen it might be convenient. Inputs and outputs in the same place... cut down on unnecessary walking and no one would invite themselves over for dinner." I pondered that, staring at the steam billowing out of my mug. It would be efficient, but not hygienic unless you had a handwashing station and mandatory exit rules. "Eh, better go with in the house but not the kitchen. I don't need any accidental toaster baths and also no one has probably designed such a house."

"Yeah, cuz that is what's wrong with that." She delivered an eye roll and poked some parts of her screen with gem encrusted acrylics that stuck out at least an inch beyond the tips of her fingers. "For budget you put unknown?"

"Correct."

"How is that correct?"

"I don't know my budget. Mostly because I don't know how much I make." I shifted in my chair from butt cheek to butt cheek, scratching Ruger on the chin. "My card doesn't get declined when I buy pet food or snacks and the auto pay utilities haven't gotten shut off, so... enough to survive and maybe buy?"

"Girl, log into your bank account and check that!"

"I can't."

"What do you mean you can't?" She was about to jump to her stilettos and spill coffee on my floor, forcing me to let loose a warning growling. With an impressive feat of tonsil power, she chugged the liquid and set the empty mug on my desk. "Open the banking website on your computer!"

"No, I mean I can access the site—" My cell phone started vibrating across my desk again and I saw it was a call from my mom. "But I lost the password. And then I got locked out of my email, so I couldn't reset it. Then I tried to go to the bank, but the woman at the desk threw a fit because I brought Winnie with me and she stole the lady's doughnut. I think it would have been fine, but the lady was eight months pregnant and on the verge of a homicidal rampage and that doughnut was the only thing between her and America's Most Wanted, so I threw some cash for a new doughnut on the floor and ran."

Silence followed my story, and I glanced at the Princess. Her mouth was hanging open, horror in her eyes, and I wasn't sure if it was the theft of food from a pregnant woman or the realization she got all dolled up and came over here for someone who had no idea how much money they made.

My money was on the latter, because stealing food was a Winnie special.

"You might not want to let your mouth hang open like that too long, bugs can fly in." I gestured to a fly floating through the room. My phone went off again. "While you... come to terms with my life choices I'm going to answer my mom."

Picking up the phone, I stabbed the green button and held it near-ish to my face.

"The seniors want to know why you've ghosted their chat!" She yelled into the device, and I put it back down onto my desk.

"I didn't ghost the chat. My phone died. Then while it was charging a real estate agent came over to tell me about what's available without stairs, that has a yard and preferably a kitchen with an oven and no bathroom."

"What? Why do you need that?" She was somehow louder, and I moved my phone even farther away from me. "If this is about everyone moving, you can't leave this town, Cynthia! There are-"

"Ma! Pause the tirade. Remember I need to move for Ruger? He can't do the stairs in this place as many times a day as we do. It's aggravating his stab wound scar tissue and the tendon's already partially re-torn. I also have to get rid of my Jeep, which isn't so bad since it still has the glitter pink steering column, but I can't get into my bank account so I don't know how much rent I can afford. As you can see, there is a lot going on and I need financial access, a real estate person, a car person and... I don't know, a personal assistant to manage my phone but the one who was handling that got diarrhea."

"Your dog has a stab wound?" Princess Liana choked out and I looked up at her.

"Yeah, that one. He got it when this crazy lady who was grossly involved with her son kidnapped his owner and tried to eliminate both of them... that man." I pointed to the board where Trigger's somber juror repose hung. "Someone killed him on that trial. And I'm going to find out who... Right after I get info from the medical examiner or... I don't know, hopefully someone who took a blood sample so we can confirm toxicology and that the blood on the marble dresser was his. Hopefully took some pictures to see if there was bruising on the chest like someone shoved him... or a tattoo he left on his thigh inked in blood that says 'this wasn't an accident and X person did it' which would be both convenient and gross..."

"You don't think he fell either? I thought everyone was buying the party line."

My mom stuttered and then stopped what she was about to say across the line.

"Clarence?" she asked, and I shook my head.

"No, mom, this is Princess Liana," I corrected her, but the real estate royalty disagreed.

"No, ma'am, I'm also Clarence. Medical examiner for the state. I examined Mr. Sampson when he came in. They claimed he must have fallen out of his wheelchair and hit his head on the table. Showed me scene photos and expected me to rubber stamp it. Nobody wanted my report after, either. But his muscular structure and time in the chair didn't align with a person who would just fall out."

Princess Liana seemed to have folded back inside, and I could see the man underneath. I'd have placed him at thirty in drag, but the lines around his eyes said he was fifty. A pair of round glasses appeared from his handbag, and I watched them add a couple more years to my estimate. He stood and studied the board.

"I hadn't looked at this properly when I came in. Thought you might be a conspiracy nut trying to solve the Marius Howser death. Or maybe a Stump supporter trying to prove how everyone was against him and he's the real victim. You knew Mr. Sampson?"

"Trigger. He went by Trigger. I didn't know him well, but I nearly cost him his life trying to help some veterans earlier this year and he trusted me with his dog. Four decades in hostile territory for his country, killing or getting information to kill, and he survived. But the civic duty of jury service was what killed him... I'd laugh if I wasn't actively plotting vengeance on whoever killed him when I find them. Normally I'm a pacifist but..." My mom snorted through the line, and I elected to ignore her interruption as a cough. "I'm tired of just letting shit go and letting the system sort it out. The system has failed us."

Clarence looked at each picture carefully, reading what I had and what I didn't.

"Juror number two is a man named Jordan Moerer. He actually lives near here in Yellow Springs, a vehicle mechanic. Served in the Vietnam war and occasionally comes by the club where he performs as Lizzy McTire. A busty blonde mechanic with a cartoon puppet who serves as her internal narrator?"

I looked at the older man in the image. The image was grainy and yet somehow, he was less discernible than every other juror. I couldn't pinpoint a nationality, an age or a hair color, but I was now certain that if he performed with boobs, they were not his. The man was barely the width of his chair with a small pooch in the belly, and if a gust of wind came by it would take him and his hair away, separately.

"I don't think he's your guy, but I can call him up and see if he has time to come by."

"That would be nice. Thank you."

"This man, number nine, he looks familiar. I can't place him, and it might not be him but his relation… I'll have to think on it, but there's something about him… and this man up here. What's under his shirt?" The medical examiner pointed at the lawyer's picture from the parking lot.

"I have a suspicion it's stolen dry cleaning. You don't think that's just a few extra pounds?"

"With the cut of that suit and the pristine shoes? If he had extra weight, you'd never see it." Clarence kept looking at the pictures, finally removing his glasses and turning back to me. "Is this what you do for work? Private Investigation?"

"Not exactly. I don't get paid for it all the time, at least not in money, but in exchange for my services to the town, Mrs. Margot lets me live above here for free. She owns the building. It's why I have no idea what my budget is. I work for The Dairy, with the animals, and a lot of my paycheck gets eaten up paying for shit Winnie destroys, so that's another issue… but…" I swallowed, trying to figure out how to word my next question. "You said you wrote up a report and did a full work up on Trigger?"

"You're wondering where that report is?" He looked at me, sliding his glasses back on to peer at me over the top. "You think I made it up?"

"No… I… think you were encouraged to misplace it. Which, wouldn't blame you, but I was wondering if there was any way a version of it still existed? The lawyer said your computer was wiped." I tried to look contrite while getting more coffee, but it was hard to do at six feet tall with a raging case of FAFO for the government that murdered your friend.

"Girl, do I look like I just fell off the turnip truck?" He pushed me out of the way and refilled his empty mug first. "When no one wanted my report, I pretended it didn't matter while saving digital and hard copies off site. Some white people come around, asking where it was and I said, 'oh somewhere, no one wanted it'. Next day, my desktop hard drive crashes at work and my home computer gets a bit of malware that eats all files stored on it? Uh uh, that's shadier than a rainforest at high noon. But it was also amateur hour, because the external drive in my desk was untouched, which is what everything gets backed up onto. My laptop wasn't touched, and the bug in my phone was so old, it was practically a fourth generation granpappy fruit fly."

I forced my eyes open wider, trying to remember population genetics. Clarence was using so many references and mixed colloquialisms, I was going to need a treasure map and a shovel to sort through them all once he was gone. The only thing that made perfect sense was the comparison of technology and fruit flies both aging rapidly but...

"Wouldn't getting rid of the bug tip them off?"

"It would, so I only carry that phone at work and on my day-to-day errands. Once I'm off the clock, it's locked up tight." He snapped his fingers, and I wasn't sure if we were back to the Princess and I should switch pronouns, or he was still Clarence. Was it the glasses or the attitude that delineated them?

"Are you Clarence or the Princess right now? I don't know which pronouns to use in my head." I decided to ask when the very thought of guessing made me want to close my eyes and curl up in a dog bed. "It bothers me to be inaccurate."

"Girl, I don't care. I'm me no matter what you call me. Now, the report." She walked back to her purse and stroked the little dog on its head. As Fluffy raised its head for chin scratches, I saw a small flat flash drive dangling from the metal D ring on its collar. Clarence worked it off and handed it over to me. "You'll find that there were a few suspicious marks on his body, a whole heap load of scars, and he was dosed pretty heavily with narcotics. I imagine if a hypothetical other medical examiner hadn't let it go, they would have said the drugs were for his many injuries, but... well, I needed a place to take my information before I knew what to make of it. The key to the lock is Dissent, with a capital D, as you know."

"What was he dosed with?" I asked, turning the drive over between my fingers. It reminded me of being handed a file by Trigger a few months ago and ending up with a target painted on my back.

Once I walked down this road, I couldn't walk back.

"Fentanyl laced trazodone, enough to take out a hundred eighty-pound man if he hadn't built a tolerance, which you might already know from the swabs taken off the point of impact. But what you might not know is that it's medical grade. There was no cut in the mixture, so whoever and wherever it came from, it was a pure and sterile, medically source."

Deanna was looking better and better.

Chapter Fifteen: Poor Sportsmanship

The Princess departed with instructions to call her once I knew my budget while Clarence offered me a weighted look and a warning to proceed with caution. My mom had hung up after the cause of death had been confirmed non-accidental and, in the silence, I pondered who the hell had jurisdiction.

And more importantly, who I could tell without ending up dead.

Stuck for an option, I called Carla.

"I was wondering when you'd call me," she said, forgoing normal greetings like hello, how are you, sorry I'm bailing on you. "Your timing isn't great, but..."

In the background, there was shouting and the high-pitched double trill of a whistle.

"Are you at a sports?" I stared at my empty coffee cup and the coffee pot on the other side of the room. It was barely noon, and I was possibly two pots in... maybe three before counting the takeaway coffees I'd gotten on the road with the money man. Or was it four?

"You're not listening, are you?" Carla grumbled and I shook my head at the empty room, since the sleeping dogs weren't exactly present. "I'm guessing you just shook your head. I said yes, I'm at a youth soccer game near Columbus. What did you need?"

"Why are you watching youth sports? Are you planning on forcing that unborn child to do group activities? Because you've met my family, the only people doing group activities are my parents and those are not suitable for children!" I shuddered at the memory of the public lewdness charge. Nothing like collecting your partially naked, fornicating parents from a police station and then seeing the artwork from the "interpretive dance and life drawing class" every time you visit.

Dance with No Pants was now on the list of activities explicitly prohibited on park signs in Sweet Pea and throughout the county.

"First of all, didn't you try and play basketball every year you were in school until eventually they had to let you when the whole rest of the team got mono?"

"From your deputy and then I accidentally set the gym on fire."

"Still, you have some level of cooperative spirit. Second, we wanted to try martial arts, but... it didn't go well, so this was the best way we could think of to work on the aggression issues... Soccer was never more violent."

"Soccer is pretty violent, but your kid isn't born yet, and Erich is pretty mellow..." My eyes widened, and I stopped staring longingly at my coffee pot. "You didn't!"

"She needed an outlet!" The whistle trilled again, and I heard someone scream the feral cry of war.

"She needs to be locked in a zoo exhibit! And you tried martial arts first?"

"Yeah... and she beat up the Tae Kwon Do instructor. He was doing a demo and wanted to demonstrate that with the right holds and moves, size is irrelevant? So, he had Sylvie do the grabbing self-defense hold... she broke his wrist in two places."

"And you thought spikey shoes and kicking people was a better idea?"

"Actually, we tried water polo next, and she almost drowned a twelve-year-old. The kid might be on America's Most Wanted in the next five years." Carla audibly winced through the line, and I didn't bother asking what new horrors my niece had unleashed. "These poor red dragons..."

Her words perked my brain, and I glanced at the board.

"Red Dragons out of Springfield?" I asked, hopping to my feet and double checking the notes on the board. "Club league?"

"Yeah... why?"

"I think one of the juror's has a kid who plays on that team. Isn't soccer season in the spring? It's fall! Don't they have to do American Football this time of year?"

"It's a club, they play year-round. Do you think we should put her in tackle football?" Carla's skepticism was overshadowed by her alarm when an audible crunch rattled through the line. "Oh god, I think she broke someone's leg. I'll drop you a pin to the field, I have to go."

The line went dead, and I stared at Meggie Elliott. Juror 8 had light brown hair, light brown eyes, rosy cheeks, and pleasant smile. Meggie's outfit showcased an ample chest, a moderate waistline, and based on the level of her head beside the other jurors, an average height.

"Whatcha lookin' at?"

I jumped out of my skin and turned around swinging. The voice right behind my ear had wisely already taken two steps back. Larry Kirby stood in jeans, chucks, and an animal science shirt that was the livestock equivalent of the Da Vinci man. His dark hair was messy, wire rimmed glasses were halfway down his nose, but the easy smile was still there.

As was his disarming heat and the freshly showered scent of soap and witch hazel.

"Considering we were recently shot at, do you think it's wise to sneak up on me?"

My phone vibrated and Carla's pin drop came through. The red dot was at an athletic complex halfway between Columbus and Springfield. Below that was a message that Sylvie had been red carded, and she'd call me later.

"Damn. I don't want to go to a children's sports game," I mumbled, and Larry rested his head on my shoulder to read the message.

"Why does it say you have 169 unread messages?"

"Because life sucks," I sighed, whistling for my furry charges to go on yet another trip to the capitol.

"How do I keep having passengers for this?" I searched for a parking space in row four of 700. The athletic field complex was filled with minivans and SUVs, all featuring some variation of stick figure families or "Baby on Board" plaques that made me think of being strapped to a backboard in an ambulance.

"There's a spot, on your right," Larry called out, and I slid into the space between a blue minivan that said, "my other ride is a Tardis" and had a series of soccer balls with jersey numbers and a cherry red SUV declaring their child was an honor roll student at Alexander Hamilton Elementary.

"Why do people with children constantly need to tell the world about them? Like, I get it, you procreated, but not everything they do needs to be advertised on the back of your vehicle!" I climbed out and opened the back door for the dogs. Lifting Ruger out, I clipped on his leash and then did the same when Winnie sleepily appeared beside him. "It's a car, not a fridge. No one cares what your kid did in school yesterday but you."

"You put expert marksman on the back of your Jeep." Larry pointed out, taking one of the leashes and walking with me toward the fields.

"That's different!"

"How?"

"For starters, it's my accomplishment." I scanned the fields and looked for something that looked red and dragon-like amid the army of miniature humans and parents. "And for finishers, it serves the larger purpose of reminding people who tailgate me that I can shoot them... with expert levels of precision."

"Do you have your gun?" Larry asked, leading us to the left. There was a subdued group of girls in blue facing off against a somehow more subdued group of girls in red and gold.

"No."

"Then you can't actually shoot anyone."

"I ask again, why are you here? No one invited you!" I tried to take back Winnie's leash as we got closer to the players and their parents.

"I invited me. You're welcome." He gave me his most charming smirk, showing off perfect teeth and the wicked glint that had conned me out of my pants more than once. "Also, I never got to tell you what I needed to say the other day."

We'd arrived at field number eleven, my feet catching slightly on the wheel indents heading toward the roadway from the red team side of the field. Beneath the somber expressions was a kind of giddy joy, the girls whispering and restless while pretending something tragic happened. Eyeing the opposite side, the girls

had the same energy. Whoever had been carted off had been...
despised.

Score one for Sylvie, I guess.

I circled the field slowly, eyeing each parent sitting in foldable camp chairs just beyond the drawn white lines. Three men in cargo shorts and hoodies with the team logo, probably mid-thirties, fiddled with their cell phones while occasionally glancing at the field. An older man had a blanket on his lap, appearing to be asleep beneath his oversized hat until he randomly yelled.

"What the hell, Kaylee? Get your head in the game!"

Two women fresh out of college were slicing oranges beside the bench with spare girls, all wearing team colors. A woman who could be their mom wielded a clipboard and visor, shouting instructions that meant nothing.

"Is this what we missed out on by being uncoordinated losers?" Larry watched a parent on the blue team scream at a little blonde girl when her kick missed the ball. Considering they were under ten, the level of hostility and commitment had to be compensation for personal shortcomings.

"Speak for yourself. This is what I missed out on for having parents who were too old and done with being parents to care what I did. This is who I'm looking for." I showed him the juror screen shot, and the social media shot of Meggie. Once I had her name, I was able to get better images, but that strategy hadn't worked for everyone on the list of names the Seniors had rooted out.

"Speaking of your parents…" Larry started, stopping short and gripping my arm as a ball rolled in front of us and a girl scampered after it. "They umm…"

"Are leaving the country to teach abroad. Yeah, they dropped that on me last night, as did Seth and Carla who are moving away, and Heidi. They told you first?" I stared at him, annoyed and then concerned when he looked like I punched him.

"They're… leaving?"

"Yeah… you didn't know?" My confusion redoubled when he searched the sideline for something and didn't see it.

"Carla never said… why wouldn't… damn-it! So you're leaving too?" He was vibrating, hands shaking Winnie's leash and face turning red. "Your whole family is moving away so I guess you are too? They bought out the Carters, so I don't owe…"

"They bought out the Carters?" It was my turn to look like I'd been punched. "They just… gave you the money?"

"Some of it… I'd saved up a lot and earned more than a decent number of tips at Eggplants. But my mom was getting out of control and your mom came to me when she heard mine telling Mrs. Margot about the giraffe nursery." He shuddered and I blinked at him.

"Are there… Do we have giraffes in Sweet Pea? Or is this about the one that birthed goo on me in fourth grade?"

"No, my mom was plotting the giraffe themed nursery for the baby I would have with Amber. There was a plan for her to either convince me to have unprotected sex while she was ovulating or ride me while I was asleep, so we'd have a baby together and be forced to marry."

I swallowed the bile that crept up my throat. Larry and I hadn't been an item for a while, but to take away his autonomy and choices... Including planned rape. She was really losing her grasp on reality if she was trying to arrange a baby trap situation to stimulate the population. I'd have to buy that woman a red hat and a pro-no-choice button for Christmas.

"That's... really bad, dude." I choked trying to not involve myself in his family drama.

"Your mom thought so too, which is why she gave me the money. Now if Amber comes near me, I can get a restraining order or something..."

"Like a taser?" I suggested, not joking. "Or a baseball bat with nails?"

I circled around a closed field, coming at the last one from behind a set of bleachers. At the very end of the row, in a double camp chair, I spotted Meggie Elliott with a blanket on her lap. She was practically hidden, the chair facing away from the field toward an empty lot, blocked from view by an easy up and several coolers, and completely obscured from the field by the bleachers. If you weren't actively looking, you might have missed the chair altogether, and most of the spectators had.

Meggie's eyes were partially closed, the maroon blanket in her lap clutched between her fingers in a white-knuckle death grip, legs holding up a large portion of the blanket. Her rigid posture gave me pause, the chair also in line with the tire tracks, and I started thinking she might have heat stroke... Except it was only sixty degrees.

Before I could call for help, she shuddered and fell back against her chair. Her arms went limp, resting in her lap, but her legs continued to form a giant lump under the blanket. Seizure followed by rigor mortis was my first thought, but I quickly dismissed it when she started stroking her belly, lips moving subtly. Still, no one seemed to see her, and she was definitely not watching the game through the eye in the back of her head between the feet of those seated in the stand.

"Is that your juror?" Larry whispered. Nodding, I started to move closer and stopped short as her legs lowered and... a man popped up behind the chair, wiping his mouth and looking extremely pleased with himself. His khaki pants had grass stains on the knees, hair mussed, and the hoodie he wore failed to conceal his excitement at what he'd just done. "Woah... did he just... in the middle of a soccer game behind the bleachers like a high schooler?"

"Yup... and that's another juror or alternate juror. Whatever you call him, he is definitely not married to her."

Chapter Sixteen: Polyamorous Adventures

"So..." I leaned awkwardly against Meggie's van, blocking the driver's door while her daughter climbed in through the slider. The blonde girl had scored the final goal of the game, clinching the win for the red dragons and she already had headphones in and a screen in her hand, tuning out the world. "I think we should talk."

"I'm sorry?" Meggie folded her arms under her boobs while grass strains walked up behind her, running his hands down her arms. "Why the hell would I talk to you?"

"Well, actually, both of you should talk to me. Because otherwise I'll need to tell the authorities what dude was doing at a children's sport's game, and then they can ask you about Trigger's murder while you register as offenders." I tried and failed to not look disgusted with them. "Then I assume your spouses will be informed and it'll be a thing..."

"Keep your voice down." Meggie's face fell and grass stains looked paler than normal. Considering he was already a balding white man with blue eyes; this put him on par with Casper. "Look, it was just a one-time thing. No one was paying attention, we were away from the area of play and out of sight, and the game was a lock. We were just a little... we missed each other, OK?"

"No, that's not OK. And I think you know it's not. So, you're having an affair, right in front of your kid?" I tried to keep my voice low. "That's so fluffed up!"

"It's not an affair!" She rubbed her temples and looked back at the man who'd recently been worshipping at her altar. "Look, let me get Libby home and then we can meet somewhere to talk."

"Who's we?" I looked at the man behind her. Larry's presence filled the space behind me, his warmth seeping in through my long sleeve shirt, reminding me the closer to nightfall we got, the colder it was. My watch said it was barely two in the afternoon, but the sun said it was night-night time. "I still don't have a name for you, jury alternate."

"Dane McKinney." He extended his hand, but I didn't take it. We both stared at it, hanging there while the implications of sanitation dawned on him. Lips pressed together, he returned it to his side, cheeks turning red. "Why don't we meet at the pizza place on Tenth? Then we can celebrate Libby's win and clear the air with all parties?"

The little girl was already zoned into the screen world, laughing happily at whatever nonsense was happening. My first inclination was to say she was happy enough in her headphones, and demand answers. But on cue, my stomach rumbled.

"We'll meet you at the pizza place." Larry stepped in, taking my hand and walking me back to the Jeep. Ruger and Winnie were already resting in the doggie hammock. "You can't persist on coffee and spite alone, Cyn. You have to eat something."

"I didn't fight you!" I complained, walking to the driver's side door and climbing in. "Why are you lecturing me when I came with you willingly?"

The minivan backed out and I did the same, following a safe distance toward the park exit.

"That's exactly why I'm lecturing you! If you'd eaten something today besides coffee and the souls of weak-willed men, you would have punched me for telling you what to do!" He had his phone in his hand and was already working the device before we made it onto the roadway. "It scares the crap out of me when you don't fight me. Want the usual on a large?"

I glanced at his screen and saw a picture of a pizza.

"Are you ordering online?" I asked, taking a turn behind Meggie.

"Yeah. You need to eat now, and no way am I risking that man asking me to share unless I see him wash his hands and his face. Just because I would climb this center console and oblige you in a second if you asked, does not mean I want some other dude's stinky fingers touching my pizza."

I swallowed, trying not to imagine him climbing over to make good on that declaration as I navigated the car through the early evening traffic.

"You're thinking about it."

"No..." I shifted in my seat, trying and failing to get slightly farther away from him. "I'm just... hungry."

"Me too," he said, gaze heated. The whole car vibrated, rumbling loudly as I briefly drifted us toward the solid double yellows. Jumping, I jerked the wheel back and overcorrected. A Honda honked at me and Larry laughed, a masculine rumble that vibrated through me as thoroughly as the roadway rumble strips. "Say the word, Cyn. I'm happy to give without taking. As Meggie said, I just miss you. Any part I can get... I'll take."

My mouth went dry, throat sticking shut, holding all the words that could emerge inside with thoughts of what we could have been. In front of us, the minivan turned on the blinker, and we turned into the lot of a small pizza place, already filled with cars featuring the same stickers I'd seen at the park.

"Is it like, a migratory pattern? Start in one place then go to the next? Everyone just... merry-go-rounds between destinations?" I watched Libby hop out of the van. Meggie followed close behind her, listening to the excited chatter coming out of the kid's mouth that I couldn't hear over the hot doggie breath blowing in my ear.

"No way. You are staying in here and eating exactly zero cheese!" I warned her, watching Winnie's ears fall flat against her head. Her brown eyes widened, pleading for all she's worth. "No way. It's too many stairs for Ruger, and you get gas. We won't be able to run away!"

Her eyebrows danced while another head appeared beneath hers. Ruger's eyes made the same pleading expression, whites showing in desperation, pepperoni smell invading the car eliciting drool from everyone. I dug into my cargo pockets and pulled out a bag of beef flavored dog treats. Giving one to each dog, I slid out of the car with a stern warning to both.

"Do not leave this car." Neither acknowledged me as they chewed on their beef treat, so I took that as confirmation.

Larry and I met at the front of the car, his hand going to my lower back to navigate me through the parking lot. My brain assumed it was for safety reasons as there were numerous trip hazards in the area, but my heart rate kicked up, remembering his offer from the car. The lower lady regions were game, but my emotions weren't down, and I stepped away as soon as we reached the sidewalk beside the short brick building.

A planter filled with ice plants ran the length, the tan bricks holding up the Cecily's Pizza sign. From the sidewalk, I could hear the deafening laughter and screeches of children inside, at least two infants crying, and a line cook dropping a metal pizza pan. An arcade game made alien pew-pew attack sounds, a collection of girls screaming to kill something, while through it all the steady hum of conversation wove through the never-ending cacophony. All of it an assault on the senses.

From the sidewalk.

With the doors closed.

"You know... I don't think I really need to know if they murdered Trigger. I have Ruger, and he's safe, and arresting them won't bring him back. It'll just maybe send some kids to foster care and..." Larry opened the door, pushing me through with his hand on my lower back. There was another set of doors between this one and the restaurant itself, giving me the first glimpse of the inside.

Red booths butting up against wooden partitions, free-standing and against the wall. A large counter for pizza retrieval, an arcade section with filthy carpet from the 90s with geometric patterns, a play area with a ball pit, and soccer kids.

Everywhere, there were soccer kids.

Brightly colored shirts and shorts. Numbered backs and high socked, cleats swapped for tennis shoes, but otherwise as filthy and grass stained as they'd been at the sports complex. Children, everywhere, and I suddenly wished I had the real Winnie and not her namesake to suck the lives out of all them.

"I can't go in there."

"Yes, you can." Larry opened the door and ushering me through. I was immediately pushed back by the noise, louder than any bomb I'd detonated, on purpose or on accident, and three times as effective at ending my will to live. "They're just children."

In a perfectly timed act of retribution, a small human with a bowl cut ran by with a ball, went to pass and kicked him in the shin.

"You were saying?"

"Just keep moving. Find your suspects while I find your pizza." Nudging me toward the dining room, he walked toward the order pick-up area. I scanned the room twice, grateful for my advanced height in the room of munchkins until one collided with my legs and latched on.

"I found the giant from Jack in the Beanstalk!" It screamed and four more ran over. "We have to knock it down or she'll grind our bones into bread!"

Two more latched on and I stared in horror at their sauce covered hands. None of them had ever heard of soap and at least one had a wart.

"Help!" I called out. "Whoever owns these, help!"

None of the parents looked up from their cell phones where they were crashed out like zombies from the Night of the Living Dead.

"Out! Drop it!" I tried all the Winnie commands I used back in the Army, but no luck.

Taking a step, I discovered they weighed less than my boots when caked in mud and manure, so I decided to ignore them and keep walking until I found Meggie, Dane, two other men and two women in a corner booth, slightly behind the ball pit.

Larry appeared beside me, holding two boxes of pizza.

"There's... children on you."

"Yup."

"Do you want them there?" His head cocked to the side like Winnie's.

"Nope." I watched the people at the table in front of me interact. Meggie had Dane on her right and the man I recognized from her social media as her husband on her left. He was beside a man, then one of the women, woman then man. All of them were touching, familiar, intimate.

A normal person might say they are familiar, but given what I'd seen earlier...

"Are any of these yours?" I asked, walking up to the table and gesturing to the ankle biting weights on my legs.

Everyone looked up at me and I studied each face, none of the rest matching any member of my jury or courthouse regulars. The woman one in from the far end had familiar eyes, but nothing else about her matched the videos or images of my female courthouse guests. Two of the men stood up and looked at the creatures attached to me, both shaking their heads and sitting back down.

"Those are the Dalton and Everly kids. Do you know them?"

"Nope. And I don't know how to get them to detach. Leave it!" I ordered, but they just giggled. "They do not obey canine commands, and I don't know any children ones."

Two of the adults laughed and one pulled out a handful of tokens.

"Why don't you guys hit up the arcade. Share these with Libby and Elsie." He handed over the coins and they whooped.

"We got the giant's gold!" My leg weights scooped the coins off the table and disappeared into the human mass of soccer shirts. "The golden goose is ours!"

I felt my lip raise in a snarl, completely over the Jack and the Beanstalk comparison.

"They aren't going to share with your kids."

"They were probably sent by our kids," Meggie rolled her eyes and gestured to the two empty chairs pulled up to the otherwise full table. "Grab a seat."

Cautiously, I pulled out the chair and Larry set the pizza box in front of me. Then handed me a bottle of hand sanitizer which I applied liberally before returning. Folding the lid under my box, I used it as a giant plate for my large sausage, olive, and tomato pizza. After shaking out my hands to confirm the sanitizer was dry, I picked up a slice and ate it in four bites. Followed by a second, when Larry returned with a cup of soda that I drank half of. He pulled a slice of pepperoni and bell pepper out of his box and put it on a plate.

Like a loser who owns a dishwasher.

"You probably know this is my husband, Kyle, beside him his partner Thorsten Meneses with his wife, Heather, and her partner Vivian. Vivian's husband Charlie is at the end." They each waved or nodded in turn, like it was normal to be a part of an endless chain of partners and spouses. Maybe in their world, it was.

"So..." I started on a third slice of pizza and carefully chewed, actually tasting this one. With my eyes firmly fixed on the crushed red pepper shaker in the center of the table, I inhaled to say all at once. "You guys are some sort of swingers, open relationship deal, and all hook up with each other and hang out and the kids are just cool with it?"

I took another bite, counting the holes in the lid of the shaker.

"Technically, we are a polycule."

The woman to my right spoke and peeked at her out of the corner of my eye.

"Polyamory is being in multiple romantic relationships. A polycule is when you end up becoming a shared dating community. Either by chance or by design… more or less." The man in front of me added, squeezing Meggie's husband's hand. "Dane was… is… new to the community but very open-minded."

The man took a drink and Dane took over.

"I met Meggie while we were serving on the jury. As an alternate, I was still sequestered, and I'd see her outside the hotel. Anxious, and freaked out, so I went to talk to her and find out what was wrong. It's when I learned she was being blackmailed."

He squeezed her thigh, and I puzzled at all this casual human contact.

"There's nothing wrong with what we do. And our children just know that we are all close friends and love each other. But the school district is full of conservative narrow-minded assholes. I'm on the PTA, and I have been in charge of allocating funds from the fundraisers as well as organizing the fundraisers. There's been pushback because I've been working on getting teachers supplies and equipment, art supplies, updated science texts, food for students, and new books for the library. There's a group who wants it to go to re-doing the sports field and putting the Ten Commandments in the Classroom. Which… OK, religion is great if you're going to follow it, but they don't love thy neighbor. Unless their neighbor can buy their own lunch, believes what they do and looks like they do."

Both men held her close, giving her affection and reassurance. It was the type of relationship people dreamed of, and she was getting it from both sides... and orgasms on a soccer field.

Color me green, I might be jealous.

"And someone threatened to out you?" I prompted and she nodded.

"Most of the PTA agrees with me on spending, but if our lifestyle became common knowledge... the community might not take it well and suddenly agreeing with me on one issue is tacit approval of everything. You know Ohio isn't exactly moderate." She rolled her eyes, and I found myself doing the same. "I don't expect people to be on board with my private life, I just expect them to separate what I do with what I do for the school. Then I get this weird jury summons to meet in the back room of a community center, and I'm told that I'm going to be on a jury, I'll vote guilty, and no one has to know about my love affairs. The irony that I'm a pawn of the same jerks I work against... the Tommy Stump piece of trash..."

"Not a fan?"

"He thinks people like me and half my friends shouldn't exist. He's the scum of the earth, weaponizing hate and hurting people for power. Those guys he sent to blackmail me might as well have been wearing white hoods and swastikas. You knew who they were and what they stood for on sight, even if they looked kind of normal."

The woman one in from the end looked heavily invested in her pizza. She kept her left hand under the table, her right lifting the slice, sipping soda, and generally keeping her eye everywhere but on the conversation at hand. Everyone else, aside from me, was cutting their slices with a knife and fork, using both hands and alternating with the soda glass.

Vivian's hand stayed beneath the table... did she have a weapon or... I glanced at the woman beside her, studying the way she used a fork, licked cheese from her lip. Nothing hesitated or trembled... but that didn't mean Vivian's second hand wasn't exploring her cave of wonders.

Silence continued for a few beats longer than natural and I shook off the speculation to tune into the questions.

"Two guys in a suit with a modified random summons that looked like a copy paste job?" I asked, repeating what Madison had told me. Meggie nodded, looking around and then lowering her voice.

"I think they were brothers and one or both of them were in the courtroom. Maybe even one on the jury. But I can't be sure."

I nodded, sliding that nugget into the folder of consistent info. I pulled out my phone and showed her the picture of the guy in the parking lot. "Does he look familiar?"

She zoomed in and out, tilting it a few directions.

"He might be the guy who did all the talking, but it's hard to tell. The lights were dim and they wore face covers, like surgical ones? It's why I recognized one of the voices from the jury, but not necessarily the face." Madison had said something similar, but the idea that men in suits with paper masks could walk into a community center without cause for question was unusual.

"What about juror seven? Deanna Schafer? Did she ever give you bad feelings?"

Meggie twisted up her face, shaking her head.

"No. I got the impression that if she cared any less about the trial or what was happening, she'd be dead. She always stank of cigarette smoke, so you could smell where she'd been after she'd been there. I always needed a shower after sitting beside her all day." Her lips pursed, and I felt a weird sense of disappointment. There hadn't been any mention of cigarette smoke in the report about Trigger's room, and it would have stood out. The knowledge bumped Deanna down my list.

"So, what about you?" I asked Dane, a piece of pizza halfway to his mouth. Two toppings fell off and landed in his lap. He tried to wipe them off and knocked over his mostly empty water cup, scattering ice everywhere.

"I was randomly selected. I work in airport maintenance, fixing runway lights. I'm... not super coordinated." He blushed and I had a mental memory of a trial video of someone stepping on Ruger's tail and then falling out of the jury box.

"You stepped on Ruger," I commented, eyes narrowed. A fake serial uncoordinated man could dose someone with drugs. It would be easy to slip Trigger something while "falling". Dane went redder and nodded.

"Right before I fell out of the box. That was the night I went to talk to Meggie."

"He fell in the hotel's pool, fully clothed," she mused, a smile on her face. "Ruined his cell phone, soaked his wallet..."

"Still not as embarrassing as that time I tripped over a runway light, disturbed a nesting Canadian goose and ended up getting attacked," he groaned. I raised an eyebrow, and he gestured toward Larry's phone. "Look up John Glenn Airport worker accidents."

Larry opened the video service and put the terms in the search bar. Four dozen videos with half a million views each showed a life of accidents, disasters and…

"Ouch," I flinched, and he shook his head.

"Whichever one you're watching, I'm sure there are worse."

Two sharp barks cut through the din of the pizza place, and I shot up. Experience had taught me Winnie near a food establishment and barking meant I was about to owe a service worker an apology or a bribe.

Usually both.

"Excuse me," I shouted, running through the restaurant. Children got out of the way, servers danced out of the way and parents were unceremoniously shoved. Bursting through the door, I ran toward my Jeep to see a man in a black suit holding a rock beside my window.

"Hey!" I shouted, running closer. A man with a red bag containing pizzas turned, blocking the sidewalk. We collided and I toppled over, rolling over to land on my back a few feet from my Jeep when the window shattered under the rock. "Hey!"

The man turned, blinking in recognition before he took off across the lot. His sharp nose the most obvious feature, but his hair was longer and less kempt than the man in Patterson's parking lot.

Juror number nine?

"Hey! Wait! What are you…"

I gave chase, babying a scraped knee and bruised hip as I tried to dart between cars with the same efficiency. I emerged between two minivans in time to see him roar off in a black sedan with deep tinted windows and government plates. On the ground beside his parking spot, a capped syringe lay abandoned.

Taking a receipt from my pocket, I picked it up and stared at the semi-clear liquid inside. It was unlabeled and there were no dosage markings anywhere on the barrel.

"Get off! What- Help!" A man yelled and I stuck the syringe in my pocket.

Turning, I ran back toward the Jeep and saw the delivery man, staring in horror as Winnie raided the fallen pizzas with Ruger watching pathetically from the back seat. Resigned, I opened the door and carried him to the sidewalk over the broken glass to join her.

"Just... charge it," I sighed, handing him my card while Larry stood there laughing. Through the window, I saw Dane and Meggie watching me. They shifted and Vivian appeared, her dark glare piercing me with a razor sharp edge of malice. Fumbling in her pocket, I saw her draw her cell phone out of her pocket, holding it in her unmoving left hand. Before I could get a better look, they walked away, leaving me pretty sure who ratted me out to juror number nine.

Chapter Seventeen: OH, OH, This is the Way

The drive back to Sweet Pea was freezing.

Without the smashed window, the farting had begun almost immediately and required ventilation. Also, an exorcism, a scented candle, and two million genie wishes to cure Winnie's IBS.

"Do you have Gas-ex for dogs at the clinic?" I asked, looking over at Larry. The heater was on full blast, but I shivered, and I was fairly certain my nipples were about to perforate my bra and my shirt if I had to go another twenty miles with the windows down at seventy miles an hour. "Can I get some at the nearest pet store?"

He chuckled and turned a vent toward me that thawed my fingers.

"Nope. There's something at my clinic that might help her, but you'd have better luck just waiting her out. You're lucky that was a no-garlic pizza."

"I'd be luckier if someone hadn't smashed my window, set the fluffy demon loose, and allowed her to access the pizzas from the pizza man I knocked over trying to stop the aforementioned window smasher from smashing my window." I pouted into my steering wheel. The highway sign we passed said the next town we'd pass through was London and I took the exit I recognized from Thursday.

"Where are we going?" Larry glanced out the window at the strip malls and business parks. At five on a Saturday, only those selling home goods and retail items still had lights on. I took a turn off the main street and passed the Mexican food place.

"Can you check my phone, go to the Senior Swingers chat and look up Olivia Hartley. And you need to use the search feature. Can't stress enough that you want the search feature if you don't want to wish for a melon baller to scrape out your eyeballs."

Larry worked my phone and scanned the screen.

"OK, but where are we going? I don't think anything's open."

I breathed out a resigned breath. "I just want to check something."

We pulled into the parking lot and my suspicions were confirmed, even before the officer exited her cruiser. Red and blue lights bathed the already shabby lot, bringing the cracks into sharp relief and causing the shattered glass to glitter in a duotone mosaic. Three cars sat in the lot, including the police cruiser whose lights painted the scene in front of us.

Crime scene tape decorated the front of the smashed lawyer's office window. The shared lobby door was mangled in its frame and the angry Korean woman from earlier was screaming at four young men tasked with sweeping up the shattered glass. I parked near the cruiser and got out.

"Excuse me, ma'am, but this a crime... What happened to your window?" The Asian officer looked at my back window.

I rounded the car but left the engine running. Larry had remained seated inside the car, scanning my phone while I tried to look into the darkened lawyer's office.

"Someone tried to stab my dog with a drug needle. It's already being investigated. What happened to the attorney in that office?" I moved slightly closer, noting the absence of any of the furnishings present just two days ago. File cabinets, mail, and the battered technology had all been removed and all that remained in the space was a dark stain in the middle of the floor. "Is that blood?"

"We're waiting on confirmation of that. What do you know about that lawyer?" She flipped open a notebook and I hesitated. Glancing between the vacant storefront and the dogs peeking out of the shattered window behind me, I weighed the pros and cons of truths and half-truths. "He's probably dead if that helps?"

"It does not..." I propped my hands on my hips, looking at the irate dry cleaner. "He had a gambling problem, was past due on rent, furniture rental, equipment rental, alimony most likely, and was being blackmailed to read a will I was a recipient of. From? Of? Whatever. The decedent was a friend, Clyde 'Trigger' Sampson, he was serving on a jury in Columbus but doesn't live near there. We were here two days ago. Where's all his stuff?"

The officer's gaze sharpened and zeroed in on me.

"My understanding from Mrs. Kim is that the rental companies came for it when she officially kicked him out. Last she saw, it was just him and a bunch of files in boxes waiting for someone to come pick him up when his car was repossessed." The officer flipped through her notebook and then closed it. "What was left to you in Mr. Sampson's will?"

I checked her name plate, Officer Kim, and pointed to the back window. "Black dog. His name is Ruger, and I suspect that lawyer was helping to poison him before I took custody. You knew Trigger?"

"Not directly. I was part of the investigation into Mr. Howser and trust me when I say nothing that was happening with that felt good. Are you the woman who was there when he died?"

I nodded. "Geez, why does everyone know that? Was there a statewide memo or something?"

Officer Kim chuckled. "Might as well have been. You're hard to miss once described. Plus, YouTube."

"Stupid internet." I crossed my arms, sinking into myself. "Howser said Trigger was refusing to deliver a vote unless cases were opened against Geissinger and Stump, that an officer had agreed to do it. Was that you?"

Her eyes widened and she held up her hands, taking a small step back. "No way. I wouldn't go near that. My family would end up deported."

I swallowed and moved on. "Have you checked Patterson's house? Talked to his son?"

She hunched her shoulders, then straightened them when she realized I was not a threat. In the car behind her, the radio squawked about a convenience store pump that was charging people before they started pumping gas.

"He was living in the office. My aunt, Mrs. Kim, said she made him pay an extra twenty dollars for the space. I told her it was illegal, but my auntie terrifies me." She didn't need to elaborate. The woman probably terrified a lot of people. "His ex-wife and son haven't seen him since Tuesday. Mrs. Kim said some brutes came by, smashing monitors and making threats. She chased them off with a push broom."

We snickered.

"Think she'd talk to me?" I leaned in to ask quietly, worried the older woman would hear me and hit me with the push broom.

"Do you speak Korean?" Her lip quirked upward and I didn't have to answer. "What do you want to ask her about?"

I asked Larry for my phone and pulled up the picture of the man in the suit.

"Can you ask her if this guy was in her dry cleaner? As a customer or as a nuisance? And if anyone's drycleaning went missing?" I swiped to a picture of the plastic bag in the prison office. "Possibly with an ID card? Or... something that would get a person into a federal prison?"

"Shit. You sure you don't speak Korean?" Her face had lost all humor. "I know this suit went missing, with an ID card, and the man threatened her with calling ICE. She's here legally and had me come out. He's a doctor, but a bad one, out at the federal prison. Who's the man in the picture?"

"One of the guys who blackmailed Patterson into reading the will and also promised him money. I think this—" I zoomed in on the pooch in the front. "Is the suit being smuggled out? I don't know if he found the lawyer following the dry cleaning theft with the plan to use it to kill Howser, or if he found the dry cleaner and the lawyer at the same time, or if all of it just came together one day like magic..."

Officer Kim shook her head and rested her hands on her gun belt. "Trigger's only been dead a week. The dry cleaning went missing around that time. But he only brings it in once a month and unless they knew ahead of time it would be here, there's no way to have timed it that well by coincidence."

"You think they followed the doctor, found this was his cleaner, and discovered an attorney next door. Probably spotted his weaknesses and figured he was an in to return, also a useful tool in their box, then coincided the will drop with dry cleaning theft?"

The officer waggled her hand in a kind of gesture.

"It wasn't quite a theft. They had the claim slip. But I think he had to hide the cleaning because the owner showed up probably two minutes after that guy collected it? If it had been visible, the whole thing would have failed."

Two more marked cars pulled in and I bid the officer a good night, climbing back into the Jeep.

"Learn anything?" Larry asked, shivering slightly despite the heater. He had the address to the two O.H.'s programmed into his phone and we were ten minutes away.

"Yeah… it's a good thing I never get anything dry cleaned."

"What do I need to know about them before going in?"

We'd pulled up in front of a duplex with a yellow VW Bug parked in front of black shuttered windows on the left, and a white Honda Civic in front of grey shuttered windows on the right. Both had doormats on in front of their doors on a shared dark blue covered porch. One featured pumpkins and bats, the other a generic welcome.

"Says Dalton's cousin who lives in London knows the goth chick who does historic tours. She has an orange cat and a yellow VW beetle. They're on Pine Ave and the guy who looks like a mop lives next door. They're always fighting about… historically accurate sex positions?"

"I'm sure they made that up. Those seniors are gross." I stared at the door mats a little longer.

Oliver was officially the human version of dry toast, and I was quietly grateful his windows were dark. Olivia's had lights on in the front and the second floor, a hopeful indicator that someone was home, if not her than maybe a roommate or live-in partner who could let me know if she was blackmail-able for any reason.

"You can wait here with the dogs if you want." I shut off the engine and got out. In lieu of responding, he got out and joined me on the pathway leading to the four-step wrap around porch. I paused in front of the door, listening for sounds inside. A slightly raised voice, music and the scrape of wood against the floor.

Larry knocked twice, loudly, and then stood slightly behind me.

"Wimp," I muttered. The music paused and the voices went silent. I knocked again, a little louder, and shouted. "Hello?"

Above us, a window slid open, and a curly haired head poked out.

"Can I help you?" His deep voice resonated with gravel, touching a register my ears had forgotten existed. The flopped bangs drifted in the breeze, and I saw clearly the boyish face of Oliver Hartman, shirtless, with a sheen of sweat on his brow.

"Yes." I cleared my throat, unprepared for the abs and pecs hidden under the baggy clothes he'd worn to the court. "I need to speak with you and Olivia."

"About what?" He asked again, pausing to look over his shoulder. Disappearing from view, I expected this was it and I was SOL on getting answers out of this pair. Raised voices came from the open window, the feminine a smooth husk to his deep timbre and I was starting to think maybe the Swingers were not actually exaggerating.

Olivia's head popped out of the window, her long hair braided and a thin black robe covering her long, willowy frame. She peered at me through thick glasses, and I tried to remember if she wore them to the trial.

Behind us, a low whimper came from the Jeep, and I turned to see Ruger looking out through the smashed window, his tail wagging in the semi-darkness. Olivia and Oliver shared a look, smiling at the dog when Winnie's head poked out beside his.

"Is that Winnie?" The human mop asked, and I looked between him and the dog.

"You two know each other?"

"No, but I love her videos! Wait, does that mean you're Cyn?" He squinted down at me, but my eyes stayed on Olivia, her polished fingers pressed to her lip with her eyes fixed on Ruger.

"Yeah. Olivia? You want to tell me about Trigger?"

Her eyes drifted to me, and she nodded, looking like a woman who'd seen a ghost.

"Yeah, I'll be down in a minute... Can you bring the dogs inside? I need to give Ruger love."

***

Oregano stared down at us from his perch on the top of the fridge, green eyes blinking and long tail twitching. The cat watched us from above as we sat at the kitchen table, Olivia holding Ruger's head in her lap and Oliver attempting to get Winnie to destroy something for a social media live.

The wooden table was old, but sanded smooth, with carefully restored chairs. A worn sofa with a floral print sat against one wall with a brown corduroy recliner beside it. Bookshelves filled with old TV Guides, photo albums and paperbacks lined one wall and there was no TV anywhere I could see.

"Olivia, whose house is this?"

I turned back to her, seeing her eyes water. Oliver took her hand, but her other remained threaded in Ruger's fur. She brushed it back and forth, looking at the colors underneath before letting it slowly domino back into place.

"It was my grandma's," she whispered. A few tears streamed freely down her cheeks, streaking eyeliner and mascara that had appeared invisible before the tears. "She got sick while I was in college, so I came down here to help care for her. But I wasn't well, and I stole her medicine. That's what they used against me."

She wiped her nose on the sleeve of her flannel pajamas, ignoring the tissue Oliver offered her.

"I used to do cheerleading and sorority. *Tied Together with a Smile* wasn't just a song for me; it was my life which sounds so dramatic and extra. I just wanted to numb the pain, the feeling it was all absolutely pointless." Olivia was openly crying now, and I held Winnie against my leg, grateful she was here. "It was just a pill here and there, but then she stopped filling the prescription and suddenly there weren't any more. Then she was hospitalized when it became too much. They said... they said that the medicine had been keeping her quality of life where she could live at home and when she found out I was using the medicine, she stopped filling it. She... she said she did it to save my life. The guys in suits told me that if I didn't do what they wanted, they'd tell the police and they'd have me investigated for drug abuse and... murder."

I swallowed, holding Winnie a little tighter. Larry took my hand, and I gripped his back.

"She died?"

Olivia nodded.

"They told me I killed her. That it was my fault she's dead and if I didn't give them all of her prescriptions and deliver the verdict they wanted..." Her voice caught on a sob. "Oliver heard everything through the wall. He used his tech job to hack the system and get himself on the jury too. I was so pissed he'd ruin everything, that I'd ruined everything. Ruger came to me the morning Trigger died. I had the room next to his, we shared a door, and I'd always left my side unlocked in case he needed help. I think it pissed him off, but also, I hoped maybe he felt a little... I don't know. It was self-serving maybe."

"He was a stubborn asshole, but... he was our stubborn asshole," I filled in for her and she nodded. Hand shaking, she picked up the water in front of her and took a drink that splattered against the table.

"When I told him about my grandma one night, he started letting Ruger come over at night when he heard me sobbing. The morning he didn't show up to jury duty, I heard him stumbling around his room. Then there were voices, two men... maybe three in the hall. The door opened and Ruger came through, but then it was quickly shut before I could see anything and then it was locked. I heard... the voices, the sound of something heavy falling, the hall door closing, and silence. In the argument, they mentioned me and my grandma's medicine. That they'd be back and make it look like it was me."

Warm spots of water blossomed on the back of my hand, and I swiped at the tears streaming down my face.

"I... I stole a housekeeping key card and saw him dead. Ruger wouldn't leave his body, but I needed to show up for jury duty or they would know. I called him in on my way, as an anonymous I heard something. I don't think they were able to come back."

Her frame collapsed against Oliver. Winnie drifted away, sniffing her way around the living room and disappearing through a doorway. The room felt heavy, and I wanted to leave this in the past.

"Do you have seizures, Oliver?" He nodded, pulling out a medical alert bracelet. "Did you bring anything special into the courtroom for them?"

"No, my medication is preventative. They offered to let me bring it in, but... it's pointless unless I forget. And I don't forget."

"Ever?" I asked, thrown off by his certainty. I wasn't even certain if I remembered deodorant this morning.

"Not since they prescribed me the right stuff. Why?"

I shrugged, mentally checking the box.

"Do you know why they wanted to kill him?"

"Trigger?"

"Ruger. If he wasn't in the room..."

"He knew the voices. I could hear them asking about him, saying the dog would know their voices. The third guy called it idiotic, but... I think it would hold up in court." She swallowed and shook her head. "I knew one of the voices... two of them maybe. But I was only certain of one."

"From the original meeting and threat or..." I didn't want to lead her, but I also still needed to ask about juror number 9.

"I think one of them was on the jury with us. The dumb one who got easily annoyed and tried to keep Trigger quiet…" She shook slightly and shook her head. "Number nine. Hated that guy, I can't remember his name though… if he ever said it all. A lot of us did casual intros, but maybe he never did."

"Colton," Oliver supplied. "When I hacked the system, I memorized all the names. He was listed as Colton Pierce. Nothing about him on the internet anywhere but I wasn't doing a deep dive."

"If you… happened to be in whatever systems you access for such things and stumbled upon some additional information about him… would you be willing to share?"

He nodded his agreement while I filed the name away, planning to give it to Carla. I reached into my pocket and pulled out the syringe with the receipt still wrapped around it. I wasn't ready to dig back into Olivia's past, but I needed to ask.

"Was this from your grandma?"

She shook her head, leaning in but not touching.

"No, she only had pills. Where did you get that?"

I hesitated; not sure she needed to know. Above us, something heavy landed on the floor. Olivia and Oliver shared a look, and I searched the room.

"Winnie!" I groaned and took off. Through the doorway, I found an old staircase and ran up it with the two O.H.s hot on my heels.

"You don't…"

"It's probably…"

I rushed to the open door and experienced déjà vu.

Winnie, holding a ball gag, in a room full of restraints with a giant wooden X in the center. A chest of open sex toys, a closet of paddles, and an open armoire filled with leather costumes. Olivia's sheer robe was draped on a cushioned bench, sweat and what I was pretending was sweat, shining on the cushioned stockade near the wall.

"Oh, my dog, why?" I glared at the dog. Outside, tires screeched on the pavement and a vehicle bottomed out on the drainage dip in the road. A series of cell phone rings cut through the otherwise silent night, before the woosh and a blast of heat came in through the window. The whole house shook, and Oregano shot through the room to land on Olivia's shoulder.

Ruger had just made it into the room and Winnie dropped the ball gag at Oliver's feet, crouching into puppy pose to play.

Scared to move I looked at Larry.

"Can you please go see what's on fire?"

He nodded and slowly walked toward the sheer curtains, glancing out into the orange tinted night as the first siren wailed in the distance.

"It's your Jeep."

I looked down at the dogs who would have been in the car if Olivia hadn't asked me to bring them in, a fresh wave of dizziness and nausea washed over me.

"I think..." I turned around, spotted a bathroom and ran to throw up a large pizza in the toilet.

Chapter Eighteen: No Progress Report

Winnie's tail slapped my cheek, someone else was breathing hot breath on my neck, and a boa constrictor had captured my waist. The air was pure noxious fumes and doggy breath, warm, humid and familiar but the bed... the bed was wrong, and the undercurrent of bleach and coffee was missing. Also missing was the familiar traffic of Main St. Sunday morning pastry seekers, the screech of happy or murdered children, and the retina burning stream of light from the alley window I couldn't find a curtain for.

The tail paused and then started slapping me again with a fresh *pooft* of noxious gases directly applied to my face.

"Euck," I choked, coughing and pushing until I could get her fluffy butt away from my face. The boa constrictor tightened and grabbed at it, alarmed when I felt the fuzz of arm hair and not the smooth scales of snakeskin. Grass, sand, and fresh linens filled the room, and outside the world was quiet. "What?"

"Shhh... We're sleeping," Larry whispered from the great beyond. His voice was muffled, and a quick head bob said another dog had stolen the pillow section and placed his giant head between me and my ex. I made a mental note to give both dogs treats for ensuring this was the least sexy sleepover we could be having.

Carefully as I could, I wiggled myself out from under Larry's arm. When his grip tightened, I muttered "bathroom" and slunk into the adjoining space. Dawn hadn't yet broken, the dim light coming through the raised window not enough to read by but enough for me to see that I was wearing my shirt and little else. The rest of my clothes were folded on top of the toilet tank and I pulled my stained cargo's on, stuffing my bra in the pocket as I went.

A scratch in my throat was a reminder of last night's vomit, and the explosion of my car that led to it. My heartrate kicked up, and with blood pounding in my ears, I reached for the mouth wash and nearly toppled it with my trembling hand. Air slid past my lips in a low rasp, catching on the dried spittle, while I worked at calming myself. "We're OK. They're OK."

But it was too close.

I swished the minty liquid around and spat into the sink, following up with a deep breath and holding it for a five count before blowing it out and repeating the process. Heart rate slightly lower, I opened the door to two furry heads staring at me while Larry was still asleep behind them. Pressing my finger to my lips, I waved them toward the door, and we tiptoed out of the bedroom and to the front door. My parent's ancient Subaru keys were sitting on the entry table, and I picked them up, leaving through the front door with my dogs.

Our family Subaru was only a decade younger than me, a sickly shade of green and possibly held together with dirt. When it wasn't parked in the driveway, I plucked a vague memory of parking behind the office from my grey matter and started that direction.

We were only a few steps in when Carla called.

"Hey." My voice came out like I dined on chainsaws. "Why are you up so early?"

"I was going to ask you the same question. You didn't sleep in your apartment, did you?" I could hear the sink running behind her and I wondered if she was also vomiting, if for entirely different reasons.

"No, I woke up at Larry's. Guessing you're the reason why?" I walked us around a fenced off section of street that declared a new gun store was being built. The public meeting to authorize the build was on Tuesday and people were not happy if one believed flyers. "I know Seth dropped off my mom's Subaru with you in the other car, but I'm guessing the whole 'don't go home' was all you?"

"Yeah. I don't think your apartment is safe. If they can plant an explosive on your car, they can put one in your building." A door opened on her end, and I thought someone screeched, but it may have been an owl. The darkness was receding fast, and the first signs of life were coming to Main St. "I take it you're at Larry's house?"

The screaming rose an octave. "I was. Have you been out-sourced for torture?"

"No, that would be your niece. She is having a meltdown about... crap, I don't remember what this one is about. Whatever it is, it's my fault. Why did you leave Larry's house?"

When we got to the front of my building, I had Winnie sniff the entrance for explosives or the scent of intruders. With her all clear, we entered, and I walked straight to the coffee pot. Winnie went toward her bed, but I called her over to check again.

Fool me once with an exploding coffee can and all that. When she confirmed only coffee was inside, I used it to fill the coffee maker with coffee grounds and water. Knowing caffeination was on the way, I decided to answer Carla's question. "Because I'm not ready to be 'wake up in bed together' friends with him. So when he went back to sleep, I snuck out with the dogs."

"Doesn't he have a guest room?" Whatever tantrum was happening on her end was now muffled, and I suspected she'd gone outdoors. "I could have sworn there was a guest room in that house."

"That's the problem, isn't it? I don't know. No matter what happens, I never end up there." I poked the power button on my computer and grabbed the dog dishes, bland dog food in the fridge, and combined the two into a canine culinary... well, they could eat it. Once it was on the floor, both dogs went to work, and I checked the front door lock. "So, you know about the dry cleaner, the missing lawyer, Olivia and Oliver, the soccer mom and her beau—"

"Still think you should let me black ops them since I think they ratted you out."

"I feel like having kids is punishment enough and we don't know they weren't the ones being followed and I just happened to be there." I walked over to my coffee maker and prepped a cup for as soon as it was ready. "Madison, the mad foreman... Did you get the syringe?"

"Yeah. It's liquid trazodone laced with fentanyl, enough to kill a dog if you can get it inserted and the dog to hold still." Her offhand comment soured something in my belly, and I felt sick again. A low ringing sounded in my ears, and I missed some of her commentary.

"What?"

"I said I'm glad they're both okay." She spoke slowly and deliberately, finishing just as the coffee maker beeped. "Still nothing on the person with the fake hand. I have someone running facial recognition but if she's not in a database, they probably won't find her."

"Anything on the County Clerks?" I poured the liquid life in my cup and drank deeply.

"Not until they reopen Monday. I'll keep you posted." The screaming started again, and she sighed heavily. "I have to go."

"May the Force be with you." I ended the call and sat at my desk. From my cargo pocket, I pulled out the flash drive Princess

Liana had given me. Tapping it end-over-end on my blotter, I considered what could be on it that I didn't already know.

The O.H.'s had confirmed liquid narcotics were probably used, the coroner himself put the official cause of death as head trauma and an injury consistent with at-force collision with the edge of the table. Looking over at the dogs, I considered my options.

"Do you think there will be something on here no one's told me before?" Winnie's eyebrows skewed left while Ruger's tail softly thumped against the ground. "What if there are pictures?" Neither dog reacted, a reminder I'd seen plenty of dead people and naked people, so their sympathy was a null set. "Yeah, we've done dumber stuff without coffee."

I inserted the drive into my USB port and waited for it to load while refilling my mug. Today's vessel featured a caricature of a cow with the catchphrase "Ya Herd?". I wasn't sure where this one had come from, after the demolition of my original collection, the newbies were crowdsourced and as cherished as they were obnoxious. The file drive popped up and I double clicked on the PDF report.

Password protected.

"Damnit. He didn't tell me a password." I pushed back in my chair and considered the blinking cursor over the rim of my cup. I switched to looking at Winnie, her white belly showing off the killer metabolism we did not share. Then Ruger, his short stocky build, was not the smallest dog in my office recently, but...

"Dog... What had the Princess said about the key to the lock when she retrieved this from Fluffy's collar?" Ruger was upside down with his paws tucked to his chest, ears flat against the floor, and lips showing off his two front canines. The little bat had a clear opposition to being upright. "Opposition? Rebellion... The key to the lock is... Dissent!"

I typed it into the box. The tiny hourglass appeared, flipping end over end while my breath stilled in my chest as I awaited confirmation that I'd understood the code. My secondhand machine hummed, the fan kicking into high gear from the exertion, a reminder that this thing had once been used for less than legal purposes and could die without a moment's notice.

The file popped open, and I glanced at the bottom corner—897 pages.

Bookmarks filled in on the side and I scanned through the tabs. Summary, images, notable markings, findings and conclusions, and the standard forms were all arranged in a logical order my brain couldn't follow. For me, this case had no logic or reason, beyond narcissism and hatred. Which meant that the perfectly organized file was insulting.

Instead of following the logical progression, I went directly to notable markings. Images and paragraphs detailing what each represented to the coroner filled the page. An old bullet wound that was marked for its bruising pattern, but I found it consistent with a person who bumped into the same thing every day. Based on the upper arm location, my guess was his desk or the shooting tables at the range.

Next was a callous on the outside of his third knuckle that was found to contain traces of oil, solvent, and metal. That was consistent with pistol magazine loading by a man without index fingers. Taking my gun out of my desk, I dropped the magazine and tried it out for myself, sliding all ten rounds out of the spring-loaded feeder, getting bit by the guards. By the time I had the last one out, blood was dripping on my blotter, and I had a new respect for the man. "Fluff! Your dad was dedicated."

Ruger sneezed his agreement and I reloaded the bullets normally, wiping each one off before putting it back in, then wrapping a tissue around the bleeding knuckle. Suspicions confirmed, I moved onto the next injury, his head wound. His point of impact was the soft spot near the eye orbital, the corner digging in and causing a fracture that put skull fragments in his grey matter. With the pictures of the hotel for reference, I looked at the two side by side.

There was no way to tell for sure if he'd been shoved into it or fallen. From his angle in the chair, the descent sideways could have been from the drugs or a shove. Olivia's assertion there were voices was my only path toward an assisted fall, and I couldn't prove it.

"Would be great if your dog ears spoke people and heard what they said." Ruger's eyes were closed, and I stepped around him and Winnie for a coffee refill. Sunlight was starting to stream in above the heavy curtain covering my front window and I knew I needed to shower and get started with more interviews. The top of an image peeked out beneath the head wound and I made my way back over. It was a close up of his leg, an air bubble visible on the outside of his right thigh with a bruise ring around it. A matching bubble was found on his opposite leg without a bruise ring, this one the top of his thigh. "He didn't have feeling in his legs... if he didn't move them around, would an injection sit, slowing it's circulation?"

I zoomed in and out on the bruise, thinking of what would leave an air bubble and a bruise. Opening my browser window to search, the Courtroom Chaos scene was still on the screen, and it played automatically. After last night, my eyes went to juror nine and I watched him lean toward Trigger, slamming into his leg while their exclamations woke up Ruger.

"EpiPen guy. Mother fluffer, that's how he did the first dose of drugs." But as the video kept going, I kept watching and saw Colton stumble backward, pain on his face while Trigger was speaking toward the floor. Recess was called, the bailiff unavailable for Trigger to speak with and Colton... limped out of the box. "You bit him."

Ruger wagged his tail enthusiastically.

"It's not just about being an audible witness and all that other crap he said, you bit him. The teeth marks will match, which is why they want you dead."

Chapter Nineteen: Noah's Ark

"What are we doing?" I asked the dogs. Ruger's tail waved like a flag, majestically floating through the air while his head rested on crossed paws. Winnie puzzled with an eyebrow wiggle, pawing at an itchy spot on her ear. After a shower, fresh undies, a second pot of coffee, and three angry texts from Larry, this morning's revelation was starting to feel like a death sentence. "We should just leave like everyone else."

"And go where?"

I drew my gun and pointed it at the back doorway, ready to kill whoever walked in while hoping it was Colton. Instead, Griffin appeared in the doorway holding two paper cups from Mo's and a box of doughnuts. Glaring at him, I gestured to the closed curtain. "We aren't open. This is the second time I've almost shot you. Learn to knock!"

"That's a stapler." He placed the coffee and doughnuts on my desk, and I looked at the device in my hand. It was, in fact, a stapler. The Glock was still on the blotter beside the bloody tissue from my knuckle unloading. Griffin looked at the blood, but wisely said nothing.

"I still could have killed you with it." I tossed the stapler on my desk and stared at him. "What do you want? Why are you ruining my travel plans?"

"What travel plans? Where can you even go? Back to Colorado? Florida? Germany? You're not allowed in Sweden or Afghanistan." He extended one of the coffees to me.

"Stop knowing things about me. It's disconcerting since I don't know anything about you besides that you own a farm, do finance stuff, were in the Navy, and own an obnoxious truck," I grumbled, accepting the coffee and selecting a pink sprinkle doughnut from the box. I took a bite and several gulps of what tasted like a latte.

"What else do you want to know?" He took a reasonably sized drink from his cup, and I stared at him.

"Honestly? I just want to know why you keep showing up here and how you're getting inside."

"I can get in because you suck at locking doors. Where were you last night?"

Deciding it would help my brain, I filled him in on all of the events after he'd left the day before. From Meggie and her polycule to my pizza vomit, I gave him a complete rundown through two doughnuts and a coffee refill from my pot.

His scowl suggested I should not have.

"You said you weren't going back out to question anyone," he seethed, and I shrugged.

"The opportunity presented itself. Why are you mad?"

"Because... you said you wouldn't—"

"Besides that. Like I said, Carla called, the opportunity presented itself, and I went. I'm already panicked about how close I came to losing both dogs, so if you're going to get on me for that, I'm doing the best I can to protect them. Hell, we didn't even sleep here last night in case someone planted an explosive."

"Where did you sleep?" His nostril breaths reminded me of a bull prepping to charge, and I was a little concerned about his blood pressure.

"At Larry's house. Not my first choice, but he was there, and I guess I fell asleep on the way back into town, so I didn't have the chance to argue." I shrugged but snuck a glance at my phone where a fourth annoyed message popped up from the man in question. Griffin followed my line of sight and gave me a knowing look that didn't sit well. "Apparently if you sneak out of a man's bed before sunup, he gets... testy."

"No shit." He shoved his hands through his hair and started to pace. The irritation was out of character for the easy-going puppy. It was the first real indication he'd given me of the person underneath the veneer, and I wasn't sure how to feel about Raging Bull.

"You need to calm down. You're acting weird. I knew the whole 'happy puppy' thing was an act, but if this is who you really are, I'm not sure we can hang. At least one person needs to be level-headed and responsible at all times when it comes to my investigative cohorts, and you're giving... angry face emojis."

"Because I didn't know you were back together with your ex and a veterinarian is not exactly helpful in high stress situations."

"I'm not back with Larry and I'm not sure what help an accountant would be either, even if you used to be a spy. So... what's your point?" I snapped, rubbing Ruger's head when he came and placed it in my lap. A fifth text popped up from Larry and I growled at the phone. "You *all* need to calm the fluff down. I did not survive a war zone and Florida to come home and be forced to answer to a bunch of men with feelings about what women can and cannot handle on their own."

"I'm not saying that because you're a woman!" He swallowed. "I just... I like you and I don't want anything to happen to you." Griffin huffed out his breath and I pulled back. "You asked why I keep showing up here? It's because I like you and watching you on the farm, I always wondered if you'd be as amazing in person as you were from where I could see you. But you're right. You don't answer to me, and you don't owe me anything. I know you don't *need* my help, but I still have help, and I want to give it. Just, could you call me, please? I can help."

Winnie and I shared a look, both of us bamboozled. Ruger's tail thumped in approval.

"Did you just..." I didn't have words. A man taking responsibility for his own feelings and making a request, not a demand?

Did I die? "I was going to see if I could find where creepy Noah Anderson lives and visit him outside of the Pet Store because it is closed. You can come if you want."

Griffin offered me a small smile.

"Then maybe we can get dinner?"

"It's eight in the morning, but I guess eventually we'll need food." I refilled my coffee and picked up my phone. The display came to life with a call from my mom. "We can go over everything while we eat, or whatever. Just not pizza, since I puked that up last night."

"No, I meant on a date, Cyn."

Panicked, I pressed the green call button to get out of answering him. Sadly, my mother's shouting carried around the room and I wasn't sure this was any better.

My mother's ire took nearly thirty minutes to comprehend, and we were halfway to Cincinnati. Apparently, in the process of moving, she located the cache of snacks I kept in the basement and a small family of mice had eaten the cheese crackers. I promised to pay for the exterminator and come by to double check for any other snacks. Griffin retained his smirk while we rode up the highway in his sterile black Forrester. We'd lifted the dogs into the back, a dog hammock already in place despite his lack of a canine companion and had been on the road before the last drops of coffee had been secured in my travel mug.

"So…" He prompted and I stared out the window.

"A needle pulling thread."

"Come on, one date won't kill you and if we get blown up, I promise not to blame you."

I rolled my eyes and hid my grin. Making death jokes wasn't something I was used to the guys I dated doing. They were always of the "it's not funny" and "we're not going to die" mindset.

"Where are we going? Does he live near his zoo boat store or are we going to a nearby town…"

"Smooth. No, he lives above it." Griffin answered, changing lanes and checking his blind spot. Ruger put his head on the man's shoulder, and he wrapped his arm around the large head, rubbing his ears and giving him kisses. "Or below it. The building design doesn't show floor plans for anything beyond a first floor, but street view suggests there should be one or the other based on staircases."

"Is that legal? I thought he worked in a shopping center." I tried to pretend the two males being friendly weren't turning me into a puddle of goo.

"Probably not. But there are no other addresses associated with his name and all his mail goes there, which may be for convenience, but his dirty magazine subscription is also delivered there. Once I saw that, it seemed like a safe bet that he lived there too. Otherwise, why risk your biblical holier than thou image?" His sneering sarcasm at the end said more than his words how he felt about this man and his business.

"Freaking hypocrite. Getting Jugs and Bums delivered while probably shouting "slut" at women who need reproductive care at Planned Parenthood. I'm sure he has a hard-on for his mom, too, because she was the last one who did all his chores for him and told him he was special."

"Yeah... more like Hoses and Holes." Griffin clarified, and my jaw fell in my lap. "Right? People are super great... and in case you're wondering, I can cook my own food and do my own laundry. If I were into men, even part time, I would not hide it. I've never judged anyone who is, and my brother sends me rainbow flags from all the Prides he attends."

"Someone's interviewing for an unlisted vacancy." I checked the GPS and compared it to the street signs.

"Just making sure my resume is on file."

We turned into a parking lot that had seen better days. The cracked asphalt had scraggly weeds growing out of it and the faded paint on most of the businesses complimented the burnt-out neon and out of date posters for events that had passed.

"Cheery," I remarked as we pulled in front of the pet store. Someone had used window paint to sketch a wooden boat filled with lions, giraffes, an elephant, and a mouse with a toucan in the crow's nest. My nephew had drawn better in pre-K, but the fact both lions were sporting manes was either a testament to his lack of familiarity with the story, or his lack of heterosexuality.

Either way, his darkly tinted windows were covered in as much dust as there was paint, and a bold message declaring "Two of Everything". The unit was on the end, slightly larger than its neighbors, and the only one closed. Immediately next to it was a liquor store with metal bars, a man in a yellow-tinged white tank top who might earn the name wife-beater manning the register with a narrow glare our direction. Next was a martial arts studio, door propped open to disseminate the smell of sweat and feet to the world. The other end was a handmade glass store that specializes in bongs, pipes and was probably a front for a head shop.

Both also sported window security bars.

"If I get murdered here, you need to make sure he doesn't take my body to be his second," Griffin joked, cracking the back windows for the dogs. "And my bones don't end up as the carbon base for glass blowing."

"If you get murdered here, I will probably have also been murdered, and we should probably send someone a pin drop to save the dogs. Also, glass is made from silica crystals and I'm questioning the legitimacy of your accounting degree." We climbed out of his car, and I stared at the picture. "You know what's dumb about the Noah's Ark story? Besides the obvious no food for the herbivores and a boat full of food for the carnivores? There would be a fluff ton more birds. You can't drown birds, so there'd be just as many birds of every species as you started with and next to no herbivores because you can't grow plants on a boat."

"I have questions about your brain."

"Like why am I this smart and not in charge of everything? It's because I lack leadership qualities and patience." I paused to pick my way around what was either dried dog poop or dried human poop, and I wasn't betting on the former. "Or was it why anyone believes the Bible when it's so clearly full of improbabilities and suspended belief, but magic is evil?"

Circling the end of the row, we saw a series of rear entrance doors. The back of the complex made me miss the front, an overflowing dumpster spewing garbage and the titter of rats and raccoons. Graffiti graced almost every inch of the stucco surface, from gang affiliations to declarations of love, and a myriad of names that did not look like something you should write on a birth certificate.

Two of the three doors were propped open, a man with red watery eyes darting out of the shop on the far end. A loud shout came from the neighboring open door, confirming the martial arts studio was trying to solicit a cross breeze to save on utilities and was also the only other business without a back door video camera.

Noah's door had a keypad lock, a welcome mat with animals, and posted sign declaring No Solicitors beside a video doorbell. The device looked new and somehow exempted from the vandalism of the rest of the alley, so either the business owner had paid them to not vandalize his stuff, or he was the one vandalizing everything else.

Or a third option I hadn't thought of yet because I was still stuck on what type of solicitors he wasn't permitting.

"Go ring the bell," I said to Griffin, eyeing his black jeans and form-fitting blue T-shirt.

"Why me?" He asked, looking for a third person to suggest do it instead.

"Because you're probably his type and I'm less likely to be his type." I encouraged, nudging him toward the door. "Maybe approach backward so he can check out the assets before seeing the front-sets?"

The accountant gave me a look that suggested he would show me both, but Noah wasn't getting either. With both hands, I shooed him toward the door, and he rolled his eyes before pressing the button.

"What do you want?" The man shouted from within, accompanied by the screech of multiple animals. "We're closed."

"I'm here to see Noah?" Griffin said, trying to sound like he was unsure but interested. Instead, he sounded confused and mildly annoyed, which I think still works for hookups. "Is... does he... He said..."

The man was a freaking actor, forcing his face to look like a nervous date and not the hiding-a-laugh man I knew was standing in front of me. Part of me felt bad, thinking it was slightly cruel to make Noah think he was about to meet the man of his dreams, only to be met with questions and crushing disappointment, but the guilt faded quickly when I caught sight of his face in the video feed. Skivvy eyes were drinking in Griffin's form, and I regretted asking him to be man-bait.

The door buzzed open, filled with the lithe form of the blonde man from the jury and his website. He was wearing jeans and a polo shirt, both pressed, hair in a gelled-down side-part.

"I don't know if we've met but I'm happy to go to lunch, I just have something to finish up first." He licked his lips, and I felt my lady parts dry up like the Sahara in the summer.

I was for certain never having sex again.

"Noah Anderson?" I said, stepping in front of the accountant and using my foot to hold the door open. His immediate surprise was replaced with panic when he saw the gun sitting on my hip. "We need to talk about Trigger, Ruger, and why someone tried to blow me up."

"You... what?"

Noah's hand trembled on the door, and I took a step toward him.

"Your illegal imports that caused you to be blackmailed into being on the trial, but you didn't need to be because you support his agenda while hiding in your closet of lies?" I continued, throwing in partial truths and guesses, watching each land with mixed results. His physical response was answer enough, and I knew all my answers without asking a complete question. "I need to know what, about all of that, means you want me dead and how you're helping?"

"Helping? I'm not... Can this wait?" He asked, sweat popping up on his brow, eyes darting around. Something moved in the shadowy interior behind him, and I squinted into the darkness.

"You were going to open this door for a date. I think we can do this now," I insisted, moving further into his space. He took another step back, tripping on a snake slithering on the ground. I screamed, stepping back while he stumbled backward into the darkness.

A silenced shot rang out, entering the side of his head and painting the opposite wall red. In slow motion, the body folded in on itself and the shadow I'd seen moving before started dashing further into the building. Cages burst open, birds squawking and another snake slithering closer.

Griffin pulled me back out, slamming the door shut to keep the snakes inside. We ran to the front in time to see a man in a suit crash through the front door and get in a black sedan, peeling out of the parking lot.

"Damnit." I puffed out air, checking on the dogs. "Now I have to eat a pound of dog fur."

Chapter Twenty: Suburban Legends

It took two hours for animal control to feel confident letting us into the building and six animal transport vehicles to relocate the creatures. The Cincinnati Zoo came for at least three dozen, four of which were believed extinct and could now potentially be re-propagated in the wild.

Five news stations were camped out in the lot, two local and three national, all waiting for something to report as cage after cage was brought around the front. Unfortunately for them, the body had been loaded up and driven off from the rear. Within seconds of the shots fired call to the police, the liquor store and pot shop were closed up and the only cars in the lot now belonged to the Tae Kwon Do students and the rubberneckers.

"OK, let me try to understand," Lt. Gax said for the 17th time, and I let out an audible sigh.

"If you haven't gotten it the first ten times I went through everything, with your numerous interruptions, I don't know why going through it again will make a difference." The crime scene techs were moving all over the animal shop with headlamps and walking sticks, swabbing, photographing, and playing Marco Polo with the furniture. Every light in the facility was on, and it was still the same level of dim as a movie theatre in the back of a porn shop.

Either Noah never replaced a light bulb, or there was a secret dimmer switch he operated by magic.

In the brief lull between animal control clearing the place and the Spanish inquisition, I'd wandered quickly through the space. Metal cages were along all the walls, tanks in the middle, and perpendicular shelves of product in between up front in the public area. Behind a swinging door were larger kennels, a water filled habitat surrounded by glass, and what could only be described as a rainforest closet. Two locked doors sat on opposite ends, one I saw eventually led upstairs, but I never saw the second one open and could only guess it went to a basement full of large game or taxidermy.

The electronics sat packaged and ready to be taken in, including the recording device linked to the Ring camera. Noah had two cell phones, three laptops, and an ancient CPU coated in a layer of dust. There was an external hard drive, four routers and something that blinked a lot before it was unplugged.

Both the front and back door were propped open, but the space still smelled musty. Wood shavings, reptiles and urine. Birds, snakes, lizards, tortoises, rabbits, puppies, Noah had two of nearly every animal I could imagine and a printout of which ones were illegal like a moron.

"You're the one found in the company of a dead body, Mrs. Sharp. I don't think you have room to be giving me attitude," he snapped, pointing a pen at me with all the authority and intimidation of Winnie with a hatchet.

Startling, sure. Deadly, probably not.

"I'm found near a lot of dead bodies. I'll change my name to Black Widow if it'll shorten the interrogation."

"This is serious, Mrs. Sharp!"

"My bad, let me put on my serious pants. I forgot I was wearing my silly ones!"

"Mrs.-"

"Call me Mrs. one more time and I will knock your teeth out. It's Ms. Sharp. And if I ever get married, I'm going to still be Ms. Sharp because prefixes based on marital status are dumb and how messed up is it that they only apply to women! Now, I came here to ask Noah about Clyde Sampson's death. They served on the Marius Howser trial together and his death was as much an accident as Epstein's. I have proof he didn't just fall and hit his head. I know how and why and have a pretty good guess on who- at least partly. None of that, however, explains why some jerk keeps trying to kill me, my dog, blew up my car and... I don't have a fourth thing at the moment, but rest assured there is one!"

"You need to calm down, lady," an old white guy with slick sleeves said and I snarled at him, lunging forward only to be caught around the waist by Griffin, again. The man had a bad habit of keeping me from committing felonies and I was getting really tired of not being allowed the same privileges as our president.

If the highest office in the country could be held by a felon, felonies should be a damn free for all.

"You need to get out of here before I claw out your eyeballs with the snake handling hook in the hallway and then use it to hold up your testicles while I slice them off with the paring knife in the room over there!"

Old boy's face went pale, apparently unprepared for the very explicit outline of how he would be destroyed and with what, from where. Clearing his throat, he puffed out his chest and strode away like it was his idea to leave the room and not the request of his as of yet un-cut testicles.

"Easy, soldier. You can get cuffed for that," Griffin whispered, stroking my back and locking his arm into place. "You have a reason to be melting down. A lot of people have been murdered in front of you recently and a lot of people have been trying to murder you. But you can't retaliate by slaughtering or castrating morons who've never seen anything scarier than a pimple on their ass."

Lt. Gax cleared his throat, and I snorted like our unhinged bull in his direction. Hands held aloft, he tried to look non-threatening. Despite having a few inches on me in terms of height and several more inches of muscle, the ranked law enforcement officer appeared to recognize who held all the power in the room.

And all the potential violence.

"I'm not... I also hate that guy, OK? I tried firing Officer Deuce's ass twice, but the union helped keep him here. Between N word drops and Colonel Sanders fried chicken jokes... I get it. And I know the dead guy was on the Howser jury. All the quote unquote conservatives in the department propped up his mouthpiece because it had the R next to his name, instead of acknowledging he was a criminal, an anti-American, and anti-law. Your friend came to me to investigate."

"Howser wasn't lying? You really were going to bring Geissinger and Stump into the case?"

"It was part of the plan, now I'm working on a brand-new case from scratch since that one's been thrown out. But I can't help you if you don't explain more than just allusions and outbursts." The lieutenant was breathing heavily by the time he was done, face pale and slightly sweaty. "We just need to wait for the electronics warrant... and ... water."

"Are you OK?" I walked over and checked his neck, arms, and lifted his pant leg. A small snake fell out of his pants, twin puncture marks glowing an angry red just above his black sock. "Shit!"

"Shit!" Griffin confirmed, dancing around the slithery assailant and calling for medical assistance. I grabbed a trashcan and turned it upside down on the snake. Standing on the can, I put the officer in the desk chair and studied the rapidly swelling and hardening lump on his leg.

"Allergic," he gasped, and I started patting down his pants. In his rear pocket, a thick quasi-pen with a depressor was prescribed to Paul Gax. I pulled off the cap, shoved up his pant leg, and pressed it to the fleshy outer of his thigh that had nothing but muscle underneath.

"Stop! Don't do that!" A white guy with frosted tips shouted. His dark blue EMS uniform hugged his biceps, blue eyes radiated competent control and knowledge despite his N'Sync wannabe appearance. "It'll move the venom around faster!"

"Why have an epi pen then? How do we get his lungs open?" The guy pulled out an inhaler, placed it between the man's lips and depressed it. After four puffs, Gax was able to take a full breath.

"We need to get him to the hospital." The EMS guy stuck his inhaler back in his pocket. His eyes swung toward me, and recognition hit. With the help of his partner, they loaded Gax on the stretcher.

"I'm riding with you guys." I followed him out into the hall as we worked through the gathered groups of animal control, officers, and crime scene techs.

"Where are you going?" Griffin ajogged after me.

"To the hospital with juror number five. Meet me there with the dogs, I might know where the drugs came from."

Riding in an ambulance without being injured was a new experience. While I thought there wasn't a lot of freedom of movement sitting on the gurney, there was even less space sitting next to one. And when the person lying down was fighting for his life, you were definitely in the way.

I took four elbows to the chest as they started IV lines, cleaned the bite site, and injected something into the site. The man had an oxygen mask on, his chest exposed to allow for easy shocking in case he went into cardiac arrest, and a look of panic that would haunt my nightmares.

Indiana Jones was on to something when it came to snakes.

After an uncomfortable ride where I patted him down and took his phone, called his wife, and then tried to make myself as small as possible, I was relieved to arrive at the hospital. Gax's teammates met him there, directing his wife when she arrived, while I sat on the bumper of juror number 5's rig and waited.

People entered the ER in various states of consciousness, wound dressing, discoloration and predicted survival. No two were in the same demographic, but all of them were accompanied by concerned family and friends holding their hands or blood-soaked rags, trying to maintain hope that they'd all walk out again.

Together.

"You look like you're having an existential crisis," frosted tips said, popping a piece of gum in his mouth and offering me a stick. "Is it the family or the injuries?"

I accepted the gum but didn't put it in my mouth.

"Family. Mine is moving away and hospitals don't allow dogs in, at least not without a human holding the leash... I'm just not good with humans. If I die... who's going to take care of the dogs?"

"Yeah, the ER's great for making you think you've epically failed to account for life." He dropped onto the bumper next to me. "You're Cyn, right? You're here about Trigger's death?"

I nodded, playing with the gum wrapper.

"Almost didn't recognize you without the upside-down visor. You used your own inhaler to save that cop?" I asked, but I already knew the answer before he nodded. "Did you talk to Trigger at all?"

"Nah. I went in as Dougie Fresh, my rapper persona. I didn't want to be EMT Doug Easton, so I figured I'd try on my dream life. Couldn't livestream, but I did a little rap at the adjournment of each day, signing off 'Doug-E-Fresh'." He spoke the last line like a 90s keyboard DJ. I expected him to scratch a record and say "noice".

"Trigger thought you were a moron?" I chuckled and he nodded, laughing along with me. "Considering I've met most of the jury now, did all of them think that?"

"Most, yeah. No one really paid much attention to me besides the bailiff. She knew who I was, though. I've done transports for prisoners in her custody before. But almost everyone else overlooked me, made for great people watching, y'know? Only Olivia also knew me and she wasn't keen on revisiting our past acquaintance."

"Is that how you got blackmailed into forking over the syringes filled with fentanyl and trazodone?" Doug jerked back and I raised an eyebrow at him. "My money was on Deanna, but I watched you with the needles in that ambulance. It would make more sense for someone in and out of hospitals than a woman working assisted living."

Doug E Fresh swallowed, looking more like the twenty-five years of age I'd found on his Wiki bio. Eyes downcast, I started to suspect if my dogs had actually died, I'd be out for his blood.

"You know some of us were blackmailed. I think Marius thought more of us were in their pocket than actually were. Olivia was seated next to Trigger because of her gran, and the leverage they had against me is the same they had against her. We met in narc-anon. Both of us used pills, but whereas she took them from family, I skimmed from the hospital. They threatened me, tried to get me to give them liquid drugs, but I couldn't get them. With the opioid crisis, that shit is locked down. Then they said they'd report me to the hospital if I didn't vote their way, even though I'd already come clean. I went along with it to keep an eye on things. Deanna would be the safest assumption, but you're also right, they don't give the hard stuff in assisted living and as far as personalities go, Deanna was the hard stuff. Patients that made grown men cry were assigned to Deanna, and she broke all of them."

"Was?"

"She died of a heart attack yesterday. Her obits in the paper." Sighing, I crossed her name off my mental list while I weighed his answers. When all of them tracked, I pulled out a picture of the needle and syringe from the parking lot.

"Any thoughts on where this might have come from?"

Doug zoomed in and studied the needle and markings. Sliding it back and forth.

"It's pretty generic. These are the plastic barrels you'd get at any drug store or compounding pharmacy to fill medication doses. Screw in tip... who were they trying to use it on?"

"My dog."

He handed the phone back and shook his head.

"Assholes. Look, I get that murdering people is wrong but going after dogs..." He chewed his gum and blew a small bubble, popping it with a soft echo around the ambulance bay. "Guessing you still want to know more about the trial though?"

I nodded, thinking about what I wanted to know. Juror number 9 was somehow involved—either willingly or threatened, Noah was dead, Trigger was dead, the Foreman was nuts, Madison had been blackmailed, Olivia blackmailed with Oliver sliding in to protect her, Meggie blackmailed and still scared... Deanna dead, unrelated.

"What did you see?" I asked, finally unwrapping the gum and putting it in my mouth. A pregnant woman was being wheeled past us, breathing in a two short, one long pattern. The man behind her clutching a bag covered in giraffes looked terrified and elated, reminding me that Larry could be having giraffe nursery babies with Amber.

"Something was off in that courtroom. It was obvious a lot of the jury was coerced into being there, nervous and shifty. The prosecutors were phoning it in, like even they thought it was garbage, but didn't have a choice. Most noticeable, though, was the defendant. Whereas most look scared, or entitled, Marius looked... defeated. He walked in like it was a death sentence and never once did he look like any statement made for or against him made a damn bit of difference." Doug was folding his gum wrapper into an origami swan. "And the longer it went on, the more conflict there was between Trigger and the dude next to him. It's dumb, but no one knew his name. We all knew each other's names except number nine."

I pulled out the picture, pointing to each person.

"Brant, Jordan," I skipped three. "Noah, you, Madison, Deanna, Meggie, Olivia, Oliver, and then Dane."

"Three is Jesi Keetes. She works in international conservation, might actually be inaccessible at the moment. I know there was a trip to Australia that was pending the end of the trial. She spent most of the trial playing sudoku. If I had to pinpoint a person who wanted to be there less than the defendant, it would be Deanna and then the judge. Everyone else would be harder to organize."

I laughed.

"The judge didn't want to be there?" I asked, turning the paper over to see the taped names and images of courtroom staff. "Aurelius Benson?"

"Yeah, dude had a low bullshit meter and was getting tired of the executive branch acting like it didn't get checked and balanced. He knew what this case was, but he still had to hear it. And the evidence... it was damning. But you can buy damn good evidence when you have the leverage. And if you had the evidence in the first place, you wouldn't even have to buy it."

"You sound like you're speaking from experience."

"Let's just say working as an EMT, I've been asked by defense attorneys to rewrite history about what I saw when I arrived somewhere. Asked by insurance adjusters to make determinations or claims that would keep them from paying out. The world is full of shady people who have no qualms taking a chance on screwing each other over. People buy evidence, be it witness accounts, or destruction of proof."

"Who would he, or they, or whoever, buy it from? Do you think the state police would be on the take?" I asked, wondering who I'd call for a report and how hard it would be to track down names. "Is this all related to the OG fraud case? Is it Stump pulling the strings? His former attorney? Some random loyalist?"

"Don't know. Attempted murder can be convicted solely based on circumstantial evidence, as long as it's damning. The weapon, the prints, the history... It was more than circumstantial. Guys like that, politicians, know how to game the system. If you have all the evidence and can arrange for it to be in the right place and pay to be untouchable. Then blackmail half the jury..." Griffin appeared, a dog leash in each hand. He strolled into the ambulance bay, not yet seeing us on the rig. From this distance, I could see his critical eye studying everyone for threats. There was still that carefree boy, but it was less in the forefront. In this instance, he looked like the former military man he claimed to be, a man with skills and secrets. "That dog is a hero though. Like a legit legend when that Fox news chick started in on her shit over Elsa."

I struggled to place the name, looking away from Griffin and rebuilding the courtroom in my head. "The bailiff? How did you end up working with her anyway? Cincinnati is nowhere near Columbus. Long drive for a transport, wouldn't they be dead before you got there?" Griffin spotted us, the set of his shoulders relaxing at the sight.

Doug chuckled, waving Griffin over when he hesitated to interrupt. Looking at him in his jeans and shirt, I wondered again where he came from. How he got assigned Trigger's account, why he'd been watching me, whether or not he really owned the farm beside the dairy. At least some of those questions I could answer, but I was scared to ask.

If he wasn't who I thought he was, I really was on my own in this.

"Ugh, I don't know whether to congratulate you or trash you for ignoring the news. Elsa Woodruff used to work down here at lower circuit courts. Dead name Edward, but please don't mention I said that. She's such a cool chick, it's insulting to reference the before times and I only say that so you know what to look up if you decide to see her full service record. Talk about a freaking suburban legend, some asshole attacks her, she takes him down, subdues him, and then saves his damn life. Gets the position with the federal court legitimately earned and the governor starts trying to implement genital inspections alongside that asshole in DC.”

Ruger nosed Doug, rubbing his head against the EMT's leg until the man gave into the cuteness and gave ear scritches. Winnie nosed her way in, and eventually the guy was overwhelmed and laughing. Griffin's genuine smile disarmed me, and I dug out my phone, shooting off a text to Joseph. Taking a discreet photo of the man, I sent one more text to the Senior Swingers Chat.

“Oh man, Winnie. Another legend if there ever was one. If you ever got her, you and Elsa in the same room, you'd be the three baddest bitches in Ohio and nothing would go unchecked. I don't think I've ever known any group less likely to take shit from backwards thinking jerks than you all. When Ruger peed on Miss Fox News's shoe, I nearly cheered.”

“Well, sounds like the perfect day to make that happen. Thank you for talking with me and having Lt. Gax's back.”

My phone buzzed and I checked the display.

The seniors were on it and Joseph was headed next door to have a look.

Walking back to his SUV, I said a silent plea to the universe that just this once, someone would turn out to be who they said they were.

Chapter Twenty-One: All Rise, Thy Middle Finger

Griffin kept up a steady stream of chatter on our ride back to Sweet Pea. The dogs were asleep in the back-seat, my phone eerily silent in the door handle beside me, and the radio was playing a classic rock station lightly in the background.

Bon Jovi's *Living on a Prayer* had never felt more dangerous than sitting in the car with a man who had no reason to be. I'd been too tired, too distracted, and had allowed a stranger to infiltrate my team when we already had too much on the line. He had access to Ruger, to me, to Winnie, and knew where we were.

Except he hadn't known about the soccer game, the pizza place, or the OH's... Unless he's who Meggie called.

"What do you think?" Griffin's question cut through my swirling thoughts. I glanced over at him from where my head rested on my fist, leaving my whole body angled toward the window.

"What do I think about what?" I asked, trying and failing to not sound suspicious.

"About Italian for dinner? There's this amazing place just outside of Dayton—"

"If you say Mi Asiago Prego, I will shoot you in the foot and throw you out of this car," I warned him, naming the restaurant formerly owned by an incarcerated criminal. He'd also owned a funeral parlor where people were being murdered in the easy to hose off basement and a male strip club that was still operating under a new name. Part of me remembered the gross facsimile of Italian food being shut down with the funeral parlor, but after my date with Larry where I got drunk, fell in his lap, tried to eat his junk, and then face planted into some cake, I had no plan of ever returning.

"I think that place closed when you sent their Coast Guard owner to the clink... after he murdered a bunch of people in front of you," Griffin said casually, and I gave him my full attention.

"How do you know about that?"

"I told you; I know a lot about you. I've seen you around, been following your work..." He shrugged like that wasn't the second weirdest thing someone had told me today.

"But why?" I demanded. My phone buzzed and I looked at the display. Joseph had gone next door to the neighboring farms. One had been purchased about a month after I returned, by an LLC and while there were horses, they didn't appear to be farming anything. When I saw the name of the LLC, I felt my stomach sour. "He sent you."

"What?" Griffin shifted in his seat, and I shook my head as the seniors confirmed what I'd guessed with public records searches. The farm was owned by the same LLC who owned Cruz's Dog Training house that we stayed in while laying low.

"Cruz sent you. He sent you to watch me after I first got home. You've been acting like a friend and a suitor but you're just a babysitter! A babysitter who's what? Been asleep the past 9 months? Figured you'd watch me get abducted and blown up a couple times, see if I survived before you stepped in? You know what, I don't care. Pull over." I demanded. "Let me out, we're done playing Batman and Robin."

"We're on a highway! I'm not pulling over and letting you get out and endanger yourself and these dogs. Also, who the hell uses the word suitor? Are you in a regency novel?" He joked, ignoring my hand on the door and continuing up the road. We were about forty miles from home and doing 70 miles an hour. I couldn't jump out and I couldn't walk.

"Now's not the time for jokes, Kristy Thomas!" I yelled.

"I always saw myself as more of a Stacey McGill." He smiled, and I gave him a death glare. Knowing the Babysitters Club did not get him off the hook. "Fine. I was letting you do your thing because you didn't know me, but this time the NFCU needed someone to handle the contract transfer. I volunteered even though it's outside my job because I wanted the chance to meet you and—"

I cranked up the radio and rolled down my window to drown out his voice.

Nothing he said was going to change the fact that he was done tagging along on this investigation and I was done being manipulated by men with no regard for my autonomy.

"Hey, ma." I walked into my office to see her standing there, coffee pot in hand.

"Heard you caused quite the disturbance in the Senior's chat with that young man." She gestured to Griffin who hadn't pulled away from the curb. "There's another chat where they're speculating theories on his identity. Most popular is that he's Cruz with a different face, like that convict face movie. Then a third one where they are attempting to work out how much plastic surgery and the estimated cost to change a person's skin tone, eye color, hair color, and height. Why don't you invite him in?"

"Because I don't need a babysitter. And if he's been loitering around Sweet Pea this long out of some misplaced sense of loyalty to Cruz, or lack of something better to do, then it's better if he just goes. I don't need his help; I've gone plenty of dangerous places with just Winnie. Now I have Ruger, so I'm basically swimming in furry back up. Which reminds me, what the hell are you doing buying Larry's Vet practice?"

Lynn Sharp pursed her lips, a look that said she thought I was being an idiot and was too stubborn to see reason.

"Would you like the long or the short version?" she asked, and I narrowed my eyes on her.

"I want the version where everyone keeps their pants on."

"Where did I go wrong with you? Your other siblings are not this repressed." She pinched the bridge of her nose, greyish blonde bob shaking as she seemed to choose her words. "Though you dated Larry for a while, I did not really see you two working out long term. Larry lacks... the spirit of adventure. What he has, however, is the ability to care for and heal sick animals—something this town has no shortage of. His mother, ooh that woman, she is a nasty little hypocrite, but her behavior was threatening to push him out of town. The town elders, and the Council, wanted to make sure that we didn't lose him. While I said the money was from me, it's technically an endowment from the town. To see to it that he continues to operate his practice and care for the animals here. Despite how it may seem, it was not a long con to convince you that the pair of you belonged together."

I'd made a single serve coffee pod while she talked, taking a drink and staring out the window in thought.

"I didn't think you did it to pull a Carter family arranged wedding deal. But I was worried, a little, that you hoped to see him as your son-in-law and it was a way to keep him... close? The animals do need him though... I don't think Debbie's ever coming back from that cruise."

My mom laughed, a high-pitched sound that had Winnie tilting her head and Ruger letting off a low woooo in harmony.

"Oh, sweetie, that woman's cruise ended months ago. She's shacked up with a marijuana farmer in Oregon where they sell organic hemp-based lady lube on the weekends and are working on a form of libido enhancers that work via vaginal suppository." I stared into my coffee, wondering if it was too early to spike it with Baileys. "But her office was an examination room at the back of the animal shelter, so it's not like there's much of a practice set-up to lure in a replacement."

Her transition between lady lube and everyday labor relations was astounding.

"Sure... Maybe you should build one?" I suggested, deciding 1400 was too early and kept drinking my coffee the normal way.

"Or maybe you should. I know this place wasn't your favorite, and it always felt stifling, but I think you can do a lot of good here if you wanted." She placed an envelope on my desk, and I stared at it, expecting it to start playing *It's Raining Men*, explode confetti and then a conga line of strippers to enter my office.

Outside, Griffin had started pacing on the sidewalk. His hands were gesturing, mouth moving, but I didn't see an earbud in.

"Is he... talking to himself?" I drank more coffee, tracking him with my eyes. Winnie went over to the window, watching intently as he walked back and forth, her head tracking every move. He was her Wimbledon, and I was not sure whether she'd give him a point for staying on the sidewalk or falling and hitting his head.

"You tend to have that effect on people. Aren't you going to ask me what's in the envelope?"

"What's in the envelope, ma?" I asked, spotting a commotion outside. Several men in jeans and red hats were shouting at one of our town librarians. Griffin rushed over, trying to put himself between the men and Kaia. "Winnie, go."

Winnie and Ruger charged through the door, taking up posts on either side of Griffin. From here, I could see the first few teeth peeking from their mouths and imagined the low rumble I'd heard Ruger let loose in defense of Trigger way back when we met. Striding to my desk, I pulled out the Glock I'd just put back in the drawer safe and clipped it to my belt.

"Ma, do you mind..." She shook her head and was already beside me, marching into the line of fire. It wasn't what I had asked, but standing shoulder to... well, six inches above her head, with my mom as we faced down a group of red-faced men felt right.

"Take it down! Take it down!" They chanted, Winnie's menacing teeth and single bracing step backing the mob up another foot.

"Do you have a permit to assemble?" I asked, in my loudest command voice and a short man with beady eyes gave me the once over.

"We're doing the state's work, girly. Move aside. We don't need a permit to enforce the law!"

His compatriots cheered and I rolled my eyes.

"Technically, that's true. To enforce the law, you need a badge. Who has one that isn't a sticker someone gave them in kindergarten to be hall monitor?" To make a point, I folded my arms at my waist, resting my elbow on the butt of my very loaded, legally carried firearm. I was now in line with both canines, flanked by my mom and Griffin who bookended Kaia. "I see none. So, I'm going to need you to disperse as this is an unlawful assembly and an ugly one."

"Fat bitch, no one..." Winnie snarled and lunged, startling the man. He stumbled backward, colliding with his moronic brethren until they toppled like dominos into the street.

"See? This is why there's a male loneliness epidemic. You're all too busy climbing on top of each other while being in denial about your feelings. Get some therapy with the rest of the time you had set aside for being obnoxious." They struggled to right themselves, limbs and hats misaligned between owners. At least two not so subtle junk grabs occurred, and I was fairly certain one muttered "praise Jesus" when his hand met testicles. "This library is now only available to people who can name the three branches of government, their function, and the purpose of the US Constitution."

"It's to keep out the immigrants and make sure the egg prices don't go up! And women do as men say, like the Bible decrees!" One hollered. I made a loud "ehhh" buzzer sound.

"You are incorrect, sir. Also, I'm adding reading the actual Bible to the list of requirements for anyone who wants to use the Bible as their reason for being annoying. You can't give me chapter and verse, you don't know Jesus. Now SCRAM!" Winnie and Ruger punctuated my decree with a series of loud barks and the street started to clear. Turning to Kaia, I studied her tear-stained face and red cheeks with apprehension. It was at odds with her colorful rainbow dinosaur dress, and the woman who hosted Taylor Swift dance sessions for the town's teens and tweens who never made it to the Eras Tour.

"So... What was that about?" I asked, pulling some cookies from my cargo pocket, confirming they were meant for humans, and handing them to her. Kaia glanced at the blue package and burst out laughing.

"Do you always have cookies in your pockets?"

"Yeah... unless I've eaten them." I shrugged and then stroked Winnie's head. Ruger went over to give Kaia reassurance while I tried not to stare at the woman. Kaia was between mine and Seth's age. About thirty-five with purple chunks in her brown hair, rainbow mermaid glasses, and a few extra pounds in the middle. I'd never spoken to her before... I never really spoke to anyone besides Mo, Larry and Stella, unless they were asking me to investigate something. But she gave me a sense of peace.

Like books themselves, she was happy to just be there whenever you needed to escape.

"They want me to take down the flag." She pointed up at the four flags hanging off the marquee style awning that ran the front of all the businesses on Main St. There was a US Flag, an Ohio

Flag, a pride flag, and a weird flag that had a flower and three colors that looked like a child drew it with a crayon.

"The crayon flag is weird, but I don't know why they'd claim the state outlawed it…" I asked, staring at it far longer than warranted. Griffin had moved in beside me, my mom watching from a few feet away.

"What? No, the pride flag. Stump copied that state out west, banning non-official city flags to force cities and towns and villages to take down anything 'controversial' in the 'spirit of unity'. It's part of that follow through on the hate rhetoric that got him elected, if you don't consider voter suppression illegal manipulation of an election."

"Sounds like a first amendment violation. Also, what about that one on the end then? How come it gets to stay?"

"That's our village flag, Cynthia," my mom answered, and I blinked at it.

"A kid could draw that with just a couple of crayons… and it doesn't look like anything. But OK. Is this that Governor Small thing? The one where his name clearly speaks volumes about his…" I made a sweeping eye movement toward the center of the human body and Kaia laughed. "Just sounds like petty bullshit of a *little* man. What happens if you ignore it?"

"Well… he copied the bill word for word, and the bill had no provisions for enforcement. So… nothing. A few cities over there did ignore it," she whispered, like it was a secret. "Some people, like this group, tried to insert themselves to enforce it, but they were ignored as well."

"And what happened?" I asked, also whispering.

"Nothing. The city made it an official city flag."

I nodded, looking at my mom.

"Who do we talk to about that second part?"

"Council, I'll get the ball rolling. Should be easy enough." She pulled out her phone and started working the device like a pro.

"For the first part, I say, own that boss bitch energy and say fluff it. Let me know if you need Winnie and Ruger's support though." I gestured to the dogs who were now hyper-focused on something across the street. I followed their line of sight to the small grassy median that served as a micro park between center street parking stalls. On the sidewalk, two men in grey suits watched us, both sporting sandy brown hair, above average height and a statuesque build, noses casting independent shadows. The one on the left might have been juror number nine, but it was hard to tell from this distance. One was taking pictures, and the other was whispering into his phone.

Before I could speak, a large truck roared past with two of the men from the mob. They offered us shouted insults and middle fingers. By the time it cleared, the two men were gone along with a black sedan.

Chapter Twenty-Two: The Princess & The Puppet

"Oh good, you're here!" Princess Liana said, full regalia in place. From her sequin dress and long red gloves to the glitter tiara perched on top of her red wig, she reminded me of Jessica Rabbit going to the prom. "I have a few places I want to show you before I go into the show tonight! I'm performing and presenting down at The Hall; it's a spot out near Dayton and Lizzie McTire's on the set list?"

The real estate agent waggled her eyebrows, and I rolled my eyes with a huffed laugh.

"I'm not sure I need to talk to Lizzie, or Jordan Moerer, but yeah. I heard back from the VA, and I qualify for... some house money and a low interest rate?" I showed the princess my email and she shook her head with a low whistle.

"Definitely won't need that much for a house out here. How did they know your income?" I shrugged and offered a minor wince.

"They are the government... kind of." I tried not to finish with a sardonic comment about until they finalize cutting off their funding. "Also, I submit stuff to them for medical care, so I think it's on there."

"Cynthia, I think before you go looking at..." My mom's phone rang, and she picked it up. The princess took my arm and started pulling me up the sidewalk.

"This place is perfect for you. I really think we need to jump on it before everyone else. Just went on the market today. Your mom will understand," Princess Liana said, taking my arm in her manicured claws and dragging me up the sidewalk with strength, efficiency, and balance in defiance of her 6-inch stilettos. "Now, it went on the market as a rental originally for 5 hours, but now it's off and I think it's going to be for sale. Since you got pre-approval, I think you stand a good chance of..."

We walked two streets over and turned into a familiar neighborhood while I checked that the two dogs were keeping up. Leash laws said they should be connected to me, but Princess Liana seemed to have a different opinion, one that she'd have to change if Daniel or Barney came by to start drama about unleashed dogs after allowing a literal mob scene at the library.

Ruger was trotting along happily, not struggling to keep up with us in the least. His nails clicked on the pavement, slightly uneven gait making the out of tune clicks and clacks more in line with his tongue out pit bull smiling prance. Winnie, on the other hand, looked incredibly put out at being forced to walk. She was sniffing at every fence post and mailbox to halt our forward progress, as though I had any control over the pace or direction of this outing.

At once, we came to an abrupt halt and I stumbled into the princess, falling onto a perfectly manicured lawn with two dog snoots shoved into each of my ears.

"Cold, wet, gross!" I whined, trying to push them away and succeeding only in redirecting the licking to my eyes, cheeks, and chin. A hand appeared from amid the furry cavalcade, wrapping around my torso and pulling me free of their canine affection. Callused fingers swiped at the slobber, and I opened my eyes, inches from Griffin's face and pressed entirely against his front. "Ugh, why are you everywhere?"

"I mean... I thought we went over this. Cruz used his money and connections to get a burned special ops guy to move to the area after the second... no, third time? You were almost killed. He'd bought the property when you came back, probably as a safety measure, but I didn't move in until later. And I developed a bit of a crush, like a book boyfriend, but you were real. Then I met you, and it was somehow even better." His fingers lingered on my cheek, stroking my lips with his thumb. "I tried to tell you in the car, but you weren't interested in listening to me confess my feelings."

My throat closed and I tried to swallow, but my heart was racing.

"That's…"

"Sweet!" Princess Liana said, clutching her purse to her chest. "Girl, you need to take that man off the market! He called you a book boyfriend!"

"Aww… Cyn!" Mo said, standing to the side with Chris and looking like a heart-eyed anime character. "You're his Juliet! That's so…"

"Creepy as hell," my mom completed the sentence, and I pointed at her.

"That one. Definitely that one. You should not take someone's job watching a person and then just never introduce yourself. That's weird!" I pushed against his chest, forcing him back a step and away from me. "And I'm weird, so I know what I'm talking about!"

"I was a spy. Watching people and reporting back was sort of my job for years. It's not weird when the government pays you for it for over a decade." He shrugged, thumbs looped in the front pockets of his jeans while rocking back on his heels. "You have no idea how unfamiliar I am with the concept of normal, so weird might be *my* normal? Maybe that's why I like you?"

I rolled my eyes, but my heart rate bumped up and my palms started to sweat. The two Griffin supporters cooed and my mom's frown softened, the culmination sending a small swarm of butterflies skittering around my belly.

Back burner-ing this problem, I looked around and then faced the house we'd stopped in front of. Blue house with white trim. The American flag they'd put up when I joined, flying beside the pride flag – updated with each new inclusion. A small stained-glass cross in the window, because my parents were church-going humans who believed in an afterlife and loving thy neighbor.

More than I thought strictly outlined in The Bible, but I'd only read *Lamb* by Christopher Moore so maybe potluck kink key parties were in there.

"This is my parent's house."

No one seemed surprised by this information.

A large storage pod sat out front, men in jumpsuits carrying out labeled boxes, bedroom furniture, and what a normal person would think was a weight bench, but I knew better. No one had told me when they were leaving, part of me thought maybe I had more time. Maybe another month until Christmas, or New Year's, but the moving humans made it clear that my parents were on their way out and it was happening soon.

"You brought me here to watch you move out?" I asked, grateful when my voice didn't betray my urge to cry. "I'm not sure I need a realtor for that."

"No," my mom replied, pressing something into my hands. "I brought you here to choose what you'd like to remain in your new home. I wasn't aware Clarence was in on it, but I suppose it's better he brings you here than I try to lure you here with baked goods. I had planned on using Mo."

My friend waggled her fingers at me.

In my hands was the envelope from my desk. I opened it and flipped through the contents. Pink slip to the Subaru, deed to the house, all sets of keys, and a new bank card.

"They're obviously moving out mine and your father's bedroom furniture, and our playroom. I know the bed at your apartment belongs to Mrs. Margot, so I thought we could bring up the one from the basement. I know there's still stairs, but they are fewer, and you can spend your time on the ground level instead of in the bedrooms..."

I leaned down and hugged her, squeezing my mom and pulling my dad in when he came over.

"Thank you," I whispered. "I... thank you."

The ice cubes in my whiskey were starting to blur but I still didn't think I could black out and forget this night.

"I need another one," I told Dolly, the bartender. She had the big blonde wig, a Dallas Cowboys style tie front crop, and a six-inch beard that was braided into a smile beneath the one on her lips. Around us, The Hall was slowly filling with the glitz and glamour of patrons who planned to perform and the average person who came for the show.

And those of us who'd accidentally opened a chamber of secrets that really lead to forgotten horrors.

My parents had turned Seth's room into a library for their "research" and the bookcases were filled with tomes from around the world. Books about ancient sexual practices, Cleopatra's bee box, the origin of the vibrator (it was for men to stimulate their prostate, because of course it was), and ancient indigenous tribes' fertility dances. Sitting beside them were dark romances and bodice rippers, some I'd even read and enjoyed, the room as a whole something I wanted.

Cue Belle and her rolling library ladder dreams.

But then... oh then... I'd stumbled on a ball gag and bumped a statue that slid back a wooden panel. It was the coolest thing I'd ever seen.

Until I saw the lost and found kept on the other side.

Underwear.

Strap-Ons.

Leather straps.

Spreaders.

My browser history after I took a picture and used the internet to figure out what a spreader is.

And one lonely speculum no one could explain.

I'd fled to the drag club like it was the last safe place in the galaxy.

"You look like someone who maybe needs a therapist instead of whiskey, sugar," Dolly said, refilling my glass with cinnamon flavored Jack Daniels and coke. "You wanna talk about it?"

I took a long drink that killed half the cup.

"Do you know Lynn Sharp? About yay short, blonde hair in a bob? And Monty... not short, always looks like he just stepped out of wardrobe for old professor dude on a movie set and like his hairline is on the losing end of a war with his eyebrows?"

"Oh yeah, I've been over to their house a few times for..." I held up my hand, begging him to stop.

"Those are my parents, and I was helping clean that house so I could live there." Silently, Dolly made my drink a triple and looked at the bottle in his hand. "It was supposed to be a good thing, I guess. The dogs need a yard, but the reality, seeing all of it..."

"Sugar, I don't think I have enough whiskey for that."

"They're leaving. Tired of protesting and fighting, so I'm moving in, and I found a room... There was a speculum, Dolly." I gave her horror movie eyes and took a drink, letting them water with the burn. "A speculum and neither of them knew why it was there, or how long it had been there, and if it was used."

Dolly pulled the meter drip out of the bottle's top and set the open bottle beside me.

"I'll just refill your coke, sugar. I don't have enough liquor in my bar to help you, so if you don't pass out after that I'll put you on the list to perform. When liquor fails, sing drunkenly off key about it." He winked and I finished the cup in front of me, amazed when it was refilled with coke and I added my own generous splash of whiskey. The house lights were still on, and I watched Dolly walk away, then turned to lean against the bar and watch the room.

"If this is what dreams are made of, makes you wish the Vespa crashed," a man said from my elbow, and I turned.

Then jumped a foot in the air when I came face to face with a puppet.

"What the hell was in that whiskey?" I whispered, looking into the cup then back at the puppet. I'd grown up with the Disney Channel, and Lizzie McGuire was one of the shows I watched a handful of times, but a 3D puppet of her animated thoughts wearing coveralls with a mustache was never a dream, nightmare or hallucination I'd had.

"Don't mind my thoughts tonight, they're a little dark," a voice beside the puppet said. Squinting, I saw a thin man in the same outfit with a wig and glitter sleeves poking out. "Heard you wanted to ask questions about the case."

"Even though it's illegal," the puppet added, and I drank the rest of my whiskey. If I was going to see a bunch of strangers forgotten sex-cessories, I was not talking to a puppet sober.

"Incorrect, little Lizzie. I don't want to know about the trial. I want to know about the jury." My voice sounded a little slurred, and I decided I should avoid saying anything with an S sound. "Ssspecifically, if anyone ssshuspiciousssh or solacious was circling Trigger?"

Avoid S or use more? My brain no longer knew.

"Woah, you're wasted," Little Lizzie pointed out and I nodded at her.

"Dolly, can you give Miss Sharp some water?" Big Lizzie asked, and water appeared along with a coke refill. I added my own whiskey but chugged the water first. It was refilled and I decided to down that too before starting in on my whiskey coke. "Damn."

"S' been a week, Jordan Lizzie. Have you ever had someone watch you because someone you used to sleep with asked him too and then that guy disappears, poof, because you had him help you prevent a bad thing and the Army was like 'now you die," I tried to pull out a creepy villain voice, but I sounded like a drunken circus performer. "Then this guy shows up everywhere you are after an intro at your friends will reading and he... you... but he didn't tell you? And a dead guy says the first guy is back but he didn't say anything either?"

Dolly replaced my water and added the rest of my whiskey bottle to my coke cup.

"That the man lingering by the door?"

I followed his line of sight to where Griffin stood. He didn't blend, but he didn't look uncomfortable and I had no idea when he arrived. No matter what unusual place I went, he simply followed along and made himself comfortable. Always looking like someone's puppy having the best day ever.

It baffled.

Like he was given that assignment once and it became his identity.

"Yup. I like him. But honestly, I don't want to. I don't want to like anyone. My ex keeps hinting at getting back together even though he refuses to fully understand why we broke up. The last guy I dated dumped me because my life was too much, which is fair, and Cruz... I don't know where Cruz is but the dead guy said he wasn't dead before he died. I wonder if Griff does... But if I ask and he does... then what?" My head flopped forward, and I downed the new water and the rest of the whiskey bottle. "Ugh. So, my dead friend. What do you know?"

"Hell of a segue," the puppet answered, and I pointed the empty cup at her.

"Quiet you. You weren't at the trial, and I don't talk to puppets... normally."

Jordan chuckled under his Lizzie McTire makeup, and I tried to look like someone capable. Capable of what, I don't know anymore, nothing makes sense anymore.

"I was next to the foreman. Trigger sent us a lot of questions, requests, and notes for the judge. Brant... that man takes everything in stride and didn't care about the notes, not like the man next to Clyde did. The air on our side of the box was a lot easier to breathe, if you get my drift. The lady behind us was an absolute Betty White but gave less shits. The woman next to her looked shell shocked and horrified the whole time, and when Suits the Shithole refused to pass Trigger's notes, he just passed them to that white rapper idiot."

The room spun on its side, and I laid my head on the bar, letting everything swim in the haze of whiskey and regret. Suits the Shithole was probably the best name I'd ever heard for Colton Pierce, and a fairly accurate descriptor, but I still didn't have any leads on who he was, where to find him or why he might have killed my friend.

Or if he killed my friend.

Maybe he was solely the doggy hitman.

"Were you being blackmailed to serve on that jury?" I asked the empty coke glass. Through it I could just see the puppet's foot.

Lifting my two-ton arm, I poked the platform sandal. "Those are not OSHA approved young lady. Only close-toed shoes in the shop or you'll lose a toe."

"She's going to be hungover in the morning," Puppet Lizzie declared.

"It's cute that you think the hangover will wait until the morning," I slurred, and big Lizzie laughed.

"Damn, girl, you are a mess. Some men came to me when I got my summons. Made it clear I was to play ball or my extracurriculars would get around my place of business. The guys I work with already know, but I went along. Scary mofos."

"Let me guess, two guys in suits?"

"Nah, some deranged paramilitary looking fool in survivalist gear and a masked man in scrubs. They got into a caged transport van; it looked like something out of a post-apocalyptic nightmare movie. Or maybe a prison movie? Either way, I didn't want to end up in that van, you know?"

I nodded, but with my cheek flat on the bar, I just rubbed my face against the lacquered surface. Its layer of sticky goo caught on my skin and snagged the flesh, tugging it in different directions while drool slipped out of the corners of my mouth.

"Anything else about them stand out? Something you'd see and think 'huh... that's a characteristic'?"

Jordan considered my question after a small chuckle.

"The man in scrubs had raw hands, like he washed them repeatedly. Made me think he really might be a doctor, surgeon or ER, someone who always needed to change gloves and use harsh soaps. Despite that, his shoes were highly polished and pristine.

The other guy... his pants were tucked into his boots and his boots didn't match. One was polished, cared for, and the other looked thrifted. Like he either grabbed one from two different pairs or stole someone's boot."

My eyes slithered to the barroom floor, noting the impeccable footwear gracing every arch. Stilettos, sequined platforms, wedge sandals, fall booties... My sneakers were the ugliest pair of shoes in the room. Griffin's tan work boots a close second, only beating mine out because they weren't sporting farm stains.

"Shoes are at least something to look at. Did anything about them hint how they knew you'd been summoned? How soon after the letter did the men show up?"

"Huh..." He looked into a glass that was sitting in front of him and took a swallow. "Hadn't considered it before, but they showed up the same day as the letter. Like they'd put some kind of tracker in it..."

"Do you still have-"

"Good evening, ladies and gentlemen!" The lights dimmed and a single spot illuminated the shimmering figure in the center of the stage. Princess Liana, microphone in hand, commanded the room in her Jessica Rabbit attire. "Before we get into the evening's program, we have a special pre-show performance."

Two men dressed as Magenta and Columbia appeared beside me, each taking an arm and helping me up.

"Performing straight and singing live, Miss Cynthia Sharp. Doing *Touch-a, Touch-a, Touch Me* from the *Rocky Horror Picture Show*." The crowd erupted into applause, and I was placed center stage beside the Princess. "Miss Sharp's had a rough night, you don't want to know what she's touch-a touched. Since our bartender lubed her up with whiskey, let's see if we can get her to let it out."

The piano trilled, and a microphone appeared in my hand.

"I was feeling done in. Couldn't win." I whispered, and Columbia and Magenta backed me up. "I'd only ever kissed before."

I finished the intro, the music swelled, and I locked eyes with Griffin. Gone was the cute puppy, the innocent character he played to blend, and in his place was a man on red alert. Either there was danger, lust, or his diarrhea was back, but what I saw looking back at me was a predator on a mission.

"Touch-a, touch-a, touch me! I wanna feel dirty! Chill me, thrill me, fulfill me, creature of the niiiight!" I howled the note, drunkenly stumbling. The ground disappeared, falling, floating, until I was in the arms of an oil-slicked blonde man in a pair of golden briefs. Rocky faded into Griffin, then back into Rocky. "Creature of the night."

Griffin's face swam back in front of my eyes. I leaned into him, pressing my lips into his, and drifted away on a whiskey cloud into the blissful darkness of unconsciousness.

Chapter Twenty-Three: Who You Know Blows

An evil ice pick wielding leprechaun was stabbing the inside of my skull, and he smelled like rotten eggs and clean laundry. Coarse hair scraped across my cheek, slapping my forehead while wet sandpaper rubbed against my toes. Heat radiated up my numb right arm, the entire left half of my body pressed against a space heater that rumbled... and clawed at sides.

"Why space heat, leprechaun-assassin," I muttered, shoving at the ice picks and claws. Furry weight met my palms, and I pushed harder. "Geroff!"

Taking hold of the tail on my face, I declared it Ruger's and also the reason my arm would need amputation. Which meant the claws and the warmth were from Winnie. The tiny man stabbing the inside of my head was courtesy of Jim or Jack and his cinnamon flavored death.

Beyond the panting dogs, gentle hum of a fan, and raucous roar of my own blood in my ears, was absolute silence. The street below was silent, no early morning shoppers prepping for their workdays or grabbing coffee at Mo's. The usual screams of children enjoying their lives to the detriment of my sanity was also absent, as was the traffic and the occasionally shouted greeting of the hearing impaired.

The entire town of Sweet Pea had gone silent.

Gone silent or...

"So you are alive," a man said, his voice preceding the glorious scent of coffee into the room. Gripping the dog tail on my face, I pushed it away from my face and slid open an eyelid to look at the man on the other side.

Griffin.

"Where am I? Too quiet." I accepted the coffee.

"My house. Guest room." He quickly clarified, hands raised in surrender before I could panic. "Though I'm not sure there was enough room on this bed, you refused to take mine."

My neck craned over Winnie, and I saw her paws hanging off the edge of the bed, still twitching in sleep. "Still not sure why we're here…"

"Because I still don't think you should go back to your building and Carla agreed."

"Just because a bunch of dumbasses tried to intimidate a librarian?" I scoffed, finishing the coffee in my cup and setting it on the table beside the bed. "That's the least threatening group of people I've ever endured a threat from. You should have seen the seniors after Winnie ruined BINGO night and a B32. Doubt any of those guys knew their dick from a Glock… or have seen either in a decade minimum."

Griffin chuckled and walked into the room, taking my coffee mug and gesturing toward the doorway.

"Nevertheless. Meet me out there, I need to show you something and then we can go get your car." Winnie's ears perked and she eyed him in warning. "I have dog food too."

My former partner was on her feet, launching off my kidneys like a diving board, and darting past Griffin before he could finish his sentence. Ruger was slower to get moving, yawning and slapping my face a few more times with his tail before taking a big stretch and gracefully descending to the floor. Following his lead, I stretched and climbed out of the bed, surprised the three of us fit in a double. Water and pain medicine sat beside the bed, so I took both and then looked down.

The shirt I was wearing wasn't mine, but the underwear was. Most everything important was covered and I didn't see my pants on the floor. Water in hand, I found the bathroom across the hall and took care of my morning business before shuffling into the kitchen.

"Thanks," I told the back of Griffin's head while he tried to get the dogs to sit down before feeding them.

"For..." He glanced over his shoulder and froze, swallowing hard. Pink lips parted, I watched his eyes sweep my frame and I tilted the water glass in his direction.

"Water and meds. Don't turn your back on Winnie while..." Too late. She jumped onto her back paws and gripped the edge of the dish with her teeth, pulling it out of his hand and sending kibble scattering to the floor. The dog went to work, hoovering the food with the aggression of a killer robot disguised as a Roomba. "Rookie mistake."

Ruger sat still, eyes pleading and Griffin returned his eyes to the task at hand. Giving the black dog his food and placing the rest of Winnie's on the floor, he righted himself and let out a soft throat clear. Eyes firmly fixed on the two dogs, he shifted from side to side with his thumbs tucked in the front pockets of his jeans. "You're uh... half naked."

"I don't know where my pants are." He nodded and pointed to the coffee cups. I took mine back and started drinking, alternating between it and water. "This your shirt?" He gave me another nod and I wasn't sure if I should preen or put a pillow in front of me like a movie woman caught... well, with her pants down. "You going to tell me why I had to come here, or did you swallow your tongue gawking at my legs?"

His head shook lightly, and he returned to the planet.

"Right. I uhh…" He swallowed and reached for his coffee, skin brushing against mine and sending a flutter through me I wanted to ignore. Placing his hand on my hip, he leaned around me to grab a tablet.

But he had coffee in his hand.

"You seem very flustered. Is this your first time seeing a woman without pants? I know they make a lot of sailor-on-sailor jokes, and if that floats your boat, I respect it. But-"

"I swear, I've been with a woman before. At least three. Hell, I'm older than you by four years!" He dropped his head to rest on top of mine and I reached up to pat him gently on the crown.

"Unless you started having sex at four, not sure how that's relevant, but bully for you." He laughed against me and pressed a kiss into my hair.

"It's just… been awhile. And it's you."

"Yup, just me." I assured him as he lifted his head. Squeezing my hip once, he let go, moving away to grab the tablet and take a seat on the couch and gesturing for me to follow. Winnie's dish was already empty, the floor around it spotless, while Ruger was still working methodically around the dish in a circle. I scratched the spot between his shoulder blades and redirected my raptor to the couch. She took the arm opposite Griffin, leaving me to sit in the center.

Of a leather couch.

With no pants.

"What's wrong?" Griff asked while I stared at the empty spot on the couch.

"I don't sit flesh to leather on a couch."

"Why not?" He asked, already lifting the cover of an ottoman and pulling out a fleece throw blanket. Spreading it out, he put half on the empty space and half on Winnie. Sitting, I stole the part placed on Winnie to cover my lap and stroke her fur with the hand not holding coffee.

"Because skin sticks to leather and it's uncomfortable and disgusting. Only men and influencers who never sit down think leather couches are a good idea." I tucked a leg under me, slightly invading his space to better see the tablet in his hands. "Now, what's so dangerous and scary."

He blinked at me a few times, decided whatever he was going to say was dumb, and moved on.

"When we were at Noah's Ark, after you left with the LT, I was wandering around and heard a man talking about how it would be better when you met your natural conclusion." His jaw ticked, fingers swiping across the screen. "It was the man whose nuts you threatened with a paring knife, so I thought he was just running his mouth. But I put a listening device on him, and... well..."

There was an app that looked like a heart monitor with a play button in the middle. Queueing up a file, he pressed the button in the center, and a green spectrum wave appeared. It began as a flat line, static and silence overlapping the steady crunch of Ruger's chews. Then a voice spiked across the screen.

"Did they succeed?" He asked, and I compared it to the voices in my memory banks.

"No. The dog and that man deterred them. It would seem your supporters are... inadequate and chicken shit." A smoother voice intoned. His polished English was more in line with the east coast and private education. "We can't allow this to continue to chance. I'm running out of time to clean up this mess."

"Now I kept her out of the place, arranged the snake on that negro who wanted to reopen everything." A third man chimed in, and I gripped my coffee mug tighter. It was that asshole officer who made Colonel Sanders jokes against Gax and I threatened to castrate. I glared at Griffin, considering he was the reason Officer Deuce still had balls. "If she wasn't such a bitch, I could have used the chaos to take her too. Why the hell she went in the ambulance—"

"Is irrelevant." The second man came back on, soothing everything over. "My brother failed to silence the dog, the mob did not create a disturbance for us to try again, and that man doesn't allow her or the dogs to be anywhere alone."

"Who is he?" Officer Deuce cleared his throat with a thick mucus hack.

Silence stretched between them during which something fell in the background, and the first man shouted about his friend being a bully on the internet.

"I don't know. None of my contacts have been able to find anything on him, but I'm sure we'll learn something soon. Put down your phone, Tommy," he scolded, and a scuffle ensued after which the first man whined loudly.

"But I need to comment back to this fool who challenged my greatness! How else will everyone know that I am the smartest, most powerful, governor—the best ever really, if I don't respond?" His foot pounded the ground, and I felt my lip curl, coffee sitting unsteadily in my stomach.

"It needs to wait, sir. You brought me on to fix this, and we will, but one problem at a time. Did we clear the problem out of Noah's?"

The officer cleared his throat.

"We couldn't get the door open. There hasn't been time to go back, but it's locked down. No one can get in there who isn't us either."

My eyes close against the voices, the deterioration of the conversation into a tantrum no longer of interest to me. I'd walked through most of the pet shop, the large animal cages, the small ones, the tanks, the space that may have held an alligator...

"The door." I was already on my feet, chugging my coffee and putting the cup on the counter. There was a doorway off the living room that led to a dining area, half the adjacent wall taken up by a slider, and the one facing me held a heavier door that might lead to a garage. Striding through, I opened it and saw a garage, the annoying truck and the SUV parked side by side.

"What door?"

"The one in the pet shop."

Closing the garage door, I turned around and started to walk back in, colliding with Griffin in the middle of the room.

"What are you looking for?"

"My pants." I walked around him and went back toward the kitchen and down the hall. The bedroom I slept in was on the left, the bathroom on the right, another door on the left, and an accordion style door on the right. Pulling on that, I found the washer and dryer, and opened the dryer.

My shirt, pants, and socks were inside.

"Success!" I pulled on the pants, added the socks and looked down at the shirt. "Damn. Was I wearing a bra?"

I looked at Griffin who was just standing in the hallway, his mouth hanging open.

"What?"

"You... bent over. In your underwear." He shifted from foot to foot, hands running up and down the front of his pants. "I saw... your..."

Laughing, I brushed past him and found my bra beside my boots. With a final head shake, I started to close the door.

"Never change, puppy."

Monday morning before ten was too early for the liquor store and the weed shop to be doing business, but a martial arts class was going when we pulled into the lot.

"Pull around back," I told Griffin, forced to give up driving and the idea of going solo by last night's alcohol choices. He drove down the alley, carefully skirting broken bottles and smashed pallets that had accumulated in the less than twenty-four hours since we'd been here. If someone had said this drive aisle doubled as a rage room, I'd believe them just based on the debris.

"Was all this here yesterday?" Griffin voiced my thoughts.

"I don't think so. It looks like someone had a fit."

We pulled behind the last door, pointing the car toward the exit to partially obscure our activity from view. Without the electronic doorbell, the steel door was indistinguishable from its neighbors... aside from the crime scene tape and the blood splatter on the doormat no one had removed.

There was no doorknob on this side, just the electronic lock and a metal handle. Leaning against the window, I eyed the gutters on the roofline and saw the cameras on the pot shop and liquor store were still in place. I couldn't determine the exact range of either, but it looked like they were most likely directed to only view visitors to their shops, the crime equivalent of don't ask, don't tell.

"Do you have a plan?" I curled my lip at him, horrified he'd learned nothing this past week. "Right, sorry, I forgot. Can you pick locks?"

I shook my head, still looking at the door. The liquor store had bars on the front window, as did the other two businesses, so vandalism was out. Cars usually had pry bars... But how tough was an electronic lock bolt? And would anyone from the Tae Kwon Do studio notice?

"Even if you get inside, what are you going to do if you find something?"

"Turn it over to... good cops?" I continued searching, half distracted. "That plus your audio file..."

"Are inadmissible."

"Way to be glass half empty." I decided popping open the door with a pry tool would be the best option, I just needed a cover. What reason would two people need for tools in an alley...

"I don't like the expression on your face." Griffin inched away from me, but the car wasn't that big and he didn't get far.

I smiled like Harley Quinn.

"Get your spare tire and pry bar out, put it on the right front quarter panel. We're going to pretend to need to change a tire… and I'm going to scope out that lock." Jumping out of the car, I looked down at the Subaru tire and tried to look concerned in case the cameras picked me up. Griffin had the tailgate open, the cargo covers off, and the metal tools in hand while he considered the tire. Wandering closer to the door, I studied the keypad and saw three numbers were more worn than the others, with number two being the most abused key.

Two, five, six… I pulled out my phone and looked at the letters beneath the numbers. ABC, JKL, MNO… Was Noah the type to make a word? And if he was, what word would he…

"No… it can't be that easy…" I whispered, entering 2625. The light flashed green, the bolt snapped back and set the door free. "What a perv."

"Did you crack the code?" Griffin asked, still holding the metal tire tools. His breath ruffled my neck hairs, and I shivered.

"Yup… and I'm going to pretend he's really into roosters." Turning on my phone flashlight, I pulled open the door and slipped inside. I was immediately met with the smell of rot. "Oof, something's going bad in here."

Griffin followed behind me with Winnie and Ruger, passing me Winnie's leash. I also relieved him of the metal tools and slid them into my cargo pockets.

"Where's your gun?"

"You saw me without pants on! You know I don't have one!" I hissed back. "Where's yours, super spy?"

He palmed a Glock from the back of his pants.

"Ruger and I will be lookout." I nodded, trying not to ogle his piece, and going into work mode. Winnie's paw rubbed at her nose, and I patted her head in apology.

"Seek," I ordered, and she went to work. Her nose worked along the wall, my flashlight checking the ground for broken glass while she checked for explosives. Past the prep kitchen, the smell of decay grew stronger. We jogged right, away from the apartment and toward the door that hadn't been open. Winnie's nose worked fast, my eyes starting to water with the smell and the dust particles floating in the air.

We got to the door, and when Winnie confirmed it was secure, I tested the handle. The cheap golden handle wiggled, but was definitely locked. There was no deadbolt, and pointing the light at the cross-wrench, I inserted the pry tip between the wall and metal plate.

It wiggled some more.

Turning fully to the side, I leaned my full 275 pounds against the bar and felt the door latch pop free with a snap.

"Yes!" I did a little dance and then secured Winnie, raising the bar in defense and opened the door. Light shining, I whipped it open with the beam sweeping the room and the weapon raised.

Odors of rot and decay, along with sulfur and feces, assaulted our noses.

Instead of a basement, we were in a storage room that had two rows of metal racks. Animal carriers, spare animal food, and accessories were haphazardly sitting on the shelves. A trail of food pellets sprinkled the floor between the racks, and I leaned down to see if anyone was still here.

Winnie's hackles went up and she let out a soft growl.

Whipping toward the second aisle, flashlight at chest level, I prepared to take on an assailant. Her rumble advanced to a grumble and I searched for something to explain her reaction. But the darkness wouldn't lift to show me the threat. Fumbling toward the wall, I walked her back, slapping at the space by the door for a light switch.

Catching the plastic switch, I flicked it up and was met with the white striped butt of a skunk, poised to strike.

"No!" I shoved Winnie out of the way, slamming the door shut as the first spray doused my center. Tears fell from my eyes and I stumbled toward the wall, barreling into it harder than I meant to.

It crunched beneath me, popping out like a Murphy bed, sending me to the floor beneath the sudden weight. My eyes cleared and I met the dead man's stare of Patrick Patterson, the former attorney, a bullet in his head and part of his skin already starting to decay. Bile burned the back of my throat, the two smells mixing together in a heady concoction that made my eyes water while I tried to swallow back my puke.

"Griffin!" I shouted, but choked, when the skunk sprayed me a second time.

Chapter Twenty-Four: Bailiff-ed Out

"No way is she getting in my car," Officer Chicken insisted, stepping another foot back from me toward the overflowing dumpster.

"I'm not taking her!" Sgt. Stupid countered, moving closer to the bagged-up Winnie poop that a raccoon had thrown out of the dumpster.

"Well, someone has to take her in for questioning!" Officer Obvious announced, though, why he felt the need to say that to his watch commander was bamboozling.

Meanwhile, I was sitting on the brick wall that partially separated the rear drive aisle of this strip mall from the neighboring one. Griffin had moved the car, safely placing Ruger and Winnie where I could not singe their nostril hairs... or entice them to lick me. As usual, he managed to loiter invisibly near the group actively discussing who should relocate me to the police department for breaking and entering.

Considering nothing was broken to enter, they were going to end up having to cite me for trespassing and getting smooshed by a dead body. A body they hadn't known was dead, weren't looking for, and the discovery of which was making national headlines because an "unknown source" sent pictures to the media. Patrick Patterson's link to this case wasn't widely known, but it was about to be when paired with another Cyn Sharp disaster.

I'd like to take credit, but the source was as unknown to me as if I would ever not smell like skunk and decomposing corpses again.

Animal control had come back and taken the skunk. She was pregnant and severely dehydrated from being locked in a storage closet. Even if I would never breathe clean air again, it was worth it to know I helped a skunk, and she hadn't gotten Winnie.

I could burn my clothes, but Winnie fur was staying firmly attached forever.

An engine revved behind me, but I didn't turn around. The whine was on par with a 750cc motorcycle and I didn't know anyone who rode, which meant whoever it was either snuck through for a story or was trying to kill me. Since I wasn't giving a story or getting rid of the smell, I didn't see the point in turning around to get murdered.

Like cattle farming, the meat is softer when it dies without having time to tense up and be worried about it.

Heavy boots made their way over to me in the silence left by the engine. None of the tell-tale sounds of a round being chambered met my ears, which left knives and poisons. I met Griffin's eyes from across the lot, and he gave me a small nod. A weird way to tell me a hitman was behind me but...

"Heard you might want to talk to me," someone spoke, and I turned slightly around. My eyes scanned jeans, a waist length leather jacket, and a short, bobbed cut around a round face offset with sharp brown eyes. Her build was trim, muscled, and imposing, but there was a subtle softness that lingered around her eyes.

"Elsa?" I asked, unsure if I was hallucinating the court bailiff.

"Yes. And if you knock five times and ask me if I want to build a snowman, I'll kick your ass. Let's go." She gestured over her shoulder, away from the group of officers still fighting over who would be unlucky enough to touch me.

"Go where?"

"Does it matter? You can't really want to stay here with these clowns?" Elsa Woodruff was passing some serious judgement on the group assembled in front of us. Considering she worked and lived up near Columbus, I was equally confused by why she was here and how she already knew she hated them.

"Kind of a rough assessment, but yeah, it matters. I don't get in cars with strangers."

"It's a bike, and that sounds like a lie." Elsa slid on her aviators and crossed her arms, the position making me feel like I had a bodyguard. "And I know those guys. They suck."

It was hard to argue with her since I'd met them. "I might be under arrest... and I smell?"

"That's why I brought the bike. And they can't arrest you, but if they have questions, your man is still here." She nodded toward Griffin who somehow gave a thumbs up with his eyeballs. "He can answer any questions about what happened."

"He's not my man," I argued, turning around and setting my feet on the opposite side of the wall. "He's a man... Who has my dogs in his car. Crap, the dogs!"

"They're OK. My wife has eyes on them, and she'll keep having eyes on them. Doug said they were in danger when he called last night. I saw the news, made some more calls... Officer Kim sends her regards." She offered me a helmet, and I pulled it on. The cargos I was wearing, and the long sleeve t-shirt wouldn't be great if we went down, but at least most of my skin was covered. She led us to an upright touring bike, with hard saddles and a tall windscreen. After climbing on, she slid forward so I could do the same and we both pulled on the helmets. "Hang on."

Elsa started the engine, and I gripped the metal rod on her seat back. She exited the lot, made a right and zipped up the road, hopping on the freeway and merging toward the suburbs, with soccer fields similar to the ones near Columbus. Tall buildings turned to short housing tracts and then faded into farmland on the side of the now two-lane highway, somewhere above Cincinnati and east of Dayton, where she exited and turned us toward a small farming community.

Wooden fence posts lined both sides of the road, rolling in gentle hills along with the road. Horses and cows dotted both sides of the road interspersed with corn, tall grass, and wheat. Aside from a lone pickup from the 1980s in a powder blue, no other drivers appeared along the route, giving the illusion that we were far away from civilization, though I estimated only about fifteen minutes had passed. Normally, I'd be concerned about a stranger driving me into the quasi wilderness with no observable witnesses, but it was peaceful.

Time slipped away in the autumnal countryside, the cool air drying my sweat, skunk spray, and decayed man smells. These clothes were toast, but above the rumbling engine of Elsa's motorbike, the reality wasn't suffocating... or nauseating. While I'd considered getting a motorcycle endorsement at some point, the idea had always been nixed for various reasons by both family, friends, ex-lovers, and two strangers who'd seen me race a Mini Cooper on a Vespa in Europe.

They were the only two with a valid reasoning—but I suspected I should adhere to it.

As Elsa wound us down the highway, I imagined a bike with a sidecar. Winnie and Ruger could wear doggles, their ears and tongues flapping in the breeze. We'd rev our engine at muscle cars and then force them to eat our dust while Griffin waved a little coffee bean flag in a tube top.

"You good?" Elsa looked over her shoulder, helmet off and a single eyebrow raised. There was humor and twinkle in her eyes that said some of my musings were written on my face and I'd missed a question while lost in my daydream. I nodded and pulled off my own helmet. Every arm movement crunched the shirt against me, confirming that whatever had dried was not exclusively liquid. "Good. Hang onto that for a second."

The bailiff held the bike steady, jerking her head to the left in the universal exit signal.

My leg lifted, but there was nowhere to go. Forward and I'd kick the driver, backward was the rear backrest of the bike and I wasn't that bendy. Putting that leg down, I tried rotating my hips until my pelvis was perpendicular to the seat. Leaning back, I slid toward my back leg, holding on to both back seats until solid ground was beneath my shoe.

Or I thought it was solid ground.

A loud squawk cut through the air, and I jerked my leg back, but I was still sliding. My grip slipped, and I landed in a heap on the ground at Elsa's feet with a chicken fluttering her wings in distaste near my head. With a well-aimed peck, she stabbed my cheek and sashayed away with the air of a queen.

"Might have taken off the helmet too soon." Elsa looked down on me with a crinkle at the edge of her eyes and a pinch in one cheek like she was biting it. "That's Hen-solo."

I huffed out a breath, held up the helmet and considered the grey sky above us that was blocking the sun.

"Do you only have one?" The dirt below my head wasn't the most uncomfortable place I'd been today. Now that both my feet were free of the bike, I wasn't all that motivated to get up.

"No. The other one is Princess Lay-a-egg." The bailiff secured the helmet beside her saddle bag and then extended a hand down to me. Calluses graced two of the fingers on her palm, and her thumb had a healthy spot that reminded me of Beth, the armorer in Afghanistan. Hers was from loading two thousand rounds a day, and I was now slightly concerned I'd gone with a stranger, unarmed, to the middle of nowhere. "It's mostly snake shot. We get a lot out in the fields by the horses."

A bailiff who reads minds... creepy.

"I don't read minds; you said that part about calluses out loud."

"How do you know I thought you read minds, then?" I accepted her hand and let her pull me up. Standing side by side, I was about four inches taller than her and a few dozen pounds heavier. Silhouetted against her was a red and white trimmed farmhouse with a small porch and large windows that looked out at a dirt and grass yard with two towering willow trees that brushed the ground.

"You said that out loud too." She started around the house, and I followed, noting that in addition to the vicious hen there was evidence of hoof stock and... cats, maybe. The prints looked like Winnie's, only smaller and potentially deadly. "I get the feeling a lot of your internal thoughts take a stroll into the outside world."

It wasn't phrased as a question, so I elected not to comment and incriminate myself.

Behind the farmhouse was an expansive yard leading to corrals, pastures, and whatever else she kept at her house. Immediately behind her back door was a horse trough tub and ten jugs of tomato juice lined up on a low table below the window. A black dog with white tipped toes stood guard, eyeing me with the same suspicion I gave people who said they didn't eat cheese.

"Not to be forward, but you can either strip to your skivvies or hope this works on your clothes, but no one's letting you into their car or house until you stop stinking." Grabbing a hose, she pointed it at me. "I promise to tell you everything I know while you soak. What's it going to be?"

"Ugh." I toed off my shoes and set them beside the tomato juice table. I set my phone on the top and started unloading my snacks, wallet, and the pry bar I forgot I still had. Once they were all empty, I tossed my shirt and pants beside my shoes and stood before a stranger in a sports bra and underwear. "Hit me with your best shot."

Frigid water slammed into my belly, sweeping up and down from my hair to my bare feet until I was chattering with water forming icicles on the tip of my nose. With a circling finger, Elsa directed me to turn around and I followed her instructions with my arms wrapped around me, my nipples threatening to tear my bra open and slice my arm to get the warmth from my blood to keep us alive... and then eventually dead, but we'd briefly be warm.

"Hop in the tub." I followed her instruction, shivering and hopping on my bare feet toward the big black tub. Once inside, I made myself as small as possible. The once comfortable fall chill was now a biting cold, frozen death looked me dead in the eyes and mocked my life choices. A reel of failures played before me: moments where I failed to act, moments where I acted too quickly... All the coffee I wouldn't get to drink.

Boiled water followed, then the acidic burn of tomato juice. It hit my toes first, the water and fruit level rising to my ankles, then my calves before I finally raised my head and saw a hose running from inside the house. Presumably it was attached to a dual temp faucet set to scalding, but as feeling returned to my limbs I found that it might have been a contrast issue. Three containers of juice had made it in with me, and the hose looked as natural hanging out of my tub as it did when I watered horses on the farm. "Hadn't meant to take that long. Jackie called to say she was on her way back with your man and pups. She's also bringing Percival and George for some reason. Though they're taking their own cars because, and this is a direct quote, your dog's farts make the skunk you pissed off smell like roses."

I snickered into my tomato bath, "Griffin must have given her cheese when I wasn't looking. He screams weak link. And he's not my man."

"So you've said. Sounds like a case of the lady doth protest too much." Elsa disappeared briefly and my tub stopped filling with warm water. She reappeared to get the hose and wound it up to take back inside. "He spends a lot of time with you for someone who isn't yours."

"That's just poor judgement." I dunked my head under and let it swirl a bit before bobbing back up. Elsa was now seated in a camp chair, feet crossed in front with hands folded over her flat belly. "And it's not protesting too much. If you'd ever met me before, you'd know I protest a hell of a lot more than this about things a lot less... just less."

Elsa chuckled, face turned to the sky, and I saw the first peep of an Adams apple that I'd not noticed before. It was the first and only visual I'd seen of what Doug called "the before times" and I wasn't too fond of knowing that personal detail.

"So, what do you have left that you want to know?" Her eyes remained closed, but the tight set in her jaw spoke to an awareness of my scrutiny. "Doug's given you the rundown on nearly everyone and I heard you've talked to more than most. Can't give you any more on juror nine than you already have, Colton Pierce, and I've also had feelers out looking for the one-handed witness. Heard Deanna died, though considering she smoked more than a BBQ pit, I'm not surprised."

I leaned against my tomato tub and considered her question. "Tell me about that day. I haven't talked to the defense attorney, Jackie Abramian, yet. I heard she was tight lipped on who that guy shouting at her was, but you ejected him, so maybe you got a name? I mean, you have to put something on the Do Not Return order, right? Then he came back... tell me about that."

"Man's name was Kelley, didn't get more than that, though. Some uniform comes by blustering about how he has it from there and escorts Kelley away. Most of the trial was pretty uneventful from a court security perspective. From the perspective of an actual trial, it was a dog and pony show without the pageantry—names neither side had heard of ending up on the witness list, actual witnesses disappearing, along with their depositions, evidence popping up like a rabbit out of a hat with no chain of custody or motion to file."

"Is that where Jennifer Doe came from? Why was she allowed to testify if no one knew her?"

Elsa shifted and took a sniff near my head. "Jackie wasn't the first attorney on the case. She inherited it the week jury selection was due to end. Half the files disappeared with the old lawyer, and no one had a complete list of testimony recorded. It was an absolute shit show."

"Who was the first lawyer?"

"A man named Patrick..." A large vehicle roared up the road and Elsa stood, checking her watch and then glancing toward the front of the house. "It's too soon. That's not them, not yet."

She grabbed the hose, and I stood, the freezing spray eliminating most of the red tint on my skin. A towel hit me in the chest. "Neighbor, maybe?"

"I don't have any neighbors, Sharp. Dry off, we need to..." The engine cut, loud music replaced by heavy footprints while Elsa went into the mudroom and appeared with a shotgun. Two men rounded the corner and before she could cock the round, taser prongs shot into each of us from each man and we went down into the darkness.

Chapter Twenty-Five: The Brothers Pierce

"What do you mean the dog isn't here? This is your cock up, find him!" The smooth polished voice from Griffin's recording was the first sound to greet my ears. In the wake of ten thousand volts, small abnormalities stuck out of his speech, a lisp corrected and overcompensated. Heavy footsteps and lighter treads worked through the room around me; my face stuck to a woven rug that scratched a soft patch of skin beneath my neck and my exposed chest and belly.

Damn it! I worked an eye open and glanced down. Aside from my tomato-stained bra and undies, I was wet and mostly naked in a stranger's house. With a small shift and a finger wiggle, I confirmed that I wasn't tied up and put that in the good news column.

So far, that column had not completely naked and not tied up in it.

"Get her up, and find out," a woman snapped. She sounded somewhat familiar, but in a way you wish you could forget. Like a human genital wart, someone you'd be better off never knowing about or having in your life. "Now! What are you waiting for?"

"She's naked."

"Well, whose fault is that?" This was the fourth voice in the room, and the third male. Silence stretched between them, a timid shuffling of steps brushing air along my bare legs, and then the second man spoke.

"Excuse me?" He poked at my shoulder, one or two fingers probing the soft flesh and sending my body rocking from side to side. A limp strand of hair half-covered my eyes, acidic tomato and wet hair mingling with just a hint of skunk to keep the would-be assailants at bay. Two fingers came into view, pressing harder into my shoulder. "Excuse me, ma'am?"

"What the hell, Charles!" Trainers stomped over, a two-inch manicured claw sliced my upper arm in a firm grip that dragged at the skin and pulled me over, leaving me flat on my back. Air swished near my torso, a swish beside my cheek.

A crack cut through the silent house, the burn against my cheek secondary to the alarm brought on by the sound. She drew back again, and I caught her hand.

"No." Grip tightening, I pulled her toward me and shoved back, the woman toppling onto her ass with a squeal. Shoving my wet hair out of my face, I glared at the woman on the floor and watched her scramble backwards on all fours. Every time her left hand grazed the floor, it made a hollow thump against the wooden floor. "Jennifer Doe... no." I looked at the man who'd shoved my shoulder. The blonde hair and vacant expression. "Charlie and... Vivian? The polycule couple? Where's Elsa?"

"We didn't need him." A man in a suit sauntered in, the ramrod straight posture putting steel plates everywhere to shame while the light gait beneath his feet didn't make so much as a tap. He was definitely the man in the video shouting instructions, Kelley, and I looked down at his shoes. "So, he's been placed out of the way."

They were polished leather and perfectly matched. "She." I corrected, a nerve in my jaw ticking. Behind him was juror number nine, feet slapping the ground in an irregular pattern. Left leg dragging slightly behind his right, each clomp more petulant than the one before it. His shoes were also perfectly matched, but in place of boots or loafers, he wore sneakers with a small logo on the side that might be impressive if I understood brands. "What's number nine pouting about?"

Colton scowled at me, his face twisting upward under furrowed brows. "You're fugly. I mean, I knew you were fat but without clothes..." He shuddered.

Vivian let out a high pitched bray, and I let my gaze shift to her. As a witness, she'd covered her long black hair under a curly blonde wig, put on glasses, and changed the shape of her nose... prosthetics maybe? Did Meggie recognize her? Or was she the one blackmailing her in the first place?

Charlie stood to the side, eyes wide and unfocused. Movement caught his attention but couldn't hold it, his eyes sliding from one thing to the next without any real understanding. I let my eyes wander down to his feet, combat boots that didn't match.

"Why are you all just standing around? If the dog has an audio recording device that links him to my brother, we need to find the dog and eliminate him. Where is the dog, Sharp?" I saw his hands resting on his knees, the red, raw skin consistent with overly washed skin.

"Not here, obviously." Another crack broke through the room, and I was sideways on the floor. Unlike the first time, Kelley hit with force and the metallic taste of blood coated my tongue under the throbbing ache of my skin. "You hit like a bitch, but I guess doctors need their hands. What's wrong with your husband?"

Vivian rolled her eyes and glanced at Charlie. "He's not my husband. I needed an in with the Clerk's office. Though he got laid off a month ago, they don't clear access to their systems all that regularly. We just went into the system as him and did what we needed to do... useless drug addict." With a sigh, she pulled out a gun and shot him point blank in the head.

Ears ringing, I stared at the blood, brain, and bone shards that now painted one wall of the otherwise pristine farmhouse. Charlie's body continued to stand somewhat headless for several beats before gravity caught up with the loss of muscle tension and he folded into a heap on the floor a few feet away from me.

Through the urge to scream, I saw Kelley shouting at Vivian. One hand cocked on her hip, she argued back but their words were drowned out by the blood whooshing in my ears under the ringing silence that follows a small caliber weapon being fired at close range. Kelley gripped the top of the weapon, ripping it from the woman's hand and stuffing it in his own pocket.

Leather loafers rounded on me, and I blinked, staring at Kelley's moving lips but no sounds registered. "What?" His lips flapped some more, but still nothing made it through the remaining din rattling around inside my head. "What?"

Kelley rubbed his temples, head leaned back whispering to the ceiling.

"Where's the dog?" His whispered question came through, a low hum in the tide of sound. "I need the recording."

"He's a dog!" I shouted.

"Where?" Colton limped over, hands fisted on his hips. "Where is the dog?"

"Dogs can't make recordings!" The hum faded and my voice was too loud to my own ears but yelling at them brought me a small amount of joy. "They don't have phones!"

"I... I know dogs don't have phones. Trigger put a recording on the dog of Colton dosing him with the drugs. And one in the room when we were cleaning up the mess. I need that recording." Kelley was now speaking through clenched teeth, eyes looking up at the ceiling for the secret to not strangling witnesses. "Where is the dog with the recording?"

"Ruger doesn't have a recording. He's a dog, where would he keep it? In his dog-kets? Pockets for dogs? Or do you think somehow Trigger ordered him to bury it with his dying breath in a hotel made of concrete?" I joined him in looking for reason hidden on the ceiling, but all I saw was a daddy long-legs in the upper left corner. "What are you looking for?"

"I'm not..." He pinched the bridge of his nose. "I'm praying for patience but there isn't enough on this planet for the level of incompetence in this room. It's probably on a flash drive on the dog's collar."

"There's nothing on Ruger's collar. I took it off and cleaned it after you assholes were trying to poison him." A shadow crossed one of the windows and I held my breath. It wasn't just a tree. "Is that really your brother?"

"Yes... unfortunately. He lacks discretion. I should have had him arrested, then at least I could have kept an eye on him in the county prison system. Far easier than trying to keep him alive on the outside. Paying off lawyers, arranging jurors, organizing the theft of dry cleaning from psychotic Korean women, and making sure that fat ass officer in Stump's pocket didn't kill that police lieutenant. Thank you for the help with that, by the way."

"No sweat. Prison doctor? That explains the van you drove to threaten Jordan and how you blended at the federal pen. I assume that was you?" He nodded and I shook my head. "So, what, Stump used your brother to blackmail you into cleaning up the mess? And then you break your back to keep it from getting bigger and people end up dead like Patterson?"

"No, Patterson was another example of morons going rogue. Though my blood brother was certainly a measure of protection for the fascist POS, it was another brotherhood that dragged me into this." Heavy boots stepped into the room, and I looked up at another marine. If being a law enforcement doctor had kept the first fit, then being a politician's attorney had made the second look like the walking dead.

"I thought the plan was just to kill Howser... there's been so many additional murders, Kelley." Milton Geissinger grew paler at the sight of the dead man on the floor. "I just wanted to be free of that man, needed help escaping. How did it turn into this?"

"Colton." Kelley seethed. "Just like when I was overseas and had to go AWOL to get him out of being cut up by a biker gang, now I have to clean up the mess he made as a juror trying to get out of Stump's debt. Now this bitch won't give me the recording so we can be done with this!"

Kelley kicked out at me, but I was out of reach. The spool of thread holding him together was unraveling faster and faster. Vivian wrapped her arms around Milton, letting him lean into her.

"Don't be like this, man. Take a breath. Elsa's good upstairs."

"You mean Edward?" Vivian sneered and Milton shook, trying to step away from her but lacking the strength.

"Don't do that. Don't be like those assholes who put us here. We fought for more than just to be pawns in someone else's power grab."

"And look where we ended up? All that's left of the unit is here, we'll make it out of this but it's us against everyone else now." Her hand stroked his shaved head and I saw cuts and bruises on his skin. "We got you out of jail, we got you out of that hole he tried to bury you in, and we'll get Colton out of this. Then we can be done. Give us the recording, Sharp."

I shook my head. "There's no recording. I don't need a recording. Everything he did during the trial is on the internet, including falling over Trigger's lap to stab him with the EpiPen."

Kelley snapped to attention, rounding on his brother. "You're on the internet?"

Colton gulped and shook his head. "You can't see anything. Mostly just Vivian's hand flying into the jury box and..." Kelley punched his brother in the jaw, sending the man down to one knee.

"You absolute cockup. If you weren't neck deep in debt to Stump's casinos, I wouldn't be in this god forsaken mess and now..." He kicked out and his shoe ended up in his brother's gut. "I was in the military for decades and haven't encountered this much stupidity. I built and disarmed explosives less volatile than this mess! We could have taken care of this yesterday if you'd been smart enough to place the bug better!"

He kicked his brother again.

"Kelley!" Vivian wrapped her arm around his torso, her hand offering a massage to one of his shoulders while her lips tickled his neck. "If there's no recording, then we're in the clear. Just kill her, the bailiff, and be done. We don't need the dog. We can put their bodies in the apartment and detonate it."

"Do more people really need to die?" Milton tried to right himself but his limbs lacked the strength. "We aren't the bad guys. When did we become the villains? After all we survived?"

I felt bad for the lone voice of reason leftover from a time when the world had rules. Milton had been a soldier, but one who'd looked for a better way. The two beside him had lost that way.

Trigger would have helped them find it.

Except they decided to kill him instead.

Colton wheezed on the floor, and I laughed. No longer sure if I was biding time until Griffin and Elsa's wife arrived or I just wanted to watch this group implode. I was past the point of wanting justice, I wanted to watch them burn. "He didn't tell you the truth?"

Two malicious pairs of eyes zeroed in on me. Colton pled with me from the ground not to say a word, panic, blood, and spit dripping down his face. He had orchestrated the death of my friend, tried to poison my dog, and blew up my car. His life choices brought him here, and I was tired of being the better person, tired of keeping people talking and letting the cops handle it. "Ask him about his leg, Kelley."

"She doesn't know what she's..." Colton tried to back away, but Kelley took hold of his throat and dragged up his pant leg. A black dress sock went halfway up his calf with just the tip of a white sterile bandage peeking above it. Without mercy, the doctor ripped the sock down and tore the bandage, half his brother's leg hair coming out with it. A perfect replica of Ruger's jaw, partially infected, was stamped on his calf. "You piece of shit!"

Colton flew across the room, head smacking with a bone rattling thwack against the wall. He crumbled to the ground beneath a small smear of blood and didn't get back up. Kelley whipped around, landing a kick in my ribs that crunched and stole my air.

"What difference does a bite make?" Vivian asked, and Kelley rounded on her.

"What difference does it make? Dog bites are unique, they line up. Colton getting bit by the cripple's dog is irrefutable. No matter how it's spun, it puts Colton in the position of triggering a canine companion. He shouldn't have been near that dog, and now he's wearing it's damn calling card! All of this, the covering up and trying to keep our covers intact. We should have run!" He stomped over to his brother. "Get up you worthless..."

Colton didn't move.

"Colt?" He shook him again, sending his head to the side at an unnatural angle. Vivian let out a scream and the door burst open. Columbus PD and the State Police flooded the house, Griffin, Ruger, and Winnie behind them.

"Cyn?" Griffin crouched beside me while I watched Kelley get pulled off Colton's body and placed in cuffs. Ruger and Winnie cuddled in close, my arms instinctively clutching both of them while Ruger spared a brief growl for Colton's lifeless form. Vivian resisted, screaming about how she was a second cousin to a chief of police in Mississippi, and they'd pay for touching her, but she still ended up cuffed on the floor. I waited for relief, satisfaction... some sense that this was over to wash over me.

But I felt nothing.

The heart of the problem was still beating in the state capitol.

"Elsa's upstairs... And I need some pants."

"Aren't all your clothes at your parent's now that it's your house?" Griffin walked with me up the alley behind my apartment, holding Ruger's leash and questioning why we were here.

I shook my head, holding tightly to Winnie's lead as she fought me to get to dumpster after dumpster. Elsa had a pair of coveralls that went on loose enough I could manage for a car ride, but with a sports bra, coveralls and tomato-stained skin, I was a few teeth above being classified as a hillbilly. "Never made it that far. I think there's a few outfits there from laundry the other day, but most of my wardrobe is still here."

My ribs ached. The EMTs had fought to transport me, but I pinkie promised I would transport myself and they gave me a couple pain meds. Since I didn't plan to go, I probably owed them a severed pinkie and a repayment on the pills.

"You're going to regret not letting me walk Winnie when those meds wear off." Griffin laughed, angling toward my back door, but Winnie was pulling away and blocked the path. Her nose worked toward the door, body shielding us from the door. Ruger's nose joined her, and I looked between them.

"Seek." I pointed at the door, letting her check the handle and the stoop. She sat, whimpering, and trying to pull us away from the door. "Shit. Take them both to the end of the alley and call for backup." I reached behind him and took the gun from his pants holster.

"Just come wait with us-" he started, but I pulled open the door and went inside before he could finish. I knew it had been locked, and a quick glance into the ransacked office space confirmed someone had been in here.

My conspiracy murder board was on its side, the heavy curtain that usually hung in front of the window in tatters beside it. The PC was smashed on the ground, monitor in a heap beside it, but a visual sweep didn't show any place an explosive could have been concealed. Ducking back into the atrium, I studied the stairs.

Carpet was intact on each step and the paint on the walls was consistent. Whatever Winnie detected wasn't here, and I ascended to my apartment with my gun at the ready. I paused at the top of the stairs for a quick visual sweep, Glock in a two-handed grip at low ready. From right to left, my kitchen was the most destroyed, then the bed had been stabbed with all the blankets cut into ribbons, coffee table smashed, and one couch cushion laying on the floor beside the turned over armchair.

Each item had the potential to conceal a device, but my money was on the bed. My clothes were beside the window, so gently as I could, I stepped out of the coveralls and tossed them and the gun on the couch, careful not to look at the shattered remnants of my beloved and trusty coffee maker.

The gun bounced off the cushion and fell onto the exposed base underneath. A click resounded around the room and I stared, temporarily paralyzed. It ticked once, twice... I ripped the nearest clothes off a hanger and ran back for the stairs. Soft clicks joined my racing heart counting down until a weighted silence filled the staircase.

I paused, thinking maybe I'd been wrong.

Air sucked into the space behind me and filled with fire. The heat shoved me forward, singeing my back, and toppling me over into the wall. I burst through the door and slammed it shut behind me. Pressed flat against it, the windows blew out and glass rained down on the alley, a mirroring sound on the street out front along with a symphony of sirens.

Chapter Twenty-Six: Stump then Fall

The hotel room mirror wasn't doing me any favors.

My new plain black suit was constricting the two broken ribs that hadn't healed in the past three weeks, and my bra rubbed against the second-degree burns running up my back. What had felt like a bitch slap had managed to bruise my face, and tomato juice plus peroxide makes dishwater blonde hair look like a children's volcano made with red Kool-Aid on top of my head. And underneath all of that, I still smelled faintly of skunk.

A brand-new suit and a silk shirt made zero difference.

"You ready?" Griffin asked from where he was seated on the second queen bed in the room. Tomorrow was Thanksgiving and instead of spending it listening to my mom give my dad explicit instructions and a list of illicit consequences should he fail, I was sitting in the same hotel Trigger died in, preparing to testify at Kelley Pierce's preliminary hearing. Vivian and Milton would be arraigned in two weeks, but this one had been rushed for some reason only the accused knew.

"I guess... are they witnesses?"

Winnie and Ruger were on the other queen bed. Ruger had been in a depressive state since we arrived, Winnie's head on his back rising and falling the only certainty I had he was still alive. "Yeah, they're expected in the courtroom... You sure you're up for this? We can video your testimony."

I glared at him. "I did not put Ruger through being back in this hotel, put a bra on, and do my hair to back out now. Maybe the head is still sitting comfortably seated on the body of the beast, and we couldn't find anything in my ruined apartment or car to link the corrupt cop, but I'm seeing this through. We're doing this, and then I'm going to see if every person I know can come over for Thanksgiving, so I don't have to celebrate alone."

"I'll be there. If you want me." His ears turned pink, and I smiled. The man was constantly waffling between respecting my boundaries and trying to let me know he was there for me.

"I want you there." A dimple popped out in his left cheek, and I shook my head. The man was adorable. "Ready to get this over with, puppy?"

Ruger and Winnie rose before Griffin, prepping themselves at the foot of the bed to get leashed. After I checked twice for my room key, cell phone, and chewing gum, we walked down the hallway, and out into the chilly overcast morning.

Beyond the hotel drop off, I could see the federal courthouse looming two streets over. Dozens of cars honked up the street, snow tires plucking the barren streets that hadn't yet seen the white flakes of the season. Somewhere out of sight, a bus honked, and someone's brakes squealed. I slipped my hand into Griffin's, each of us holding a leash as we crossed the lot and walked to the corner for the traffic signal.

"What do you eat for Thanksgiving food?" Griffin asked, squeezing my hand as we crossed the street. We made it to the opposite corner and started up the next street. "Are you a turkey person? Ham? Maybe roast beast?"

We skirted an open manhole, the cones knocked over by the stiff wind working its way through my blazer. "Are you accusing me of being the Grinch? Is it because I have dogs and like... two friends?"

Griffin snort-laughed, stopping us at the next intersection. Ahead, the courthouse steps were adorned with two dozen video cameras and a podium. None of the media logos were familiar, with the exception of Fox News and CNN. Four black town cars lined the curb in front of and behind the media vehicles, each with a dark tint and government plates.

"Shit." Ruger growled his agreement while Winnie put on her best FAFO face, looking like the once highly trained military police canine she had been. Officer Deuce from Cincinnati stood beside the front door in uniform, smiling the gleeful gloat of a killer who'd never be brought to account for his crimes. "This isn't his jurisdiction and I hate him."

From the street corner away from the steps, I could see his gaze sweeping the gathered news people . As soon as the Fox News blonde was in place, front and center, he escorted the Governor to the steps of the courthouse, careful to slouch so he wouldn't appear taller than the man.

"Hello, yes. I am here," he said into the microphones and Ruger's growl kicked up in volume. My gaze bounced between the governor and canine.

"Do you think he was in the room?" I leaned into his chest, the soft fabric concealing my face while we quickly ascended the steps beside the self-gratifying cuckold on display. Officer Deuce was being derided by the man before him and the look of pure bliss on his face would likely satisfy him more than water-based lube and a tissue. "And can we use that whole recording thing to get him and officer awful jailed?"

"My recording is inadmissible." Griffin reiterated, steering me toward a wooden bench. We were outside court room number four, and I sat down. My ribs ached and I tried to take shallow breaths to get the pain under control.

"Not the actual recording. The one Kelley believed Ruger was carrying around in his dog pockets." He considered the suggestion while I watched Elsa escorting Jackie Abramian toward the courtroom. She had a hand possessively held near the woman's lower back and while I wasn't one to tattle, the sight reminded me Elsa's wife had watched my dogs. "Sup?"

Elsa nodded, but Jackie extended her hand. "Sorry, I didn't make it in to meet you when everything went down. Jackie Abramian-Woodruff, I know we didn't get to speak but—"

"You married the defense attorney?" I gaped at the bailiff, pieces of the prosecutor's statement clicking into place. "No wonder they thought you'd rip Kelley's head off. Are you here to testify… in uniform?"

"No." Her curt response was said through pursed lips and I looked back at the attorney for an explanation.

"I'm defending Kelley. He's going to make a plea deal." She patted Elsa's shoulder, and I sighed. "I know you came all the way here to testify in his arraignment hearing, but if the judge doesn't go for it you'll still be needed so please don't leave…"

"There's brain matter on my wall." Elsa shook her head, leaving the group and entering the courtroom.

"Her point is valid. What's the deal?" Cameras clicked in the hallway, and we all turned to see the governor parading his paparazzi toward us. "Should we…" I gestured at the door.

Everyone nodded and we slipped inside. Griffin and I took seats on the far side away from the jury box, watching Jackie take her place at the defense table and begin to set up her papers. Percy and George walked in from the judge's chambers, nodding at her and offering a minute thumb up. Jackie relaxed slightly and I could see Elsa do the same from across the room, both of their shoulders dropping another inch from their ears.

"I think that means the plea deal is happening." I leaned against the wall, trying to take the pressure off my ribs. "Guess this was a waste."

The wooden door banged open, bouncing off the wooden bench at the rear of the room. Stump filled the doorway, flanked by the news anchor and Officer Deuce. Strutting down the aisle like it was a red carpet, he waved at the few people seated in the galley and placed himself on the bench behind the defense table.

"Twatwaffle." The word slipped out and empty eyes flashed in my direction. My urge to flip him off was held back by my inability to lift my arm. "Wish I had a snake hook and a knife."

Griffin squeezed my hand, giving me a laughing smirk as the judge entered the room and Elsa ordered us to all rise. Then sit. Silently, I cursed her with a thousand inconveniences on par with unnecessary standing and sitting with broken ribs and second degree burns on my back.

"Bring in the defendant." Judge Benson's voice boomed out into the courtroom. The door beside me opened, a bedraggled and broken Kelley was led in wearing cuffs. His hands and feet were cuffed, the orange jumpsuit not replaced with fashionable clothing for his court appearance.

Placed at the table, he leaned in to whisper to Jackie who nodded back.

"I've been made aware of a plea deal. In exchange for information on involved parties, Kelley Pierce has asked that he be allowed on an escorted outing to attend his brother's funeral and a pardon for Milton Geissinger who's committed no crimes beyond those of association. Given the subject of this information, I am willing to conditionally grant the plea deal. You will provide us with the information necessary to prosecute the actual attacker of Ms. Charrish, the accomplices to the murder of Mr. Sampson, and we will allow you to hold a funeral for your brother."

"You worthless coward!" Stump roared, shoving to his feet. Benson banged his gavel, but Tommy already had Deuce's service weapon pointed at Kelley's chest. "You have nothing! You are weak! I should have killed you when..."

A shot rang out and Winnie charged forward, teeth clamping around the man's wrist and dragging his arm down. Ruger moved in and tripped him into falling while I struggled to stand and help. Elsa was right there, cuffs ready and a second beside her, eyes on me, she nodded. "Winnie, out."

She let go and both dogs came back to me while Stump and Deuce were placed in cuffs. Beside Jackie, red blossomed in the orange of Kelley's jumpsuit, face frozen forever in an O of surprise at his own death. Screams resounded around the courtroom, the two cuffed men shouting while newscasters fought for prime viewing to show the world how unstable the leader was. My phone was already pinging with notifications and tags of yet another Cyn Sharp disaster.

"It's good about Milton. He... he wasn't bad. Trigger would have liked him." I stared down at the dog in front of me, petting his head. "Maybe May will let him work at the range."

"I'm sure having a lawyer around would be good for the cause. At least this administration is over." Griffin gestured to the now empty seat the former governor occupied.

"No getting out of murder in front of a judge." I leaned against the wall, watching the chaos with the same indifference I watched ants when Sylvie kicked over an anthill. "And we're not getting out of here for at least an hour. I should probably be horrified but... I'm too busy being relieved that those two are going to prison. Also, I'm really tired and I don't know if there's a vice governor or we have to hold an election."

"Then lean on me and take a nap. I'll look that up while you rest and provide a full Hamilton style rap."

"Be prepared to cite your sources in iambic pentameter."

"Obviously. Rest, Cyn. I got you."

I cuddled close and Winnie jumped up beside me while Ruger laid across his feet. As my eyes started to drift closed, I realized that I believed him.

"Thanks, puppy."

He had me, and I had them. New car, new house, new pots and pans probably.

We'd survive starting over—together.

About the Author

E. N. Crane is a fiction author writing humorous mysteries with plus-sized female leads and their furry friends. She is one of two authors under the Perry Dog Publishing Imprint, a one woman, two dog operation in Idaho... for now. My dogs are Perry and Padfoot, the furry beasts shown above. They are well-loved character inspiration in all things written and business.

If you are interested in joining my newsletter, please subscribe here: https://e-n-crane_perrydogpublishing.ck.page/578ed9ab 37or on my website, PerryDogPublishing.com

You will receive A Bite in Afghanistan, the prequel to the Sharp Investigations Series, as a thank-you for joining. I only have one newsletter for mental health reasons, so both romance and mystery are on there! If you only want one in your inbox, follow Perry Dog Publishing on all socials to stay on top of the latest news... and pet pics.